"I've learned to be wary. To tell the truth, I doubt now that I shall ever marry."

Emily looked at Rosa with the beginnings of a smile. "And do you know? I didn't feel like a cool fish yesterday. That stranger's kisses were far more exciting than any I've known before. Isn't that scandalous?"

* * *

Miss Winbolt and the Fortune Hunter
Harlequin® Historical #300—January 2011

SYLVIA ANDREW

has an honors degree in modern languages from University College, London, and before ending up as vice principal of a large comprehensive sixth-form college taught English for foreigners in Switzerland, Cambridge and in Compton Park, an international finishing school for young ladies, which was housed in a beautiful country mansion leased from the Devonshire family. The house and grounds have provided inspiration for several settings in her novels. She and her husband, Simon, now live in the west of England, in a small market town full of the Georgian architecture they both love. And just a few miles from their home is the marvelous Dorset Jurassic Coast World Heritage Site. In 2000 Sylvia wrote a historical celebration of the town's splendid fifteenth-century parish church in a millennium son et lumière, which was a great success.

She and Simon belong to the Georgian Group, the National Trust and English Heritage, all of which help them to satisfy their love of historic houses and wonderful landscapes. Simon lectures all over the place on architecture and wild orchids, while Sylvia tries to do nothing, and usually fails, since she is heavily involved in the local museum. She just can't keep away from old maps, newspapers, photographs and census returns! Her other passion is theater performances of Shakespeare. She and Simon have one married daughter, whom they visit quite often, and a very precious grandson called Joe.

Miss Winbolt
and the
FORTUNE
HUNTER

SYLVIA ANDREW

HARLEQUIN®

TORONTO • NEW YORK • LONDON
AMSTERDAM • PARIS • SYDNEY • HAMBURG
STOCKHOLM • ATHENS • TOKYO • MILAN • MADRID
PRAGUE • WARSAW • BUDAPEST • AUCKLAND

Recycling programs
for this product may
not exist in your area.

ISBN-13: 978-0-373-30609-1

MISS WINBOLT AND THE FORTUNE HUNTER

First North American Publication 2011

www.eHarlequin.com

Printed in U.S.A.

This one has to be for Simon, and my friends at
Crewkerne & District Museum

Chapter One

Berkshire—May 1820

'You must find a husband and set up your own establishment, Miss Winbolt. Marriage is the only answer. Nothing else will serve.'

Emily put her cup down very carefully. 'Mrs Gosworth, I feel this is hardly a matter…'

'I feel for you, my dear,' her hostess continued. 'Your brother's marriage must have made life very difficult. After years of being in charge at Shearings yourself, it must be galling to have to hand over the reins to his new wife.'

Annoyed as Emily was, she had to laugh at this. 'Nothing could be further from the truth, I assure you. Rosa and I are the best of friends and we deal very well together. I'm sorry, ma'am, but you are quite wrong to suggest—'

Mrs Gosworth was not about to abandon a topic she found so enjoyable. 'Your sister-in-law would say nothing to upset you, of course. But the servants at Shearings are accustomed to receive orders from you. How will the new Mrs Winbolt establish herself as their mistress, while you are still in the house? Such a dear, sweet, biddable girl is sure to find it difficult, if not impossible. You are so decided in your opinions, Miss Winbolt, that there must be a risk that your brother's wife will become a cipher in her own home!'

'My dear ma'am, you are quite mistaken about Rosa's character,' Emily said, still smiling. 'She is far from being the spineless creature you represent. Her manner is gentle, but she is perfectly capable of asserting her authority wherever and whenever it is needed. As indeed she does.'

'Dear me! Two women of character in the same house? You are bound to fall out.'

'I doubt very much—'

'Perhaps you could set up house on your own? But, no! Your brother would never permit it. And what would the rest of the county say if he did? They would blame his wife, of course. No, marriage is the only answer. You must find a decent man and secure him without delay.'

Emily's resolve to hold on to her temper was beginning to wear thin. She called on her sense of humour and confessed with a deceptive air of meekness that she knew of no one and asked if Mrs Gosworth had a suitable candidate in mind. Humour, along with refinement or concern for others, played no part in Mrs Gosworth's makeup. Yellowing teeth showed in a triumphant smile as she said, 'Not at the moment, but it shouldn't be too hard to find someone. It's a pity that your looks are no more than passable. Your brother is a very handsome man and no one in the neighbourhood could match his wife for beauty, but you...' She shook her head. 'It is a real pity. However, the case is not a hopeless one. Running Shearings has given you experience in household management and that would appeal to some men—especially one looking for a wife endowed with as handsome a fortune as yours.'

At that point Emily very nearly walked out. But, determined not to give this woman the satisfaction of seeing how very angry she was, she shook her head mournfully and said, 'Alas, it looks as though I shall remain single, after all. I have no desire for such a husband.' She got up. 'Thank you for inviting me today, ma'am. It has been…an altogether delightful visit. Now, if you will excuse me, I'm afraid I must go. I have an appointment elsewhere.' Then she curtsied and added, 'You are very kind to be so concerned about how I deal with my brother and his wife. But pray let me set your mind at rest on one point at least. If I ever do decide to set up my own establishment, I shall not be leaving Shearings because of any difficulty in my relationship with my sister-in-law, I assure you. Good day, ma'am.'

Berating herself for her stupidity, Emily made her way back to Shearings. She knew that Mrs Gosworth was an embittered old woman with a desire to make mischief wherever she could, but she visited the old lady partly out of pity and partly out of curiosity to see what she would say next. But this time it had been too much. Now, as she went through the gate leading into Three Acre field, she asked herself why she had taken the risk. Mrs Gosworth's malice might have missed its mark by a wide margin, but it had raised a question that had been haunting Emily for some time—the question of her future. Bitter experience had taught her that a

fortune-seeking husband was the last thing she wanted,
but how else could she reasonably find a home of her
own without causing distress to Philip and, more particularly still, to Rosa? As she shut the gate behind her
and set off across the field, this thought was still plagu-
ing her. Much as she loved her brother and sister-in-law,
she felt a growing need for independence. But how was
she to achieve it without seriously upsetting them? She
walked on, absorbed in her thoughts, and it was not until
she was about halfway across the field that she became
conscious of the black shape over to the left.

When she looked round and saw what it was, Rosa,
Philip, Mrs Gosworth's malice, her own doubts and
painful memories, and everything else were wiped clean
from her mind. Pritchard's bull, large, black and powerful, was standing not twenty yards away, regarding
her with a malevolent eye. Her heart missed a beat as
stories about this animal flashed through her mind. Will
Darby came to Shearings with a fresh tale every day,
each one more gruesome than the last. Black Samson
was as wicked as he was handsome. He had already
savagely gored and killed a couple of stray dogs that had
dared to come too near. Quite without provocation he
had attacked and tossed Job Diment, one of Pritchard's
farm workers, and the man was still laid up with a badly
mauled arm. There were others who had escaped even
worse injury only by the skin of their teeth....

For a second she was frozen to the spot before an
instinct for self-preservation took charge. She looked
round the field. Black Samson would catch her long
before she got to the gate on the other side. She must
find a refuge somewhere else. Where, where? The giant
oak over on the right was nearer. It might serve. She
took another quick glance at the bull and saw that he had

apparently given up interest in her for the moment. The temptation to run was strong, but it would undoubtedly be better to walk as unobtrusively as possible towards the tree and hope that he would continue to ignore her. She took a few nervous steps, but couldn't resist the temptation to look back again. When she saw that Black Samson had raised his head and was now advancing purposefully in her direction, she lost her nerve. Without any idea what she would do when she got there she gave a little scream, took to her heels and fled towards the tree. It was the worst possible thing she could have done. Made lazy by the heat of the afternoon the bull had only been slightly curious, but this was too much of a challenge! Roused by flying feet and fluttering skirts, he lowered his head, horns at the ready, and took up the chase.

Emily ran for her life, and soon she was sobbing and gasping for breath. The tree was too far, she would never reach it in time! The bull was gaining ground fast—she could almost feel the animal's breath on her back. She stumbled just as she reached her goal and for one paralysing moment was sure she had breathed her last. But with a final desperate effort she threw herself at the tree and grabbed at its lower branches. Her foot was still dangling when the bull reached her, but the tip of his horn caught her bonnet, which had been hanging by a single ribbon down her back. He paused to shake it clear and this gave Emily the all-important moment to scramble to safety. One branch, two... She didn't care about her dress, paid no heed to nails and fingers. All she saw was the haven of the branches above her. At last she reached one broad enough to shelter her. She lay sprawled uncomfortably across it, lungs bursting and heart racing—but safely out of the bull's reach.

She stayed there for some minutes, exhausted and almost afraid to move, till after a while she recovered enough to sit up and edge along the branch so that her back was resting against the trunk of the tree. She was trembling all over as she took stock of her situation. Her legs were scratched and smarting and felt as if they would never hold her up again. Her stockings were in shreds round her ankles and she removed them and put her shoes back on. It was a painful process, for her fingernails, where she had scrabbled frantically up the trunk of the tree, were broken and the tips were bleeding. But when she looked round she saw that at least she was safe! This oak was broad, and as long as she took care there was no danger of falling. She looked down at the bull and was shocked to see what had happened to her bonnet. It was lying torn and tattered in the dust and the bull, shaking his head in angry frustration, was slashing at the poor remains. Emily felt sick as she watched. How could she have been so stupid as to forget about Pritchard's bull? She, not the bonnet, could have been lying there underneath Black Samson's hoof.

Turning her eyes away with a shudder, she tried to pull herself together and think what to do next. One thing was certain—she wasn't going to go anywhere near that bull again. She had been unbelievably lucky to escape. The village were already muttering about the beast and Farmer Pritchard was under pressure to get rid of it. Now, too late, she remembered that Will Darby had told her yesterday that Pritchard had moved the bull to Three Acre field because it was further away from the village and protected by stouter fences and hedges. But the field was on the route to Shearings, and after her conversation with Mrs Gosworth she had wanted to walk off her temper before she saw Rosa. She had sent her groom and the carriage back ahead of her and set off alone across the fields. Between her fury at Mrs Gosworth and preoccupation with her own major problem, she had not given the bull a thought. What an idiot she had been!

Though she was hardly able to move a muscle, she tried to regain some of her usual calm good sense. It would be more useful to stop blaming herself for what had happened and to plan instead what she should do now. How could she get away without climbing back down into the field? Looking round her, she saw that the branches of the oak overhung a thick hedge, which bordered the field. On the other side was a grassy pasture, which sloped down to a stream. She knew the area. It shouldn't be too difficult to drop down from her branch into the pasture, and so on to the footpath that ran alongside the stream towards the back entrance to Shearings. She was really not too far from safety. Encouraged, she edged slowly far enough along the branch to be able to see over the hedge. But the slope was steeper than she had remembered, and the drop from the tree much too great. She couldn't possibly get down without help.

Severely disappointed, Emily was tempted to give way to tears, but she told herself sharply not to be so poor-spirited. Anyone might be a little worn by such a frantic dash through the field and the hasty scramble up the tree, but that was no excuse for despair. Nor were her various aches and pains. The footpath was not much frequented, but if she could just hold on a little longer Will Darby was bound to pass by on his way home from Shearings. A treacherous little voice inside told her that it might actually be a good while longer—it was still early in the evening, and Will was never in a hurry to get home—but she refused to listen to it. She must keep up her spirits. Meanwhile, she could try to make herself more comfortable... But the branch creaked ominously as she wriggled along it, so she gave up the idea and prepared herself for an uncomfortable wait.

Time passed very slowly and before long she was beginning to feel dizzy from the strain of holding herself upright. Then, just as the pain was becoming unbearable, she saw someone walking along the path in the direction of the village. The relief was enormous. Will must have decided to come home early for once!

'Will!' she shouted. 'Will, help me!' He hadn't heard her—he wasn't going to stop! 'Will!' she shouted again. 'I'm so glad to see you. I'm over here! This way! Stop, please stop! Are you deaf? For heaven's sake, man, don't be such a fool! I've been stuck in this tree for hours and I need your help!'

To her relief Will Darby stopped, looked around till he saw her in the tree, and climbed up the slope. But when he stood below her she could see that he wasn't Will Darby, after all. He was a complete stranger.

'Well, well, well,' he said. 'A damsel in distress, by heaven. Calling me by name, too! I don't know you, do I?'

The stranger was no farm servant. He was dressed somewhat carelessly, with his coat unbuttoned and his shirt open at the neck. But his boots and breeches, though dusty, were of good quality, and his accent was that of a gentleman. 'No,' said poor Emily, conscious in spite of her distress that her hair was tangled, her dress was torn and that she was exposing a shocking length of bare leg. 'I... I'm afraid...'

'Then how did you know my name?'

'I... I th-thought you someone else,' she said.

'I see,' he said. 'What the devil are you doing up there?'

Emily was tired and sore and she had no time for stupid questions. 'What do you think I'm doing?' she said with something like a snap. 'I'm stuck. I can't get down!'

He took his coat off, then jumped up to take a quick look over the hedge. 'Why can't you get down the other side? It looks as if that would be much easier.'

'Because there's half a ton of bull waiting for me behind the tree. His name is Black Samson and he's famous for his wicked temper. I have no desire to be gored to death.' Her voice rose as she went on, 'And, whatever your name is, unless you or someone else don't stop asking useless questions and help me down from this tree, really quite soon, I shall fall down all by myself.' Her voice quavered on these last words—she was perilously close to tears.

'That would never do. We'll have to see how we can manage it. I've rescued many a cat from a tree in my time, but a grown woman is an altogether different matter.' He examined the hedge, which was full of brambles and thorn bushes, looked down the slope and eyed her perch. 'I can't lift you down,' he said doubtfully. 'You're too far out of my reach. I really ought to fetch more help.'

'No!' Emily was near the end of her tether. 'I couldn't possibly wait that long. The nearest place is much too far away! You must help me now!'

'I see. Well, in that case, we'll just have to do our best. Can you edge a little further till you're clear of that thorn hedge? I think we can do it if you lower yourself down very carefully and trust me to catch you for the last few feet. I'd say the ground here was level enough for me to manage it. Just about. You'll have to go carefully, mind. Gently's the word. Otherwise we could both end up rolling down the slope. Gently... that's right. That's the way! Gently now, gent—'

There was a crack, a scream and a shout of dismay as Emily's branch snapped and she fell precipitately into her rescuer's arms. He struggled to keep his balance, but the angle of the slope was too much for them. Together they rolled down, jolting over the rough ground and slithering where it was smooth. But he held her firmly throughout, shielding her from the worst of the bumps. They finally ended up in a grassy hollow, where they came to a stop. They lay there in silence for a moment or two. Then he said, 'That was exciting. Are you hurt?'

Dazed and winded Emily lay, still wrapped in his arms, not sure whether she was or she wasn't. After the buffeting and bumping of the previous minute, the hollow was strangely quiet. The world seemed to have retreated, leaving them alone in a haven of peace. She lay there almost dreamily, surprised and pleased that her various aches and pains appeared to have vanished. After a moment she shook her head.

'Are you sure?' He was leaning over her, his face close to hers. It was a nice face, she thought hazily. A kind face. A face full of humour. A tiny fan of wrinkles at each corner of his dark blue eyes gave her the impression that he laughed quite often. Or was it because he spent a good deal of his time out of doors? He was quite tanned. His nose was slightly crooked, and he had a firm chin, though it looked at the moment as if it needed a shave. He wasn't laughing at present— his expression was serious, a small frown between his brows. How pleasant, she thought. He's really concerned about me.

She was surprised at how comforting this was. She regarded herself as an independent creature, but recently she had begun to feel lonely, even amongst the people she loved best in the world. And Mrs Gosworth had stirred up doubts about her future, which she would rather have forgotten. She was in need of comfort. It was very agreeable to be regarded with such concern and, though the sensation was new, it was very pleasant to have someone's arms holding her so…so protectively.

'Would you like me to help you to get up?'

She considered the question. This feeling of intimacy, this new awareness of a man's body close to hers, was strange, but definitely attractive. 'I'm really quite happy where I am, thank you,' said Emily, giving him a sweet smile. 'I don't think I want to move.'

Afterwards, when she thought over what followed, she told herself she must have hit her head as she fell. It was the only explanation. Or perhaps she had been so shaken by her fright with the bull that she had been temporarily out of her mind. Whatever the cause, she had certainly not been herself.

Emily Winbolt had a warm heart and a lively sense of humour, but outsiders were seldom aware of either. Her manner to them was usually cool, even distant—that of a perfectly well-behaved, perfectly brought up, perfectly well-bred young lady. She was a devoted granddaughter, an openly loving sister to her brother Philip, and when he married had given her new sister-in-law the same affection. But several unfortunate experiences had made her cynical about most members of the opposite sex, and only her strong sense of humour had saved her from lasting bitterness.

Her behaviour in the hollow, for whatever reason, was so shocking, so completely out of character, that those who knew her would never have believed it. She later concluded it must have been caused by a fit of madness following her fall.

But while she was with this stranger it seemed altogether natural.

He frowned slightly. 'All the same, I think we should at least check whether you're damaged at all. Can you move your arms and legs?'

Still in the grip of this strange emotion, she stretched luxuriously like a cat then smiled again and wrinkled her nose at him. 'You see? Apart from a few scratches I'm perfectly sound.' The movement brought her into closer contact with the body next to hers. Her cheek was resting on his chest, and she could feel the warmth of his body, a slight roughness of hair, through the thin lawn of his shirt. His heartbeat was strong and it was growing faster...

He smiled back and it was just as she had suspected—his eyes wrinkled at the corners, laughter lurking in them.

'You've collected half the hedge in your fall,' he said, carefully picking leaves and twigs out of her hair and smoothing it back from her forehead. Emily gazed at him in delight, filled with a sense of well-being, her loneliness and other anxieties quite forgotten. This man might be a stranger, she might never see him again after this meeting, but she had not felt as close as this to anyone else for a long, long time. His eyes met hers again and she knew he was going to kiss her. Far from being shocked, she was warmed by the thought. He put his finger gently under her chin and tilted her face to meet his...

At first the kiss was tentative, as if he was not sure what her reaction would be, but as he felt her response it deepened and grew more intense, though still gentle. It seemed to go on for a long time. Emily was lost in its sweetness. When he would have lifted his head, she put her arms round his neck and pulled his mouth to hers again.

'Well, well, well,' he murmured against her lips. 'I little thought when I lost my way this morning that I would end up with an enchantress in my arms. What is your name, lovely one?'

Even in her present dazed state Emily had no wish to tell him who she was. This was a magic hour, a time out of reality. Emily Winbolt, spinster, had no place in this enchantment. He saw her hesitation and laughed. 'You're quite right! I shouldn't have asked. Though it's hardly fair—you know mine.'

'Will,' she said softly. 'Though I didn't know it was yours until you told me.'

'Who is the other Will in your life?'

She could have replied, 'One of my brother's servants.' But she didn't. She didn't want him to know where she lived, or what her name was, any more than she wanted him to know that her brother owned the land all around them, and they lived in a handsome residence in the Palladian style quite close at hand. She didn't want to talk about her brother's wife, gentle, loving and very, very beautiful. Emily wanted for once to be Miss Nobody from nowhere, not rich Miss Winbolt, sister to the local landowner and an heiress in her own right. And, more than anything, she didn't want to be reminded of the problem that had been gnawing at the back of her mind for weeks, and which had been brutally brought to the fore by her conversation with Mrs Gosworth.

'He doesn't matter, Will,' she whispered. 'Nothing

else matters at the moment.' She smiled at him dreamily, 'Will,' she said. '*Will.*' And she pulled his head down to hers again. This time the kiss was passionate from the start. He held her so closely that she felt every part of his strong, muscular body, and delighted in it. He smoothed her hair again and kissed her brow, her eyes, and then returned to part her lips with his. Emily's heart was racing once more, this time with a feverish excitement. She had been kissed before by a man she had been about to marry, but never like this. Never before had she been so aware of her blood running through her veins with such singing delight. Her skin tingled wherever he touched her. She realised now how bloodless, how meaningless those other kisses had been. Nothing in her experience had prepared her for this. She felt overwhelmed by a need to be held by this man, caressed by him. He was no stranger to her—she belonged to him. Nothing existed except the two of them, and the hollow where they lay hidden from the rest of the world in an enchanted, magical world of their own. His lips found her throat, her shoulders, her breasts...

A sound of whistling broke into their idyll. Will Darby on his way home! She stiffened and firm hands gripped her. 'Lie still,' he whispered. 'He won't see us if you lie quite still.'

The magic vanished into the air, as reality broke in on Emily's dream. She lay rigid and silent until the footsteps died away in the distance, then, overcome with shame, she struggled to be free of him. 'It's Will Darby,' she said, as she scrambled to her feet and straightened her dress. Avoiding his eye, she stammered, 'They'll be wondering where I am. I must go.'

He got up, and when she turned away from him put

his arms round her waist. 'I'll come with you,' he murmured against her neck.

'You can't,' she cried in panic, pushing him from her. 'I have to go alone. You mustn't come with me.'

'I don't believe it!' he said, half-laughing, half-serious. 'That's too much the cruel enchantress. You can't appear out of nowhere, bewitch me, and then just... disappear! I won't let you.'

Emily, torn between shame and a treacherous desire to stay, said desperately. 'Please, you must let me go. I...I cannot stay any longer. Don't look at me like that! I...I don't...don't know what came over me...' She couldn't finish the sentence. With a little sob she turned and stumbled down the slope to the footpath, picked up her skirts and ran for dear life towards Shearings. When she threw a hunted glance back, she saw to her relief he was making no attempt to follow her, but stood where she had left him, ruefully shaking his head.

After she had disappeared round a bend in the footpath the stranger stood for a while, then shrugged and went to pick up his coat. The village where he had left his horse and pack couldn't be more than a few minutes walk away. It was too late now to see Charlwood again tonight. He would put up at a local inn or camp out in some hedgerow or other. The thought didn't disturb him—the night would be warm, and he had done it often enough in the past. And as he walked he shook his head over what had just happened. It was altogether something new in his experience! Such passion, followed by such an abrupt departure! Why had she gone? Was the other Will her lover, or even her husband, perhaps? He rather thought he would never know. He shrugged again and went on his way, deciding to dismiss the episode from his mind. Unless Charlwood proved to be more suitable than he had thought at first sight, he wouldn't be in the area for long. It was most unlikely their paths would ever cross a second time. At this thought he felt a fleeting regret. There had been something about her that had attracted him as he had not been attracted for many years. Not her looks—he could hardly remember anything about the way she looked, except for a pair of silver-grey eyes. Her legs and ankles had been good, too. He grinned as he remembered his first sight of her, those long slender legs dangling from the tree... But there was something else... Something about her had appealed to him at a deeper level. She had been such a strange mixture of abandonment and innocence...

He shook his head, and stepped out more briskly. No, she was just a passionate little flirt. She was probably a consummate tease, too. Life was too short to spend a second thought on her. But, by heaven, she knew how to stir a man's blood!

Chapter Two

By the time Emily reached Shearings she was exhausted. The bruises and scratches she had forgotten a short while before had returned to plague her, and she limped painfully through the garden room door in the direction of the back stairs. But, though she went as quietly as she could, she was not quiet enough. Rosa had obviously been listening for her.

'Emily! Dearest! Thank goodness you're back! We were worried about you, after the carriage returned without you. But why have you come in this way—?' She stopped short and regarded her sister-in-law with astonishment. 'Heavens! What on earth have you done to yourself? No, don't waste time on that now—you can tell me later. We must get you upstairs to your room first.'

Emily was helped through the hall and up to her room at the top of the main staircase, and was soon sitting in a chair being ministered to by Rosa herself and by Mrs Hopkins, the housekeeper. Mrs Hopkins had been with the Winbolt family for many years, and had known Emily since childhood. She gently removed her torn clothes, exclaiming as she did so at the state of her hands and legs. Rosa meanwhile fetched salves and lotions from her own room, then disappeared again to return with a glass of Philip's best brandy. After a short while Emily was lying on her bed, propped up by pillows, her hands bandaged and the scratches on her legs bathed and soothed with ointment. Rosa sat beside her on the bed and held the brandy to her lips.

'Drink it all,' she said with a reassuring smile. 'Every drop. You'll feel better.'

When Emily hesitated, Mrs Hopkins nodded her head. 'There's nothing like a drop of brandy, Miss Emily,' she said firmly. 'You do as Mrs Winbolt says.' They waited until Emily had finished the brandy, then the housekeeper said, 'If you don't need me any more, ma'am, I'll go about my business. The master will be back soon, I dare say.'

After she had gone out Rosa said, 'She thinks you'll feel able to talk more freely in her absence, but she could have stayed. Mrs Hopkins wouldn't dream of gossiping with the other servants. She is the soul of discretion.' She paused, then said hesitantly, 'I'm very anxious to know what happened, Emily. If you feel well enough to tell me, I'd like to hear about it.'

Emily took a breath. Discretion was a good word to use. She would have to use a good deal of it herself.

'You know that I visited Mrs Gosworth this afternoon...' she began. She paused.

'I did warn you,' said Rosa. 'She is one of the unkindest people I know. Oh, Emily, I should have gone with you. Did she upset you?'

'She tried,' said Emily with a small grimace. 'But I'm afraid she was disappointed. I was angry rather than

upset, but I managed not to show it. I even thanked her
for a delightful visit!'

Rosa clapped her hands and laughed. 'Wonderful!
She must have been furious. How long did you stay?'

'Not a second more than the correct time, believe
me. But you can't imagine what I did afterwards. I must
have been mad.'

Rosa raised an eyebrow. 'You? But you are the soul
of good sense!'

'Not today. After talking to that woman I was so very
angry that I didn't want to be driven home. I needed
to work my temper off. I needed exercise and air, so I
walked home across the fields. And…and I forgot all
about Pritchard's bull and came through Three Acre
field.'

'Thr-Through' Rosa looked at her aghast. 'I don't
believe you! You *can't* have forgotten. Weren't you
listening when Will Darby told us he'd been moved
there?'

'Yes. But it had gone right out of my mind. I didn't
think of the bull until I was halfway across the field and
saw his eyes on me.'

Rosa was shocked. She got off the bed and walked
about the room in agitation. 'Good God, Emily, when
I think what could have happened… What has already
happened to others…' She turned and looked at Emily
in bewilderment. 'How can you have been so foolish?
It's so unlike you! That bull…' She came back and
took her sister-in-law in her arms. 'We could have lost
you.'

Emily laughed shakily. 'There were a few moments
when I thought you had. But I ran faster than I've run
in my life before and reached a tree by the hedge just
before the bull caught up with me.'

Rosa gently took Emily's bandaged hands in hers. 'I suppose that's when these got so damaged. What happened then?'

'I found I was stranded and waited for a while to see…to see if anyone would come to rescue me.'

Emily was not used to lying, especially with Rosa's clear blue eyes, wide with sympathy, looking at her. She took a deep breath and went on, 'But…but no one did. So…so I jumped down.'

'Emily! That was so dangerous!'

'Yes. Yes, it was. The branch broke, and I…and I rolled down the slope. It was steeper than I had thought.'

'You could have been killed! I shall certainly have something to say to Philip when he comes back. I asked him to go when the carriage arrived back without you, but he said you'd be perfectly safe walking home. He really should have gone to look for you.'

Emily gave a weak smile and tried not to show how profoundly grateful she was that her brother had refused. What he would have said, or done, if he had discovered her in that hollow, lying in the arms of a perfect stranger in an intimate embrace, was too awful to imagine.

'But where was Will?'

'*Who?*'

Rosa looked puzzled. 'Will Darby.'

Emily, who had been thinking of quite a different Will, tried to speak naturally as she responded, 'Will Darby… Oh, yes, of course.'

'He must have been on his way home about that time. Didn't you see him?'

''Er…no. I didn't,' said Emily, avoiding her sister-in-law's eye. She could feel her cheeks getting hot.

There was a slight pause, after which Rosa said, 'You

must be tired. I think you should have a rest now. Are you hungry? I'll have some soup or something easy to eat sent up.' Bending over to kiss Emily goodnight, she said softly, 'A night's sleep will work miracles. We'll see you in the morning.'

Emily lay awake for some time after Rosa and the maid had gone. She was still bewildered by what had happened that afternoon. Will—Will the stranger—had called her an enchantress, but judging by the effect *he* had had on *her*, it was far more likely that he was the sorcerer. She grew warm as she remembered how she had behaved. Wantonly. Shamelessly. Other words came to mind to torment her. But when she finally fell asleep, her last thoughts were oddly comforting—a stranger's arms protecting her as they rolled down the slope, a strong body holding her so close, laughter in a man's eyes as he held her and kissed…her…so…sweetly… And her dreams that night were surprisingly pleasant.

The next morning Emily got up, determined to put her encounter with the stranger and her own inexplicable reactions behind her. She nodded reassuringly when Rosa raised her brows in a silent question as she entered the breakfast room, and held up hands now free of bandages. Philip had apparently been told an edited version of her arrival the night before. He asked about her injuries and she assured him they were all purely superficial. He frowned when she told him of her visit to Mrs Gosworth, then said, 'I can't understand what possessed you to go through that field.'

'Philip, I can't tell you. I don't know! I agree it was madness, and that I was luckier than I deserved.'

'Perhaps I should have a word with Pritchard.'

'Please don't. I'm sure the field is perfectly secure. No one else in the village would be so stupid!'

They talked of other things for a while, but then Philip asked, 'By the way, did you happen to see any strangers on your way back? They were saying down in the stables that some fellow or other was wandering about round here yesterday. From what they told me, he arrived halfway through the morning, left his horse at the inn in the village and went for a walk. Odd sort of thing to do, wouldn't you say? Did you catch sight of him, Emmy?'

Emily's cheeks grew warm, and were even warmer as she felt Rosa's eyes on her. She replied with commendable calm, 'No, I don't think I did. Did he...did he go back to the inn?'

'Yes, but quite late. He claimed to have lost his way. But he must have come back along the stream about the time you were there.'

'Is he...is he still at the inn?'

'*I* don't know! I haven't seen Will Darby this morning. Why are you asking? There's no reason to be afraid. They all thought he looked like a gentleman. I don't think he's dangerous.'

Now *that* is entirely a matter of opinion! thought Emily with a wry smile, hastily straightening her face when she saw Rosa looking at her again.

Philip went on to talk of other matters, and the stranger was not mentioned again. Emily hoped he was forgotten. But afterwards Rosa looked Emily in the eye and said firmly, 'It's a lovely morning. Do you feel well enough for a walk in the garden? Or shall we sit in the small parlour? There are just the two of us here this morning. Philip has to go over to Temperley.'

Philip said, surprised, 'Aren't you coming with me to see your father?'

'Not this morning, my love. It's a business call, and you'll do much better without me. No, Emily and I are going to have a comfortable chat in the garden. Aren't we, dear?'

'I thought I might go...'

'You mustn't disappoint me, Emily,' said Rosa, with smiling determination.

Rosa was the sweetest, gentlest girl imaginable, thought Emily, except when she's looking as she does at the moment. She gave up. 'No. I see that I mustn't. Very well. The garden it is. I should like a walk.'

'And a talk, I hope,' said Rosa with another charming smile.

It was a beautifully sunny day and the two ladies, wearing wide brimmed hats and carrying parasols, went out into the garden. They walked for a while, and then sat down in the shade. Emily looked around her. She had helped Philip so much here when he had first inherited Shearings. Their Great-Uncle Joseph's chief interest had been in new methods of farming, and Shearings's gardens had lain neglected. She and Philip had worked so hard that first year to create this haven of flower beds and shaded walks, arbours and fountains. Emily sighed. She was genuinely happy that Philip had found Rosa. They were ideally suited. But it was sometimes difficult not to be nostalgic about the past.

Rosa snapped her parasol shut and turned to Emily, who saw the militant look in her sister-in-law's eye and braced herself.

'Now!' she said. 'Now you can tell me just what happened yesterday, if you please.'

'I...I've told you.'

'So you did. And I believed you. But that was before I heard about a stranger. A gentlemanly stranger.'

'What...what has he to do with me?'

'That is what *you* are going to tell *me*, Emily dear. I know you. You're a bad liar. And I have a strong suspicion that you not only saw this "gentlemanly stranger" yesterday, but probably talked to him, too. Is that what made you so late?' She stopped and looked closely at Emily. 'Dear heaven, I hadn't thought... He didn't attack you, did he? Is he the cause of those bruises and scratches? Tell me, Emily, don't be afraid.'

'No, no! You're quite wrong. I told you the truth about those. I got them when I climbed the tree. Most of them.'

'And the rest?' Rosa's lovely face was unusually stern.

Emily heard the determination and realised that she was not going to get away with less than the truth.

'You see too much, Rosa. I should have known you'd guess. Very well. I climbed up the tree as I told you and saw that I couldn't get down. That was true. But you're quite right. I didn't tell you everything.'

'Which was...?'

'It seemed like hours before I saw someone coming, and when I did I took it to be Will Darby. I knew he would pass by on his way home so I called out to him and he came over. But...but it wasn't Will Darby, after all.'

'I knew it! It was this stranger,' Rosa said.

Emily nodded. 'He agreed to catch me if I jumped, but the branch broke, and we fell and rolled down the slope. That was when I got the rest of the scratches.'

'Was he hurt?'

'I…I don't think so. He didn't seem to be. He…he's very strong.'

Rosa watched, fascinated, as Emily's lips curved up in a small, reminiscent smile. 'What…what happened then?' she asked carefully.

'I was dazed, of course. He waited until I felt better, then…' Emily glanced briefly at Rosa and said, 'Then I left him and came home.'

'Alone? He didn't offer to see you home safely? What a strange man he must be to leave you to find your own way after such a fall! He can't have been much of a gentleman.'

'No! No, you mustn't think… He…he wanted to bring me home. I wouldn't let him.'

'Why ever not?'

'He…he…he kissed me.'

'Against your will? The heartless wretch!'

'No… It wasn't like that. It wasn't at all like that!'

Emily got up and walked away. Her voice was muffled as she said, still not turning round, 'I let him kiss me. Willingly.'

This surprised Rosa so much that for a moment she couldn't say anything. Then she stammered, 'I can't believe it!'

'Neither can I! Not now.' Emily stood a moment with her back towards Rosa. When she turned round, she had a look of desperation on her face. 'I don't know what came over me, Rosa!' she said in a stifled voice. 'I'm not normally so…so idiotic. Perhaps it had all been too much for me—Mrs Gosworth, the bull, then falling from the tree…I don't know! But, whatever the reason, I behaved like a…like a wanton. I must have been mad. How will I ever forget it?'

'Of course you can. You were dazed, in shock. Don't

get upset, Emily! It was probably more difficult than you think to refuse him.'

'But afterwards…I should have been angry, should have fought to get away from him as quickly as I could. But I didn't.' She fell silent and her face softened into a smile of remembrance. For a moment she looked… vulnerable. 'I enjoyed it. He was so kind…so gentle… I felt so…so safe with him…so cherished… I didn't push him away. I wanted him to kiss me again. And he did.' She shook her head in a gesture of repudiation. 'I'm still…so ashamed.'

Rosa got up and said softly, 'Dearest Emily, you mustn't be. I think it quite likely that the shock of the fall affected your behaviour yesterday. You were grateful to him, as well as dazed. I shouldn't worry about the state of your morals! But there's more to it than that.' She thought for a moment. 'Let's go for a walk.'

As they walked through an avenue of trees planted by Philip's great-grandfather nearly a hundred years before, Rosa said, 'Mrs Gosworth can be very cruel indeed. I suffered at her hands quite badly. My first marriage, as you know, was an unhappy one. Stephen, my husband, was involved with some very disreputable people… Mrs Gosworth somehow or other heard about Stephen and when I visited her shortly after our marriage she hinted that I had ruined Philip's life by marrying him, that the Winbolts' reputation was irreparably damaged by associating with me. Philip had to work hard to reassure me afterwards that it was all nonsense—she can be very convincing.'

She stopped and looked at Emily. 'You are one of the most level-headed people I know, Emily, but yesterday you were so angry with Mrs Gosworth that you forgot about a very dangerous bull and could have been killed.

And afterwards, when you were telling me about the stranger, you said you had felt "cherished". That's a very unusual word for you. You are much more likely to insist on your independence. You must have felt the need of comfort quite badly. Tell me, Emily—what did Mrs Gosworth say to upset you so?' When Emily said nothing she went on, 'Was it about me? Did she suggest that your reputation had suffered because of your relationship to me? I must say, I thought Philip had put a stop to such talk when he saw her earlier this year.'

'No, it was nothing like that.'

'Perhaps she tried to suggest that you were unlikely to find a husband? That's a favourite ploy of hers to any girl over the age of twenty.'

Emily said bitterly, 'On the contrary. She suggested that I ought to marry as soon as possible. It shouldn't be too difficult, she said, to find a husband for someone with a fortune like mine, even if they have little else to recommend them.'

Rosa was as angry as Emily had ever seen her. She said something under her breath, walked on a few paces, then exclaimed, 'That woman is poisonous. She should have been chased out of the neighbourhood years ago! Little wonder that her own family refuses to go near her. Why the county continues to receive her I do not know! Emily, she is not worth a second thought.'

Emily did not reply for a minute. Then she said quietly, 'But it's true, isn't? I learned that before I was twenty from the man I had been about to marry. I had thought we loved each other, but he only loved my fortune. I heard him say it. "Of course I'm not in love with her, Caroline," he said. "You know I love you. But I need her money. Good lord, why else would a man tie himself to a cool fish like Emily Winbolt? I'd sooner go to bed with a block of ice." It was quite a shock.' Emily gave a bitter little smile and went on, 'He was furious when I called the engagement off.'

Rosa put her hands on Emily's shoulders and shook her. 'I didn't know the young man, it was before I knew you, but you were well rid of him. He could never have made you happy. Emily, you are an intelligent, caring person with a delightful sense of humour. The sort of man you could love would have to be someone special. And he would be proud to have you as a wife.'

'Where will he be found? I've met many men since, but never one I wanted for a husband. Most of them found my fortune more important than I was. I've never fallen in love again, never felt the least stirring of desire for any one of them. Half the time they didn't understand what I was talking about. Even if they had cared. And very few men appreciate what you call my "delightful sense of humour".'

'Very few men see it. You are always too guarded.'

'I've learned to be wary. To tell the truth, I doubt now that I shall ever marry.' She looked at Rosa with the beginning of a smile. 'And do you know? This will probably shock you, but I have to confess it. I didn't feel like a cool fish yesterday. That stranger's kisses were far more exciting than any I've known before. They stirred me more than Harry Colesworth's ever did. Isn't that scandalous?' She laughed. 'Don't look so worried, Rosa dear. I know I couldn't marry the man—he was little more than a vagabond. Certainly no one a respectable spinster like me could ever consider as a husband! No, I don't think I shall marry, whatever Mrs Gosworth says.' She paused, and then said hesitantly, 'In fact, I have a different plan for the future. You could help me with it, if you would.'

'Of course I will,' said Rosa. 'But what is it?'

'If Philip agreed, I should like most of all to set up house on my own. Near at hand, of course. You could help me to persuade him.'

Rosa was deeply shocked. She turned on Emily. 'What a dreadful idea! I won't do anything of the sort. I wouldn't be at all happy with such an arrangement and neither would Philip. This is your home, Emily, and the only good reason for you to leave it would be with a man who loves you and wants to marry you.' She stopped short, and continued more slowly, her voice revealing how hurt she was, 'What have we done that you should prefer to live alone, however near at hand? I thought you loved us.'

Emily sighed inwardly and wished she had said nothing. It was just as she had foreseen. And Philip's reaction would be just the same. How could she explain to two of the people she loved best in the world that she often felt lonely in their company, often felt like an outsider, a hanger-on, however kindly they treated her? She loved them, enjoyed their company, and would always want to spend time with them. But she would never be really content until she was mistress of her own establishment, creating a garden again, planning improvements. In that way she would feel independent enough to spend as much time as she wanted with them, without feeling she was intruding on their idyll. They were so happy together. She sighed again. They would never understand. It was an impossible dream.

Meanwhile Emily's stranger had arrived at Thirle, where he was staying with Lady Deardon, his godmother.

'Really, William, you are a disgrace! What the servants think of you I cannot imagine.'

'Good God, ma'am, since when have we had to worry what the servants think? You don't pay 'em to think!'

Lady Deardon tapped her stick impatiently. 'Your life in South America has spoilt you, my boy. Mark my words, you'll soon change your tune when you have an establishment of your own to run here in England. Good servants are to be treasured. Your man arrived some time ago with your baggage. I cannot for the life of me call him your valet. Anyone less like a gentleman's gentleman would be difficult to imagine. But I suppose he knows what to do. Do go and put some respectable clothes on before Reggie sees you. You know what a stickler he is, and he'll be back for dinner soon. Then you can tell me your news.'

'There isn't much,' William said briefly, as he went out. 'I haven't seen anything I'd call really suitable.'

Emily would not have recognised him when he at last came downstairs again. Not only had he washed and shaved, but everything about him, from his carefully brushed hair to his gleaming evening shoes, his immaculate shirt and perfectly tied cravat, his beautifully fitted coat of blue superfine and snowy white pantaloons, pronounced him to be a gentleman of some distinction.

'I must say you scrub up well,' said Lady Deardon. 'Why you choose to wander about the countryside like a tramp I cannot imagine. Reggie has just arrived. He's dressing now, so there's time for us to have a talk. Have you heard anything more about the children?'

'The latest news is that they will stay in Jamaica with

the Warburtons until they can all come to England some time in the autumn.'

'Who are these Warburtons?'

'Good friends of mine from my days in the Navy. When John died so unexpectedly, they took the children in.'

'Poor little things. I take it that Juana's family still refuse to have anything to do with them?'

'When Juana ran off with my brother, the Lopez family didn't simply refuse to acknowledge her marriage to him, they cut her out of their lives completely. The children don't exist as far as they are concerned. Juana's family will never relent, even though her children are now orphans.'

'So they are your responsibility. What are you going to do?'

'What else can I do but find somewhere to live and make it into a suitable home for us all? The children are safe enough for the moment, but it's hard to say what effect the events of the past year have had on them. It will be better when we are all together in a house of our own.'

'Have you found anything?'

'There's only one possibility in the district. I came across it today. Charlwood. It's a handsome estate not too far from here, and the land is in good heart. The house itself looks ruinous, but it could be rescued. It is basically sound and it has plenty of rooms. The gardens and park have real potential, too. They've obviously been laid out by a master hand. I liked it.'

'So it's for sale? I know Charlwood quite well. It was once a lovely place, but there was some sort of dispute over ownership when the old man died, and it's been empty for years.'

'That's the drawback—the whole place has been neglected too long. It would be months before the house was habitable. A year even.'

'It's in a beautiful situation, William. It sounds as if it could be just what you're looking for.'

'It certainly came close. But the children will need to settle down as soon as possible after they arrive here.'

'It's a wife you need, if you're to look after those children properly. Have you thought of that? A mother for them is more important than four walls and a roof.'

'I know, I know. I haven't the slightest wish to marry, but I suppose I must. To be honest, it's a devil of a mess.'

'Bringing up two orphans won't be easy. They need a mother and you haven't even found a wife yet! It isn't every woman who would be willing to take on a ready-made family such as that.'

'Since they are the only reason I would even consider marrying, any wife of mine will have to accept them. John was my brother and his children are now my responsibility. There's no alternative.'

'Well, if you do wish to hold on to them you must find a decent, well-bred young woman and marry her! That is far more important than any house.'

'How the devil can I ask anyone to marry me when I haven't a home to offer her? What should I say to her? "Madam, you can have my heart, my name and two orphaned children, but, alas, we shall have to live in a field!" I can't see any sensible woman accepting such an offer, can you?'

'Don't be ridiculous, William! Of course she wouldn't. But now I come to think of it, there's a very pretty Dower House at Charlwood. Is it included in the sale?'

'Yes.'

'Well, then, you and your family could live there until the main house is ready. I know it's a little small—'

'Extremely so. That was why I have almost decided not to consider it.'

'Is it as much of a ruin as the main house?'

'No, a few months' work would put it in order.'

'It could surely house you all till Charlwood itself is ready to receive you.'

'I suppose it could—if it could be made ready in time…'

'Reggie and I are going up north at the end of October, but you could all stay with us till then if it wasn't quite ready for you. There, that's settled. Here comes Reggie. We shall go in to dinner.'

Later that evening Lady Deardon returned to the question of a suitable wife for her godson. 'I've been thinking over dinner how to set about finding you a wife, William. It is essential you find one before long. I don't imagine a débutante would suit you?'

'Not at all! The ones I've met since coming back to England seem to me to be remarkably silly. They don't appear to understand what I'm talking about half the time.'

'As I thought—you need someone older.'

'Preferably intelligent. And, if possible, with a sense of humour.'

'Aren't you being a little too particular for a man in such desperate straits? I suppose you'll tell me next that you're looking for a woman with a fortune, too!'

'The very thing!' exclaimed her godson with a grin. 'A rich widow would be best of all! Putting Charlwood in order will cost a mint of money, and now there's the additional expense of the Dower House. I shall certainly need a rich wife!'

'My dear boy, you may not find it so easy. Rich young women who are looking for a husband do not grow on trees.'

William was visited by a sudden vision of the young woman he *had* found in a tree. Warm, responsive, breathtakingly passionate… Rich or poor, in her teens or in her thirties, he was most unlikely to find anyone among the ladies of polite society nearly as exciting as his wild girl of the tree…

'William!'

With an effort he put the girl firmly out of his mind and said cheerfully, 'I shan't give up hope yet. There must be someone somewhere.'

'You talk as if any woman would do! Have you no feelings in the matter? No heart?'

'Any heart I had was battered out of me years ago, ma'am. No, I want someone whose company I find tolerable and who will care for the children. Affairs of the heart have nothing to do with marriage. A congenial partner is what I want, and if she is rich, so much the better.'

'You are trying to shock me again. You always were a tease.'

'I meant every word. Meanwhile, I shall have another look at Charlwood.'

Chapter Three

William's casual air was deceptive. Before another day was over he had inspected Charlwood again and made up his mind. Underneath its ruinous appearance was a spacious, beautifully proportioned house which could in time be made into just the sort of family home he was looking for. Meanwhile, with a few alterations, the Dower House could house them all quite adequately. He set about buying the estate with the energy and efficiency which had served him well in South America. It was an odd coincidence that, soon after the negotiations were complete, William's lawyers were approached by another buyer, who was apparently equally eager to possess Charlwood, and was offering more than William had paid for it. But William refused the offer without hesitation. Charlwood was to be his—it was the perfect place for him and his family.

One evening Lady Deardon told him that she had met a certain Mrs Gosworth when visiting an acquaintance. 'She lives nearby in a small village called Stoke Shearings. Have you come across it?'

'I spent a night at the inn there not long ago.' William smiled reminiscently, visited once again by the memory of a woman with silver-grey eyes and tumbling hair, long, bare legs and slender ankles. She had looked like a gipsy, and had behaved like one, too. As he remembered the passion he had aroused in her, his blood stirred again... A wanton, a tease, she might be, but he still hadn't forgotten her.

'William...William, why do you keep going off into a trance when I am speaking to you? Don't you want to hear what I have to tell you?'

He returned to the present. 'Forgive me, I was thinking... thinking of...of something else.'

'Well, whatever it is, forget it for the moment. This is more important. After talking to Mrs Gosworth, I think I've found a possible wife for you! There!' Lady Deardon looked so complacent that William felt impelled to say solemnly,

'I've heard of the lady. She's in her sixties, and a harridan to boot. You're very kind, but I don't think she would do for me.'

Lady Deardon gave a laugh. 'Don't be such a tease, Will. Of course I don't mean her! I thought she was a most unpleasant woman. But she talked of someone who sounds perfect. A Miss Winbolt. Not in her first youth, and unhappy at the change in her circumstances. She lives with her brother and his wife in the big house in Stoke Shearings. It belongs to the Winbolt family. You didn't happen to call on them when you were in the area, did you?'

'No, that was the day I got lost, and when I got

back to the inn that evening it was too late for a social call.'

'Shearings itself is a beautiful place, apparently. It has some superb gardens. From what Mrs Gosworth says, Miss Winbolt kept house for her brother for years, but last January he married a rather unsuitable woman and brought her home to Shearings.'

'Unsuitable? What did she mean by unsuitable?'

'Rosa Winbolt had been married before. Her husband apparently belonged to a raffish lot in London, and died in suspicious circumstances.'

William shook his head at his hostess. 'My dear ma'am, I hope you haven't been paying too much attention to Mrs Gosworth. The new Mrs Winbolt may have once lived in London, but she comes from a highly respected local family and is very well liked in the neighbourhood. I've heard nothing but good of her.'

'Really? So the trouble may lie with Emily Winbolt herself? Mrs Gosworth did say she was a rather strong-minded young woman. It could be that the new bride wants to take over the running of the house and Miss Winbolt finds it difficult to step down. According to Mrs Gosworth, she is past her first youth and rather plain, so she can see that her chances of finding a husband are fading. She might well consider marriage as a means of having a household of her own.'

'And you think I might be her saviour? I'm not sure I like the sound of that.'

Lady Deardon looked disappointed. 'Really, William, you can't be as eager as I thought to find a mother for those children. Here is a respectable young woman with every reason to want a husband, a real possibility, and you say you don't like the sound of her! You haven't even met the lady! She certainly isn't the sort of empty-headed débutante you despise.'

'No, but I would think twice before saddling myself with a plain, strong-minded spinster of uncertain age. It seems to me that would be a recipe for unhappiness.'

'Well, why don't you wait till you see her? She might surprise you. The Winbolts are bound to be at the Langley House ball at the end of the month, so you could meet her there.'

'Very well—but I make no promises!'

'I don't ask you to.' Nettled by his lack of appreciation of her discovery, Lady Deardon added, 'After all, Miss Winbolt may not approve of *you* when she sees you! She is said to be pretty cool in her attitude to men.'

'Worse and worse! Strong-minded, plain, and now cold-hearted, too! Your poor Miss Winbolt sounds to me like someone born to remain a spinster.'

'Not *my* Miss Winbolt, William. And not *poor* Miss Winbolt, either. I saved the best till last. She has a considerable fortune of her own!'

'Really? And she hasn't found a husband for herself all these years? What an antidote she must be!'

'William!'

'There must be *something* wrong with her, ma'am.'

Lady Deardon laughed and gave up. 'Very well, I can see you are not to be persuaded. We shall say no more about Miss Winbolt.'

Lady Deardon did not give up her quest entirely. Not much later she greeted William triumphantly with the news that she had found another possible wife for him.

'She has only been a few months in the neighbourhood, so I met her for the first time today. I found her quite charming. I promise you, William, if you are as hard to please about this lady as you were with Miss Winbolt, I shall wash my hands of you. Her name is Mrs Fenton and she is exactly what you wanted—a rich young widow. Her husband died just over a year ago. She lived round here when she was a girl and has now moved back again. I'm sure you would like her. I thought I might invite her to dinner one evening.'

'Please do. She sounds more promising than Miss Winbolt. I should be delighted to meet her.'

Mrs Fenton came to dinner. In her early thirties, beautiful, poised and witty, she was just as attractive as Lady Deardon had said. William was definitely intrigued and when he heard that she, too, was to be at the ball at Langley House, he begged the lady to reserve a dance for him.

Meanwhile Emily was suffering the aftereffect of her confession to Rosa. Garden parties became a frequent diversion at Shearings, and as time went on the house saw a succession of riding parties, evening parties, and weekend parties to which Philip's former Army friends were invited, along with the more respectable of Rosa's London circle. Plans were in hand, too, to spend the next year's Season in London. Rosa, anxious to stop her sister-in-law from taking the disastrous step of living alone, had evidently decided that the best solution would be to find a husband for her as soon as possible. Emily watched all the activity, ordered some new dresses and resigned herself to waiting patiently until her loving family realised that she had made up her mind. Sooner or later she would find a comfortable house surrounded by a small park and spend the rest of her days there with a respectable female for company. Meanwhile she would watch the scene before her with her usual calm, slightly ironic, eye.

Of course, invitations were returned, among them an invitation to the ball at Langley House. Rosa was quite excited at the prospect, and as they drove to Langley on the evening of the ball the conversation in the Winbolts' carriage was of the distinguished guests they would find there.

'The Langleys have such a wide circle of acquaintances. Maria Fenton is back in the district and will almost certainly be there now that she is out of official mourning. I shall be interested to meet her again. I knew her when I was a girl, Emily. She was a few years older than I was, but she was so lovely that you couldn't help but notice her. I wonder if she changed after her marriage.'

'I shouldn't be surprised,' said Philip. 'Edric Fenton was a strange man. Who else is coming?'

'The Deardons will be there, and I expect they'll bring a guest of theirs, Sir William Ashenden. They are almost bound to include him in their party. Apparently he has just bought Charlwood.'

'I can't imagine what possessed Ashenden to buy that place. Does he know how much it will cost to put in order? A retired naval officer would need something other than his pay to make it habitable,' said Philip.

Rosa had other matters on her mind. 'I wonder how old he is…and if he is married,' she said thoughtfully.

The ball was well under way by the time the party from Shearings arrived. The ladies left their cloaks in a small room set aside for the purpose, then Philip escorted them to the ballroom, where Lady Langley greeted them warmly, 'You've known most of the people here since you were a child, Rosa, dear. But perhaps you haven't met Lady Deardon? Her table is in the far corner. I shall take you to meet her.' She added with an arch smile at Emily, 'Lady Deardon's visitor is with her. I'm sure Miss Winbolt would like to meet him. Such a distinguished man…'

So Rosa's efforts to marry her off had not gone unnoticed in the neighbourhood, thought Emily grimly. The idea was so unwelcome that, though she smiled and made a suitable reply, her manner as they were taken down the room to be introduced was distinctly frosty. Lady Deardon regarded Emily with interest, but then turned to Philip and Rosa to say she was alone for the moment, but hoped they would wait till the rest of her party returned. They agreed with pleasure and sat down. Emily gazed round.

Further down the room a gentleman, tall, lithe and assured, was leading a strikingly attractive woman on to the floor. He was smiling as he bent his head to hear what his companion was saying. Little wrinkles fanned out from the corners of his eyes… Emily's heart missed a beat. For a moment she was frozen. It couldn't be! It couldn't possibly be! She was imagining things. The likeness was purely accidental. It couldn't be Will. Will was a carelessly dressed, carelessly mannered wanderer. He wouldn't be a guest of one of the neighbourhood's most stiff-necked families, dancing with one of its most beautiful women. Of course he wouldn't! She sat for a moment telling herself to be sensible, to stay calm. But she found it quite impossible. The shock had been too great, and the ballroom was suddenly unbearably hot—she needed air, somewhere to recover. Slipping

her fan into the arrangement of flowers behind her, she
exclaimed, 'How foolish of me! I seem to have left my
fan in the pocket of my cloak. Please excuse me while I
fetch it.' And without waiting for any offers of help she
got up and made her way as calmly as she could out of
the ballroom.

But once outside she fled to the small boudoir which
had been set aside for ladies, where she sat down and
requested a glass of water. She was trembling. The man
in the ballroom couldn't possibly be Will. It was a delu-
sion. His face had haunted her dreams for weeks, and
now she was beginning to imagine it when she was
awake! That must be it. It wasn't Will, it wasn't…! She
grew cold. But what if it was? Her throat felt dry and
she took the proffered glass gratefully. After taking
several sips of water, she calmed down again and began
to reason sensibly. How could someone who was little
more than a vagabond find his way into a house belong-
ing to the Langleys who were one of the county's highest
sticklers? It was impossible. Of course it was! She must
have imagined the resemblance.

Rosa came into the room. 'Have you found your fan?
I was sure you had it with you…Emily, is there some-
thing wrong?' She took a closer look at her sister-in-law.
'Are you feeling the thing? You look a little pale.'

'I…I felt the heat for a moment. It's better now.
No, I haven't found it yet. Perhaps I dropped it in the
ballroom.'

'We'll look for it when we go back. If you're ready,
I want you to come with me to meet the gentleman
with Lady Deardon. Philip and I have been talking to
him while you were in here and I think he could be
the very man for you! He is just as distinguished as
Lady Langley said—tall, very well dressed, with such

a cultivated, intelligent air. I suspect he has a sense of humour, too. I know you will like him. I can tell Philip does. Do come.'

Emily sighed. Another candidate to save me from my doom, she thought. This time it's an elderly naval officer. How tired I am of meeting 'just the man' for me. In the last few months, ever since I told Rosa of my wish to live alone, I have been introduced to a knight, two baronets, an admiral and what seems like every possible rank of the Army from an ensign to a brigadier... And when we're in London Rosa will no doubt find distinguished men of letters, artists, poets, diplomats, any one of whom might be 'just the man for me'... I shall die of a surfeit of suitors! The thought amused her. She was even smiling as she accompanied Rosa back to the ballroom.

But at the door she paused and took a cautious look round. There were plenty of tall gentlemen, but no one who looked remotely like Will. Her imagination had been playing tricks on her. Sighing with relief, Emily followed Rosa to Lady Deardon's table.

Philip was there, in conversation with a tall, grey-haired gentleman. My goodness, thought Emily, Rosa must be getting desperate. This one is even older than the brigadier! But she smiled charmingly as she curtsied to Lady Deardon, who turned to the gentleman next to her and said, 'My husband, Sir Reginald Deardon, Miss Winbolt.'

Sir Reginald Deardon! The lady's husband! Emily had difficulty in suppressing a broad grin at her own mistake. Perhaps Rosa was not as desperate as she had feared! They exchanged a few words, then Lady Deardon said, 'My godson will be here shortly, Mrs Winbolt. He has just gone to invite Mrs Fenton to join us for a moment. I believe you wanted to talk to her. Here they come.'

Emily regarded at the couple slowly advancing towards them with horrified fascination. They made a striking pair. Mrs Fenton had pale gold hair and very light china-blue eyes. Her black dress was the very latest in fashion, her diamonds magnificent, and she walked up the room with conscious grace, seemingly indifferent to the many admiring glances cast in her direction. Emily's eyes turned to the gentleman at her side, still hoping for a miracle. Perhaps she had been mistaken, perhaps it was just an extraordinary resemblance. But her heart sank as she looked. It was a nightmare. The gentleman... She swallowed. Lady Deardon's famous guest was tall, lithe and perfectly assured, completely at home in this gathering of the neighbourhood's highest society. He was dressed in beautifully tailored evening clothes, immaculate linen, and had a diamond pin in the snowy folds of his cravat. But he was unmistakeably the man who had rescued her from the tree. Will... William... *Sir William Ashenden*.

The pair drew near. It was certainly Will. No one else could have the same lurking amusement in such dark blue eyes, the same fan of laughter lines at the corners... Her knees grew weak at an unbidden memory of that broad chest under her cheek, the feel of those long legs wrapped round hers, the sensations aroused by his kisses. She suppressed a faint gasp and clutched the back of the chair for support as a mixture of fear and this unfamiliar but powerful feeling almost undid her. Keeping her eyes lowered and her feelings tightly under control, she stiffly acknowledged the introductions that followed. Eventually she made herself look up. His eyes were amused, but she could perceive no sign of recognition in them. She took courage. Why should he recognise her? Who would connect the well-dressed, highly respectable Miss Emily Winbolt with the untidy, bare-legged hoyden, the hussy who had responded to his kisses with such a lack of restraint? She had a reputation for coolness. On this occasion she would make very sure she lived up to it. She had to!

Mrs Fenton's china-blue eyes had swept over Emily with indifference, but she talked animatedly to Rosa for a moment or two, eyed Philip with lazy interest, then, after receiving an invitation to visit Shearings and thanking them all for their kindness, she excused herself.

'I hope Sir William will see me safely back to my table,' she said, waving her fan at him with a smile.

'At a price, Mrs Fenton,' he said. 'On condition that you will dance this waltz with me first.'

'You drive a hard bargain, sir,' she said with a delicious pout. 'But I am in your hands.'

He laughed and offered her his arm to lead her on to the floor.

Emily would have been hard put to it to describe her feelings. Overwhelming relief, certainly. Sir William Ashenden had clearly not recognised her. But mixed with relief there was another less easily defined feeling... What was it? She watched the two dance up the room and decided that she disliked Mrs Fenton. The woman was too confident of her power, too obviously charming. And far too beautiful. Sir William was looking down at her with such admiration in his eyes... With a gasp she pulled herself together again. She should be thanking her stars that 'her Will' had not recognised her, not be envious of his attentions to Mrs Fenton!

* * *

After the waltz was over William returned Mrs Fenton to her companions and rejoined his godmother. He had enjoyed Maria Fenton's company, and looked forward to more of it in the future. He was by no means sure, however, that she was what he was looking for in a wife. He had met many such women in his travels, graceful, accomplished, with a gift for amusing conversation. But he was looking for more genuine warmth in the woman he would marry, someone who could not only charm his neighbours at balls and soirées, but would create an affectionate home for his orphans as well. He might be doing the lady an injustice, but he suspected kindness to children would not be a priority with Maria Fenton.

He turned his attention to his godmother's other choice. Miss Winbolt. At first sight she lacked any kind of warmth. Indeed, her manner was distinctly chilly. But she was hardly the woman Mrs Gosworth had described. She couldn't be more than four or five and twenty and, far from being jealous of her sister-in-law, their affection for each other was clear. A bit of an enigma then, Miss Winbolt. Perhaps he should make an effort to know her better, if only to please his godmother.

The Winbolts had moved on and were engaged in conversation with a group of friends nearby. Emily Winbolt was standing slightly to one side, talking to Rosa and one of the gentlemen. William examined her from a distance. It was true—compared with her sister-in-law she seemed almost plain. Her hair was drawn back into a neat knot at the back of her head, and though her dress was obviously a London creation, its severity did little to enhance her looks. But her profile had a purity of line that was attractive. And from what he could see, she had quite a good figure… At that point something someone had said amused her and she laughed. William was astonished at the difference it made in her. It was a delightfully deep laugh, full of warmth and genuine enjoyment, and he was visited by a strange feeling that he had met this woman before. She turned as he approached and the laughter died abruptly. He could even have sworn he saw a fleeting expression of alarm in her eyes before she lowered them. But when she looked up again Miss Winbolt was once more the woman who had been described to him. Her eyes contained nothing but chilly indifference. Undeterred, he went up to her and bowed.

'Miss Winbolt, I know so few ladies here tonight. Dare I request a dance with you?'

The orchestra was warming up for the next set of dances. Miss Winbolt stared at him. He thought for a moment she would refuse, but her sister-in-law said,

'Be kind to Sir William, Emily. He is to be one of our neighbours soon. Isn't that so, Sir William?'

'N…neighbours?' Miss Winbolt was pale.

'Charlwood, Miss Winbolt.' He offered his arm. 'Shall we? Or shall we look for some refreshment and have a talk about Charlwood?'

'Oh, no!' she exclaimed and put her hand on his arm. He was surprised to feel it trembling and felt a sudden, powerful urge to protect her. But from what? What was Miss Winbolt so afraid of?

He was still puzzled as they took to the floor. The urge to comfort persisted, though their conversation when they talked at all was conventional to the point of inanity. She danced well but stiffly, keeping her distance and giving him only the very tips of her fingers to hold when it was needed. By the end of the set he was ready to concede that his first thought had been right, after all—Miss Winbolt was a born spinster.

When the music came to an end William took his partner to the edge of the floor, ready, and indeed relieved, to deliver her back to her family. Then something happened that caused him to change his mind yet again, this time irreversibly.

The behaviour of some of the younger guests had become rather boisterous. And one of them, eager to reach the refreshment tables before his friend, charged into Miss Winbolt. Taken by surprise, she lost her balance and would have fallen, but William caught her. She clung to him for a moment and again he was assailed with a sense of familiarity. Everything about her was familiar, but more than that, it was exciting—the way she held him, the sensation of her body against his, even the scent of her hair. He pulled her closer. The desire to kiss her was almost irresistible…

'Sir William!' Her voice was muffled against his chest. 'You must let me go! Immediately! Please.' She looked up at him. The look of desperation on her face, in her silver-grey eyes, brought him to his senses.

He stood back and shook his head, feeling more confused and embarrassed than he had for years. What had he been thinking of? 'Miss Winbolt, I'm sorry. I…I hardly know what to say. I don't know what happened. That fellow…'

'Yes, yes. He was to blame.' She turned away quickly and started towards the doors.

'Miss Winbolt—'

'Please. It was an accident. I was shaken. That was why I held on to you so tightly. I'm sorry if I embarrassed you.'

'No, no! You re mistaken—'

Without looking, she interrupted him. 'You must excuse me. I think I've torn the hem of my dress. I must put it right.' She fled through the doors and he saw her make for the ladies' boudoir.

It was some time before she reappeared, but William was still deep in thought. She started nervously when she saw him, but took his proffered arm and they began to make their way back into the ballroom. But after a few yards William stopped and turned. 'I must make sure you have forgiven me,' he said.

'For what, Sir William?' she said stiffly, without turning her head. 'It was not your fault Edgar Langley knocked me over. You saved me from falling.'

He would have tried again, but she interrupted him as she had before. 'Pray say no more,' she said impatiently. 'It really isn't necessary. I would rather forget the incident. And now I should like to rejoin my brother. He must be wondering where I am.'

She walked away without another word. William was left a prey to an impossible mixture of thoughts and conjectures.

He was so silent on the way back to Thirle that Lady Deardon asked him if he was not feeling well. When he assured her he was perfectly fit she went on,

'What did you think of our two ladies? You couldn't have a greater contrast between the two. Mrs Fenton is almost as lovely in her way as Rosa Winbolt, though older, of course. That dress must have cost a pretty penny, and her diamonds...! She certainly put herself out to charm you, William. Do you like her?'

'Very well. She is good company.'

'I don't fancy the friends she had with her,' said Sir Reginald unexpectedly. 'Not quite county.'

'I didn't see them, but you are always too much of a stickler, Reggie. I dare say they were friends of her husband. But, William, what about Emily Winbolt? I confess I don't know what to think of her. That dress probably cost every bit as much as Maria Fenton's, but it didn't do half as much for her. She was altogether very plainly dressed.'

'Ladylike,' said Sir Reginald. 'She looked a lady. More than the other one.'

Lady Deardon ignored this comment. 'She's not as old as Mrs Gosworth led me to believe, and the story about her sister-in-law is obviously nonsense. Their affection for each other is plain. But she is definitely cool in her manner.' Lady Deardon looked sharply at her godson. 'William! Have you heard a word I've said? What do you think of Miss Winbolt?'

'I'm not at all sure,' said William slowly. 'But I intend to find out. Did I hear Mrs Winbolt issue you with an invitation to visit Shearings?'

'Yes, I asked her about its famous gardens and said how much I wanted to see them. We have arranged to go next week.' Sir Reginald stirred restlessly. 'You needn't come, Reggie. William will escort me, won't you, dear?'

'I certainly will,' said her godson. 'I would very much like to have a closer look at…the gardens.'

Chapter Four

Emily was equally silent on her way home in the Winbolt carriage, though this was not noticed as quickly. Rosa was full of the ball and its guests. 'Maria Fenton is as lovely as ever,' she said. 'But I was disappointed in our conversation. She didn't seem to be very interested.'

'My lovely, sweetest Rosabelle,' said her husband. 'It was obvious to everyone but you that Mrs Fenton's eye was on William Ashenden. The beautiful Maria wouldn't waste much time on another woman, however old a friend she is.'

'Oh!' said Rosa. She sounded disconcerted. 'I thought…I thought Sir William seemed quite taken with Emily. He was certainly attentive enough later on.'

'No! He wasn't! He can't have been!' Emily said this with such force that both Philip and Rosa regarded her with astonishment. 'I mean…' She faltered. 'I mean we only danced once.'

'Well, you may not have noticed, but he hardly took his eyes off you after that one dance. Emily, what is wrong?

Why do you find the idea that he was interested in you so distressing? I would have said he was exactly the sort of gentleman who would appeal to you. You haven't taken a dislike to him, have you? I do hope not. We are to see quite a bit of Sir William and the Deardons in the near future.'

'We are?' said Emily apprehensively. Her heart sank. How long could she avoid being recognised? She was very much afraid that William Ashenden was too intelligent a man to be deceived for ever. Sooner or later she would say or do something to remind him, and she didn't like to think of what he might do then. Added to that was this strange power he seemed to have over her. Tonight, she had lost her balance in more ways than one. When she fell against him she had had to fight an overwhelming urge to hold him even closer, to rest her head against him even longer, to hold her head up for his kiss. It had taken every ounce of determination she possessed to stand away. He must have wondered what had come over her. He had certainly been surprised and embarrassed. She sighed. She was just as strongly attracted to him as Rosa could wish. If only she had met him for the first time at Lady Langley's ball, she might have found someone she could learn to love. But that was now out of the question. She could never relax with him, be herself. It would be too dangerous. When she caught herself sighing again, she told herself to be sensible. It wouldn't have done much good anyway. Sir William Ashenden was interested in Maria Fenton, a far lovelier woman than she could ever be. Meanwhile she was living with a sword over her head. How long would it be before it fell?

Emily's worst fears were in the process of being realised. William's suspicions were already stirring, more because of his own astonishing reactions to her than anything she herself had said or done. He had been surprised at the strength of the desire he had felt for the girl in the hollow and had been quite unable to forget her. For a man who prided himself on his self-control, this was bad enough, but now, within a space of weeks, he had experienced the same degree of desire, this time in the highly civilised atmosphere of a ballroom. And not with a practised charmer like Maria Fenton, but with Miss Emily Winbolt, of all people! He had come damned close to kissing the girl in public! But on think-ing it over later, he realised how very odd *her* reaction had been. Far from being angry with him for holding her longer and more closely than strictly necessary, *she* had apologised to *him!* Why? Why had she felt the need to apologise? Miss Winbolt was indeed the enigma he had thought her.

He lay awake that night, still puzzling over her behaviour. The more he thought about it, the stranger it appeared—and not only after that dance either, but throughout the evening. Coolness might have been expected—after all, there was no reason why she should look more kindly on him than on anyone else. But fear? That was the emotion he had seen in her eyes before she had looked away, and her hand had trembled when it rested on his arm. Why? And why had so much about her seemed familiar when he had held her in his arms— her touch, the scent of her hair, her eyes…silver-grey eyes… Those eyes were her outstanding feature—clear silver grey, like the water in the stream which ran along the valley in Stoke Shearings.

The girl in the hollow just above the stream had such eyes, too…silver-grey… A thought came into his head at that point which appeared to be so completely fantastic that he began to wonder whether his obsession with the girl in the hollow was affecting his mind. It was impossible to believe that Emily Winbolt and that girl were one and the same... No, it was quite impossible!

But as the night wore on the idea began to seem no longer quite so absurd. It would explain a lot—her alarm at meeting him tonight, her reluctance to talk to him, the strange sense of familiarity... Was it because he *had* met her before tonight? Had held her in his arms before? Shearings, where the Winbolts lived, was not far from the spot where he had rescued the girl from the tree, and she had run in that direction. Could it possibly be true? If it were...

William started to smile. What a situation that would be! Emily Winbolt, born spinster, society's model of rectitude, abandoning herself to making love with a stranger in the fields! What a hypocrite that would make her! He lay for some time thinking about the two women, and fell asleep at last still trying to reconcile what he knew of them.

William had an important appointment the next morning with his architect at Charlwood. But after his sleepless night he had decided to look first at the spot where he had met the girl who had haunted him. He rose early, and instead of setting off towards Charlwood he made for Stoke Shearings. He left his horse once again at the inn and followed the path alongside the stream. The water was as clear as he remembered, the slope above it just as steep. The hedge and even the oak tree where he had first caught sight of her soon came into view. He climbed up the slope and stood beside the oak. Someone had cleared away the broken branch and tidied up the hedge, but it was unmistakeably the spot.

'You're not thinking of climbing through that there hedge, are yer, sir?' William looked down. A man was standing on the path below, shaking his head. He went on, 'I don't advise it. It'd be the last short cut yer'd take. There's a vicious animal in the field on t'other side.'

'Really?'

'Black Samson, Farmer Pritchard's bull. A dangerous beast, if ever there was one.'

'Thanks for the warning,' William said. 'I'll take note. And you are…?'

'Will Darby, at your service, sir. I work close by for Mr Winbolt.' He clambered up the slope and went on, 'I could tell you a tale or two about that bull, I could. Job Diment. Elias Carter, they'm both still laid up after 'e attacked 'em. Not worked for weeks and weeks, they 'asn't. Why, it's not long since Mr Winbolt's own sister barely got away with her life. Don't go near 'um!'

'I certainly shan't. Miss Winbolt, you say?'

'Aye, sir. You'm be looking at the very spot where she escaped. Leastways, that's what Mr Winbolt said when he told us to mend the hedge just where we're standing. Lucky, that's what she was. With the branch giving way under 'er and all.' He looked curiously at William. 'Be you bound fer Shearings, sir?'

''Er, no. Not today. I'm going in the other direction. Well, thank you, Will.' They clambered down the slope together and William slipped a coin into Will Darby's hand. 'I'll be on my way—and I'll take your advice and go the long way round!'

To William's relief Will Darby gave him a toothless grin, touched his cap, and set off without asking any more questions. He had no desire to lie to the man, but nor did he wish to explain what he was doing in that quiet spot at such a very early hour.

* * *

William Ashenden suffered from an over-developed sense of humour and a strong sense of the ridiculous. His friends frequently told him that his major fault was a desire to tease. The situation he was in the process of uncovering was so perfectly bizarre, so exactly to his taste that, as he rode on to Charlwood, a bubble of mirth was growing inside him. He was hard put to it not to laugh out loud. Ice-cool Emily Winbolt and his passionate seductress—what an unlikely combination! Soberly dressed Emily Winbolt and a raggle-taggle, bare-legged gipsy girl—what a contrast! Oh, yes! The alarm in Miss Winbolt's eyes, her fear of him, were both now perfectly understandable. Indeed, she must be worried out of her skin lest he should recognise her and tell the world what she had been up to. His grin broadened. What fun he would have with her! The little cheat deserved a bit of teasing before he put her out of her misery.

For a moment he paused. *Did* she deserve it? Was she in the habit of finding secret pleasure with strangers? Or was she indeed a respectable woman who had been under the same spell as he had been that day, unable to resist, swept up by some mysterious force? For a moment he hesitated, but then shrugged his shoulders. It wouldn't do her any lasting harm. Circumstances had forced him to be too serious lately—he felt in need of diversion. The problem of what to do with the children had been worrying. The question of a wife and a home, and the chores associated with renovating Charlwood, had been interesting, but not exactly amusing. A brief spell of teasing Miss Winbolt would provide some light relief. Not for long, though. He couldn't keep her in suspense for long. And, whatever happened, the affair would be strictly between himself and the lady. She might worry for a short while, but she would understand that the world outside would never learn from him what had happened between them one evening in May.

Rosa's invitation to the Deardons threw Emily into a panic. She realised that she would sooner or later have to meet William Ashenden again, but this seemed altogether too soon. During the intervening week she attempted to find a dozen reasons why she should not be present, but her sister-in-law frustrated them all. Rosa thoroughly approved of William Ashenden and knew Philip liked him, too. This was enough to persuade her that this was indeed 'just the man' to be Emily's salvation and she was determined to promote the acquaintance. She genuinely could not understand why Emily didn't agree, and was convinced that once her sister-in-law got to know Sir William better she would acknowledge that Rosa was right. She was disappointed, therefore, when Emily appeared just before Lady Deardon and Sir William were due to arrive.

'Emily! You have so many pretty summer dresses! Why on earth are you wearing that one?'

'What's wrong with it?'

'It's…it's so dull. And surely you'd be cooler in one that didn't fasten right up to the neck? Why didn't you wear your new pale green muslin? It's so pretty, and the colour suits you perfectly.'

'I've decided that it is cut too low, Rosa. I prefer this one.'

Rosa was not finished. 'And what have you done to your hair?' she exclaimed. 'It's more suited for a walk through a cloister than a summer afternoon in the garden!'

Emily, who had taken pains to make herself as unlike

the girl who had fallen out of that tree as possible, was pleased, but did her best to sound offended. 'I'm sorry you don't like the way I look,' she said. In fact, she agreed with Rosa's every word. Her dress was plain, in an unflattering shade of grey, and fastened up to the top. Much to her maid's distress, she had insisted on having her hair pulled back and twisted into a low, tight knot at the back of her neck. Fashionably thin sandals, her usual wear in summer, had been replaced with boots. Emily had decided not to give in without a fight. She would deceive William Ashenden for as long as she could, until she could decide how to deal with him. She heard the sound of a carriage drawing up at the door. 'But I'm afraid it's too late to change my dress now,' she said, doing her best to put a note of regret into her voice.

Philip and Rosa made their guests welcome, then led them into the garden. All five walked about in it for an hour or more, Emily using considerable ingenuity to avoid William's company. When Rosa suggested they should sit in the shade for a while Lady Deardon accepted with pleasure, and the party made its way to a cool arbour, which had been furnished with a table, chairs and one or two benches. Here they sat down—all of them except Sir William.

'You said something about an avenue of trees planted by your great-grandfather, I believe, Winbolt? I'd like to see them. Perhaps Miss Winbolt could show me the way and tell me about them?'

'What a good idea,' exclaimed Rosa. 'She knows almost as much about the grounds as my husband, Sir William. I'm sure she would be delighted to be your guide. And you must ask her to show you the maze.

The Shearings maze was once quite famous, but it was in a sad state before Philip and Emily restored it, along with the rest of the gardens.

'A maze? That sounds very interesting. Miss Winbolt?' He held out his arm.

Emily stared at him hopelessly. 'I...I don't think...' she began and then stopped. She couldn't come up with a single reason why she should refuse to go with him, except that she didn't want to!

'I do hope you can oblige him, Miss Winbolt,' said Lady Deardon. 'A large number of the trees at Charlwood are old and decayed, and will have to be replaced. William is becoming quite an expert on the subject. He has already inspected the plantations at Thirle. I'm sure he will find your avenue very interesting.'

Emily smiled weakly and took his arm. Sir William's request was harmless enough. To persist in refusing, especially after his godmother's encouraging words, would seem ungracious, and might well make him suspicious. But go into the maze with him she would not!

Once they were out of sight of the arbour Sir William stopped and asked, 'Is something upsetting you, ma'am? The sun, perhaps? Or are you tired? We could easily sit somewhere and talk, if you would prefer it.'

'No!' exclaimed Emily with more vigour than politeness. Her companion raised one eyebrow and regarded her with surprise. But she could have sworn there was more than a touch of laughter in his eyes.

'I mean...I like w-walking,' she stammered. She took a breath. This would never do. If she was to impress this man with the contrast between the gipsy in the hollow and Miss Emily Winbolt, she should watch her responses! They walked on in silence while Emily tried frantically to think of something to say. After a while she said with commendable calm, 'My sister-in-law tells me you were in the Navy. Have you seen much action?'

'When I first joined, yes. But the Navy is no place for a man in peacetime, Miss Winbolt. So I took the… bull by the horns and sold out.' Emily was startled. She almost stumbled. Had he meant anything by that pause in front of 'bull'? She stole a glance at him but he looked unconcerned, and she was reassured as he went on, 'I was in the West Indies at the time, so I went off to explore South America.'

'How interesting. Where did you go? Brazil?' To her relief the conversation that followed as they walked through the grounds was very conventional, mostly about his impressions of Mexico and Brazil. Emily began to relax.

But then he said, 'But we've talked enough about me. These trees are truly splendid specimens. Are they oaks?'

'Oaks? N…no! They are lime trees, I believe. There are one or two oaks scattered about the grounds, but they've been used as specimen trees.'

'I saw a splendid old oak the other day. But sadly, it had lost one of its major branches.'

'Oh?'

Sir William laughed. 'In fact, I met one of your brother's men there. A Will Darby. Do you know him?'

He knows, thought Emily. I'm sure he knows. But she suppressed any hint of fear and said calmly, 'Of course I know him. He's one of the grooms. Have you seen enough of the trees, sir? I think I've shown you the best of them.'

'He warned me about a dangerous bull that was kept in the field where the oak grew.'

Emily put on a puzzled frown, then said, 'Ah, yes! I think I know the one you mean. That would be Farmer Pritchard's bull. Black Samson. Shall we turn back now?'

They turned and started to walk back towards the gate to the gardens. But her tormentor was not to be put off. 'Of course I already knew about the bull,' he went on. 'I had seen it before when I was last in Stoke Shearings.'

This time the twinkle in his eye was even more marked. Was he playing some sort of cat-and-mouse game with her? Emily felt a spurt of anger. She was not about to weaken. She must keep her head and marshal her wits.

'You've been here before? I can't remember meeting you...?'

He went on, 'I had a walk along the stream through the valley when I was last here, too. It's a beautiful spot. You know it?'

Emily nodded.

'Very steep sides to it, of course. I would have called on your brother, while I was staying in the village, but lost my way during the day, and...' Emily stiffened. He shook his head and went on apologetically, 'With one thing and another, by the time I got back to the inn it was too late.'

'Really?' she said with admirable indifference.

Her adversary was not deterred. He said, 'I wish I had made the time now.'

The meaning was plain and she decided that this was the moment to stall him. 'I am sure my brother would have made you very welcome, Sir William,' she said primly. 'So would my sister-in-law.'

'And you?'

She gave him a smile full of insincere regret. 'Alas, I was not here at the time. I...I was with my g-grandfather in London.' She shouldn't have added that last bit. She had stammered. Rosa had always said that she wasn't a good liar.

The silence grew. 'Now that does surprise me,' he said at last.

'Why?' Emily asked with a touch of belligerence.

'Because...' He regarded her with amusement as she lifted her chin. Then he went on, 'Because London would have been so crowded at that time of year. The middle of June, wasn't it?'

'No, the middle of May.'

'Oh, yes. So it was. How did you know?'

'How should I *not* know when I pay visits to my grandfather, Sir William?'

'Quite! But how did you know that it was May when *I* was in the district?'

They had reached the gate at the end of the trees. Emily had never been so thankful in her life to reach a simple gate. 'My sister-in-law will be wondering where we are,' she said and hurried through, deliberately letting the heavy gate swing to behind her. It must have hurt when it hit him, but apart from a swiftly drawn breath he gave no sign, and soon caught up with her again. They were just by the entrance to the maze and she attempted to hurry past. He took her arm and stopped her flight.

'But, Miss Winbolt! Isn't this the entrance to the famous Shearings maze? You can't have forgotten that Mrs Winbolt particularly wished me to see it. She would surely be disappointed if I said I hadn't even ventured inside. Shall we go in?'

'Oh, but I...' Without quite knowing how he did it, Emily found herself being led into the maze, where they were soon surrounded by a high wall of hedges. But, she thought grimly, if Sir William Ashenden thought she was about to wander idly through the maze with him, he would find he was mistaken. The situation was far too dangerous for her peace of mind. She knew the maze inside out and had every intention of losing him as soon as she could. Within minutes she had taken a swift turn to the right, then another, then hurried along to the left. Slightly out of breath, she stopped and looked round. There was no sign of him. She waited a moment or two, then, smiling with satisfaction, she turned a corner to make her way out. Sir William was there, sitting on a bench that had been placed to rest the weary at the centre of the maze.

'There you are,' he said genially. 'Where did you get to? I've been waiting for you.'

He patted the seat beside him and Emily, whose knees had gone weak, sat down. What else could she do? 'Now,' he said, 'where were we? Oh, yes, of course! How you knew I was in Stoke Shearings in May. I'll tell you how it must have happened, shall I? It's very simple. The people at the inn told Will Darby, and Will Darby told you!'

Emily stared at him blankly. What had they been talking about? Then she said, 'Yes. Yes, of course. That must have been it.'

'A curious coincidence, that.'

Against her better judgement Emily asked, 'What is?'

'That he and I have the same name—though I am

usually called William. Only in exceptional circumstances does anyone call me Will.' He paused. '*Very*
exceptional. One might almost say *intimate* circumstances.'

Emily rose to her feet in some agitation. 'I...I should
like to join the others. They will surely be wondering
where we are.'

'They know where we are,' he said firmly. He led
her back to the bench and sat her gently down again.
'We can talk a few minutes longer.'

'But I don't wish to talk to you!' cried Emily in desperation.

'I think you do,' said Sir William softly. 'I think you
must.'

'What do you mean by that, sir?'

'Come, Miss Winbolt. Why do you think I've taken
such pains to speak to you alone? I admire your spirit,
but you can't keep it up for ever, you know. Why don't
you admit it?'

'Admit what? I don't know what you're talking
about—'

'Yes, you do, dear Miss Winbolt.' He held her eye
and repeated the question. 'Why don't you admit it?
Why don't you take our famous bull by the horns and
ask me if I have recognised you?'

'Recognised me? What do you mean?' she demanded
defiantly. 'How could you have recognised me? I don't
remember ever having met you before Lady Langley's
ball.'

'Well now, that surprises me—that you have forgotten our first meeting, I mean. *I* have found the experience quite impossible to forget. Those legs dangling
so enticingly from the oak tree, the sensations as we

rolled down that bank clasped in each other's arms, your delightful response to my kisses…'

'Stop! Stop!' Emily cried. She jumped up in a panic, her hands to her ears, and made to run away. He caught one of her hands and pulled her back.

'Admit it,' he said softly.

'Very well!' she cried. 'I admit it, I admit it! Does that satisfy you? And what are you planning to do, now that I have confessed? It must give you a great deal of satisfaction to know that you could ruin me with a few sentences. I dare say you think it would make a fine story for the gossips.'

'That's very true. Were they ever to hear it.'

Emily hid her face in her hands. 'I can't bear it,' she said.

'Don't look like that, Miss Winbolt! There's no danger of it, I assure you! It will remain our secret.'

She looked at him, not sure whether to believe him or not, but the blue eyes were sincere. There was a short silence then she whispered, 'How can I trust you?'

'I suppose you'll have to take my word for it. I'm no monster. I don't believe in destroying reputations for pleasure. Of course, I don't understand why you behaved as you did—'

'How could you? I don't understand that myself!' cried Emily in despair again. 'I still don't. But why did you tease me so?'

'I must confess the temptation was irresistible. I had heard so much about the respectable Miss Winbolt, so cool to would-be suitors, you see. And then, afterwards—it was all so ridiculously unlikely. I was enchanted by the situation. Will you forgive me?' He smiled at her, the tiny fan of wrinkles appearing at the corners of those dark blue eyes. Emily stared at him, bemused, and the smile disappeared. He leaned forward slowly and kissed her.

'No! You mustn't!' She stared at him in shock, then turned away, her face hidden in her hands again. 'I'm so ashamed,' she whispered, 'So ashamed that you should believe you can…can…' She shook her head. 'What must you think of me?'

He took her hands in his and drew them away from her face. His expression was quite serious. 'I don't know what to think of you. Which is the real Emily Winbolt? The wild enchantress in the hollow, or the cool, level-headed Miss Winbolt? How can both of you exist in the same body? And why do you have such a strange effect on me? There are so many questions. Believe me, I think you are the most intriguing woman I have met in a long time.'

She snatched her hands back. 'No!' she cried. 'I won't allow you to kiss me and say things like that. I am not any kind of enchantress! I was not myself when we met before, I don't know what came over me! If you think you can tease and torment me, say what you like to me, kiss me, because of what happened, well, you can't. I won't have it. I have never before behaved like that, and I never will again.' She took a deep breath, then lifted her chin and gave him a chilly look. 'And now I wish to go back to the others, if you please.'

He regarded her for a moment, laughter back in his eyes. 'You disappoint me.' He smiled. 'Though I suppose I should really be grateful to you—life was becoming a little dull before I met you. Now I have an additional interest.'

'And that is?' said Emily, not altogether sure she wanted his answer.

'Why, to find the real Emily Winbolt, of course!'

'I've already told you, sir. The real Emily Winbolt is what you see before you. Philip Winbolt's unmarried sister, a respectable and respected lady. There is nothing of that gipsy in her. What happened in May was a momentary madness, an aberration. It will not be repeated.'

He stood back and surveyed her dress and hair. 'Looking at you now, I can believe it. Did you have to try so hard to put me off the scent with your drab, nun-like appearance? It was a wasted effort, I assure you. That girl is still there, Emily Winbolt, however hard you try to suppress her. It may be that I am the only one to have had the privilege of meeting her, but she is there!'

His determined tone frightened her. The effect he had had on her on that hillside was something she had never before experienced. She hadn't understood it at the time and she didn't understand it now. But she wanted no part of it ever again. It was too powerful, too all-consuming. The very thought of it made her tremble. Emily forced herself to be calm as she said, 'Sir William. Since we are apparently to be near neighbours, and my brother and his wife seem to approve of you, I suppose I shall have to put up with your company. But that is all.' Her voice rose. 'However low your opinion of me may be, I am not here as an object for your amusement, to be spoken to as you please!' She turned away from him, struggling to hide how close to tears she was.

He watched her for a moment, then turned her back again and put his hands on her shoulders. 'Forgive me,' he said remorsefully. 'I never meant to upset you. But this situation... Shall we make a bargain?'

Emily looked at him apprehensively, wondering what

he was about to suggest. Was it another trick? But he
shook his head at her expression and said softly,

'You may trust me. I cannot forget the girl I met that
day in May, and still hope to meet her again, whatever
you say. But I shall respect your wish to ignore our
first meeting. And, as far as the rest of the world is
concerned, we met for the first time at the Langleys'
ball. Can we not get to know each other as ordinary
neighbours? Meet and talk as two people newly introduced? The battle between us may continue in private,
Emily, but you need not fear I shall embarrass or tease
you again with memories of past behaviour. Agreed?'

He put out his hand and after a moment's hesitation
Emily reluctantly took it. She would not be able to avoid
his company completely in the future without giving
rise to awkward questions. This seemed to her to be as
good a way forward as any. 'I agree,' she said.

This time there was genuine warmth in his smile.
'Shall we join the others?' he asked, offering her his
arm. He led her unerringly out of the maze and together
they walked back to join the rest of the party in the
arbour.

They were watched by at least two interested parties
as they came back. It has to be said that when Rosa
and Lady Deardon saw Emily's heightened colour, and
William's air of satisfaction, they exchanged a look
which in less elegant ladies would have been called
conspiratorial.

Chapter Five

Before the afternoon ended it had been decided that all three Winbolts should visit Charlwood to view the gardens there. William warned them not to expect anything like the order and beauty of Shearings.

'I have been concentrating my efforts on making the Dower House into a suitable home for my family,' he said. 'The rest of the place still needs a lot of attention.'

'Your family, Sir William?' said Rosa, with a quick glance at Emily.

'I have two wards, Mrs Winbolt,' William explained. 'They are at present in the West Indies waiting for a suitable passage, but I expect them soon.'

'They will all stay with us at first,' said Lady Deardon, 'but then the family will move into the Dower House as soon as it is ready. Later, of course, they will all live in Charlwood itself.'

'I'm afraid that day is still some way off,' William said ruefully. 'The work is going rather slowly. We seem to have had more than our share of accidents. None of them has been serious, but they delay the work.'

'I imagine there's a great deal to do. The house has been empty for so long, and I don't believe there was even been a caretaker to look after it,' Philip said. 'It's a pity. It was beautiful in its day.'

'And it will be again. But it takes time and patience,' William said.

'Not to mention money,' added Philip. 'The house and land here at Shearings had been left in excellent order, but I was surprised how expensive it was to restore the gardens. I don't envy you, Ashenden, with both to see to.'

'But worth it,' William said briefly. 'However, since I am just a simple Navy man, I must look to my neighbours for advice and help with the gardens. And from what I've seen today, I couldn't ask for anyone better to help me than you, Winbolt, and your two ladies. Do you think you could oblige me?'

'Willingly,' said Rosa. 'I'm sure we should love to do it. Quite soon. But tell me about your wards, Sir William. Two, you say? Are they…are they closely related to you?'

William turned to Rosa with a smile. It was a nice smile, but had a hint of something in it which probably only Emily saw. He's heard of Rosa's search for a husband for me, she thought, and he thinks she sees him as a possibility. But Rosa doesn't know that he would never think of asking me to be his wife—he still isn't sure whether or not I'm a hypocrite, a well-bred lady with the soul of a wanton. He might flirt with such a woman, kiss her, but he wouldn't want to marry her. As for me… I'm not looking for a husband, but even if I were he would be the last man I'd choose. After what has happened, how could I ever be at ease with him? But she listened all the same with interest to his reply.

'A niece and nephew, Mrs Winbolt. They are my brother's children and now, except for me, quite alone in the world. James, the boy, is eight, and Laura is just six.'

Rosa's tender heart was touched. 'And they have no mother?' she asked.

'No,' Lady Deardon said, and went on, 'But they need one. All children do. I keep telling William that he must find a wife before very long.'

'I intend to,' said her godson, 'but that, too, takes time and patience.'

'In that case you should start working at it as soon as possible,' said his godmother a little tartly. 'Suitable wives don't simply fall from trees, William.'

'Oh, I don't know,' said William with a smile. 'Stranger things have happened.'

Emily jumped, threw him a look, and said hastily, 'Talking of strange things, is it true that Lord Langley is selling his greys? I find that *very* strange. I can't imagine why he would, they are a splendid set of horses.'

She held her breath for a moment, wondering whether Rosa had seen the significance of William's words, but, much to her relief, her diversionary tactic appeared to have worked and the talk slipped into less dangerous channels until it was time for the visitors to go.

As he took his leave of her William said, 'I hope I am to see you too at Charlwood next week, Miss Winbolt. I look forward to hearing what you will recommend.'

'My brother and sister-in-law are the experts, Sir William. I don't think I have much to add to what they can tell you,' said Emily coolly.

'You underestimate yourself. After our walk this

afternoon—and our most instructive talk—I am sure you will have a great many ideas.' He held her eyes as he said, 'I shall see you next week, Miss Winbolt.'

At first Emily was annoyed and frustrated at this command of William's to come with her brother to Charlwood—for it was no less than a command, of that she was sure. She felt she could trust him not to betray her secret, but she had no desire to spend more time with him than she had to. He had seen a part of her nature, a passion, a strength of feeling, which no one else had ever even suspected, herself included, and she resented the hold this gave him over her.

Nevertheless, as the days went by she found to her surprise that her resentment was fading and she was even beginning to look forward to the visit. Indeed, she was surprised to find that she was happier than she had been for a long time, if only because life had become so much more interesting. After all, Sir William and she could now in fact meet on more or less equal terms. What had she to lose? She had nothing more to conceal, he knew the worst of her. She expected nothing from him except his silence. Though he might tease her, she could now be herself with him in a way that had been impossible before. And, if she was honest, she had to admit he had a quirky sense of humour which, in spite of herself, she found appealing.

When the day came even Rosa could not find fault with the way Emily was dressed. She was wearing one of her newest and prettiest dresses of pale apricot muslin, and over it a corded silk spencer in a deeper shade of the same colour. Her kid shoes and gloves, and her bonnet of Leghorn straw, were of the first elegance.

Her hair had been released from its severe knot to allow one or two curls to escape. The colour of her dress gave a soft glow to a complexion that was normally rather pale, and excitement gave her face animation. But Rosa would have been less pleased if she had been aware of her sister-in-law's motive for taking such pains with her appearance. She was not out to attract, but to impress. She had so far been at a disadvantage in every one of her encounters with William, but that was now about to change. She aimed to look every inch what she was—an elegant, well-born lady of some wealth, who could keep any man, including Sir William Ashenden, firmly in his place. It was purely coincidental that she was also looking her best.

The look of surprised admiration in William's eyes as he greeted them at Charlwood was very gratifying. Emily had half-expected one of his comments and braced herself, but his behaviour could not be faulted. He welcomed her as conventionally as he welcomed Rosa and Philip, and a little to her surprise said nothing to disturb her. Nor did he make any special effort to engage her in private conversation. On the surface at least, the owner of Charlwood was merely receiving three of his nearest neighbours for their first visit.

They went first to the Dower House, where he introduced them to the couple who lived over the stables there.

'Mrs Lilley looks after this house for me, and her husband keeps an eye on the rest of the place, including Charlwood. Have you seen anything more of our intruders, Sam?'

'No, sir, not today I haven't. I think they must have been frightened off.'

William turned to his guests. 'Several intruders

have been seen in and around Charlwood recently. Sam says they must be vagrants—but there's no sign of any damage, is there, Sam?'

'None that I could find, sir. But if you don't mind I'd like for my brother's lad to share the watch with me for a while. He's a strong, well-built boy, and he'd soon deal with anyone what oughtn't to be there. The house is too big for me to be everywhere at once. It'll only be for a short while till they fellows learn that Charlwood is being properly looked after again and they ain't welcome any more.'

'Very good. See to it. And thank you.' William turned once again to his guests. 'If you wish, I could show you a little of the main house before we start. One of the rooms has a view of the grounds, which will give you an idea of the basic plan. The house is still in a mess, but the way through to the salon at the back isn't as hazardous as it was. I'm afraid you would have to walk up the drive. It's too rough for the carriage.'

Philip said instantly, 'I'm sure we could walk. I've heard so much about Charlwood. And I would very much like to see whatever you can show us. What about the ladies?'

As the ladies were both in complete agreement, they walked up to the house. Emily was still half-expecting William to present her with some sort of challenge, but his behaviour continued to be exemplary. They conducted a very civilised conversation about plans for the garden and nothing more. Of course, it was perfectly natural for him to offer her his arm and help her over the uneven ground. Philip did the same for Rosa. He even lifted her over a pile of stones from a broken wall that was blocking their path, but without comment. If she suspected that he held her fractionally longer and perhaps a touch more firmly than was strictly necessary, she said nothing.

When they reached Charlwood, William led them carefully through a maze of half-finished woodwork and plaster to the back of the house. Here they found themselves in a large, beautifully proportioned room with tall windows along the back wall that led on to a wide terrace. Emily looked round. There was evidence everywhere of the ravages of time and neglect. The floor was littered with bits of plaster from the ceiling, which had once been white and gold, but was now a dirty grey. Torn strips of some sort of material hung down from the walls, and pictures and mirrors that had once hung against them were propped up on the floor. And yet the dust and debris could not disguise the elegance of the room's proportions, its lightness and grace. Resisting a strong desire to linger, Emily picked her way carefully through the mess, walked over to the windows and looked out at the view.

'Why, it's perfect!' she exclaimed and paused, gazing at the symphony of colour outside.

The house was built on a slight rise overlooking the valley, and from the windows could be seen meadows and woods gradually sloping up to a line of hills. The whole was a symphony of green, the soft green of the meadows and the bright greens of early summer in the woods beyond. And beyond them lay the blue haze of the downs. 'This view alone would make any effort to restore the house well worth it,' she said impulsively, turning round to the room. William pulled a face. 'Have you looked nearer to hand?' he asked, coming to join her.

It was true that the view nearer the house was not so attractive. A wilderness of weeds, overgrown bushes and trees was threatening to take over from what had been a formal garden. A broken statue covered in ivy and other creepers and surrounded by thorns stood forlornly in an untidy circle of stones, which had once held a pool. But Emily was not put off.

'Philip! The fountain is just like the one we have at Shearings.'

William laughed out loud. 'What an imagination you have, Miss Winbolt. I can't see any resemblance whatever.'

'Oh, but I do! You must look below the surface chaos, Sir William. That statue, once restored, would be as lovely as any we have. It is so right for its setting that the fountain must have been laid out when the house was first built. And it is obviously original. I hope you realise how lucky you are. And…is that the remains of an avenue beyond? Does it lead to a folly? A summerhouse, perhaps?' She turned back to him eagerly. 'Sir William, you must restore it all! The fountain would not be difficult—I am sure you'll find there's a stream nearby to feed it. And look at those urns—they are perfectly placed to carry the eye out beyond the lawns!'

Emily had always been the creative mind in schemes for Shearings's gardens, and the potential of these gardens of Charlwood had set her imagination alight. In her pleasure and eagerness she was a different person, quite forgetting her normal reserve.

For a moment William studied the animated face turned up to his, his expression difficult to read. Then he raised one eyebrow and said quizzically, 'You don't think the urns are, shall we say, a touch randomly posed, then? To me they look rather like the local lads outside the inn at the end of a hard day.'

They both regarded the urns. True, they were sym-

metrically placed at intervals round the edge of the
lawns, but not one of them was vertical. Half were leaning drunkenly to one side or the other, and the pedestals
of the rest had sunk and were half-buried in the earth.
Viewed objectively, they were a sorry sight.

Emily could not help herself. A smile appeared first,
then she laughed. 'You are quite right, of course. I can
easily imagine Job Diment and Will Darby looking as
tipsy. But I suspect the urns are still fairly undamaged.
May I take a closer look at them?'

'We can have a look at the garden as soon as you feel
you have finished here. Seeing more of the house would
be better left to later. Parts of it are still too dangerous.
We shall even have to go out the way we came—the
other doors are all blocked at present.'

'Because of the danger?' asked Philip

'Mostly. But also because of the intruders I mentioned. It's easier to keep a watch for them if there's
only one entrance.'

'What are they looking for? Do you know?'

'They could well be seeking shelter here. I can't
imagine why else anyone would be interested.'

They returned through the hall and round to the back
of the house, which lay in bright sunshine. Rosa eyed the
tangle of vegetation in front of them somewhat doubtfully, and when she saw a bench nearby which was
still in reasonable condition she spread her shawl over
the seat, sat down and firmly announced, 'I shall have
walked enough by the time we are back at the Dower
House, Sir William. I shall be very happy to sit here for
a while and enjoy the warmth of the sun while the rest
of you make your way through that…jungle.'

Emily had gone on ahead eagerly, but she turned at
this and came back. Shaking out her own shawl and

putting it beside Rosa's, she said, 'Of course I shan't go
without you if you're not feeling well, love. I can easily
see the urns another day. We shall stay here while Philip
and Sir William struggle with the vegetation.'

'You're very sweet, Emily, but I am really quite well,
just a little tired. As you very well know, I am always
happy just to sit peacefully in any garden without re-de-
signing it, or suggesting improvements! I haven't your
enthusiasm. Do go. I can guess how eager you are!'

'Yes, you go with Sir William, Emily. I shall stay
with Rosa,' said Philip. He sat down beside his wife,
kissed her hand and gave her a little smile. Without
turning, he said, 'You don't need any help from me to
give him the benefit of your ideas.'

Emily felt her cheeks growing warm. This was too
blatant! She started to shake her head.

'Please do not refuse, Miss Winbolt. Your brother
will think you are afraid to be alone with me,' said William. 'But I can assure him—and you—that you will
be perfectly safe. We shall never be out of shouting
distance.' His tone was serious, but Emily could have
sworn the twinkle was back in his eye as he looked at
her, challenging her…

Philip laughed. 'Emily is far too sensible for such
nonsense. From what I know of her, inspecting your
wilderness and deciding what to recommend would be
exactly to her taste. She has a passion for such things.'

'Really?' murmured William. 'Then I must take
advantage of it. Are you ready, Miss Winbolt? I promise not to keep you for more than half an hour.'

'Make that an hour, Ashenden,' said Philip with a
grin. 'Emily will need at least that.'

Annoyed at being thus outmanoeuvred, Emily
accompanied William in silence to the ornamental gate

which led to the lawns behind. As he held it for her he said, 'It isn't really quite as bad as it looks from the house. The men have cut a path through the under- growth. You needn't fear for your very pretty dress, Miss Winbolt.'

Emily looked at him coldly, and made no reply. Wil- liam stopped and regarded her.

'You're angry. Why? What *have* I done to offend you? I thought I was behaving impeccably! Indeed, my behaviour has been absolutely impeccable all afternoon! Wouldn't you agree?'

'Yes, but—'

'Are you annoyed that I admired your dress? How strange! I thought ladies liked to have their dresses admired.' He paused, while they negotiated their way on to the lawns. Then he went on, 'Why were you giving me such basilisk looks, Miss Winbolt?'

'Basilisk?'

'Yes, quite basilisk. As basilisk as I have ever seen. And believe me, I've seen a good many. The dowagers in every Government House I have ever visited special- ise in them.'

'Really, sir,' protested Emily, hard put to it not to laugh. 'You're not very flattering. Is this the way you normally talk to your female visitors?'

'You're the first, so I can't say. Would you like me to flatter you? I wouldn't have thought you needed it.'

'Quite! We can afford to be plain with each other. And since I am to be plain—'

'You are far from that, Miss Winbolt. Especially today. That straw hat is delightful. Very becoming. You're not at all plain, even when you're giving me a basilisk stare—it's back again, incidentally. Even worse than the dowagers.'

'Sir William!' Emily experienced an unusual desire to stamp her foot, but, mindful of the condition of the lawn, stared at him angrily instead. He raised an eyebrow, the blue eyes laughing at her. She struggled for a moment, but, however hard she tried, her anger drained away and she had to restrain a desire to laugh with him. At last she said weakly, 'I don't even know what a basilisk is!'

'Nor do I, but I am sure it gives people unpleasant looks—even people such as myself who don't deserve them.' His tone was reproachful, but the tiny fan of wrinkles had appeared at the corners of his eyes.

'You are talking nonsense, sir, and you know it. We shall change the subject!' said Emily with determination. 'Tell me, do you wish to retain these urns and the fountain?'

'Can they be rescued?'

'I think so,' she said, and went over to give them a closer look. 'There's someone in Stoke Shearings who could advise you on that. Philip and I used him a year or two ago. I think he's worth a try—shall I have a word with him?'

They went on, picking their way through brambles and branches of wild roses, studying the stone ornaments, searching for signs of a conduit for the fountain, looking for evidence of paths and flower beds, and the talk once again became businesslike. William could see that Emily had forgotten him as she wandered here and there, completely absorbed in what she was doing. Once she found a cluster of small white bells buried among the weeds and bent to examine them more closely, an expression of delight on her face. A few stalks of purple daisies were apparently another prize. But though she was clearly enchanted by those and Charlwood's other hidden treasures, she never lost sight of the overall design. He watched her, fascinated by the swift changes in her expression, as she assessed the prospect from the back of the house, examined the perspective from where the avenue of trees began, took a closer look at the fountain... Her enthusiasm was infectious, and William was once again intrigued. How many sides were there to this woman? At their first meeting he had seen her aroused by the excitement of his love-making, with little thought of restraint; at the Langleys' ball he had seen her severely self-controlled, coolly ironic, even though she must have been almost frightened out of her wits. But this was a different woman again. This woman had passion *and* control, was able to use her brain to plan and assess, even when in the grip of enchantment. Was this, at last, the true Emily Winbolt? If so, she was someone to be reckoned with.

Emily suddenly became aware of William staring at her, and stopped in the middle of what she was saying. 'I...I'm sorry,' she faltered. 'Philip always says my enthusiasm runs away with my tongue. I am very interested in garden design.'

'So I have guessed,' said William, unable to suppress a smile.

Emily's cheeks grew pink. 'You're laughing at me,' she said accusingly.

'Only a little. I am impressed, too.'

She smiled nervously, started to say something, then stopped. They stared at each other in silence. After a long moment she drew in a sharp breath and turned abruptly away, but haste made her unwary. Her foot caught in the trailing branch of a bramble, and she would have fallen if William had not caught her. He held her briefly to steady her, then knelt down to release her dress and shoe from the thorns. He inspected her ankle and looked up. 'Are you hurt?'

'No, no. I...I'm perfectly all right. It was stupid of me...' Her voice died away as he got up, put his hands on her waist and turned her round to face him.

Suddenly William felt exactly as he had at their first meeting, his heart beating faster, his breathing uneven. Here in this wilderness of thorns and roses he was more tempted than he had ever been before. It was quite outside all his previous experiences. He wanted to embrace her as passionately as he had embraced her in the hollow, to forget where and who they both were, and the promises he had since made her. His arms tightened... Then she looked up, and the silver-grey eyes were wide with apprehension. It stopped him. A false step now and he and the woman he had just got to know would never again enjoy the easy companionship of the last half-hour. If he valued her confidence in him, he must draw back. With an effort he said as calmly as he could, 'I apologise. Before we examine the gardens another day, I'll make sure the paths are clear. You could have had a bad fall. As it is, you've had a shock. Are you sure you're all right?'

The dangerous moment had passed. She straightened herself and said carefully, 'Thank you. You're very kind, but you may let me go, now. I shan't fall again.' Still avoiding his eye, she said in a low voice, 'I think it would be better if we went back.'

William paused, then made up his mind and said, 'Of course, if that is what you wish. I was hoping to show you the folly, but if you are still too shaken...' He looked at her and added carefully, 'I assure you I will take great care to see that you're not...upset again.' Another pause. 'I promise.' She looked at him uncertainly.

'Come, there's still some time left,' he said persuasively. 'Your brother gave us an hour and, to be honest, I would prefer to see you easier in your mind before you go back to them. Try to trust me.' He waited for her reply, surprised at how important it was to him.

'I suppose we could walk as far as the folly,' she said slowly. 'Rosa won't mind waiting a little longer— the sun is warm, and she is always happy in Philip's company.'

William hid his relief, keeping his voice casual as he said, 'They seem a devoted couple.'

'They are. They are exactly right for each other.'

There was an opening there for what he wanted to say, but as they walked up between the trees he was careful to keep the conversation once again on conventional grounds. This was not the right moment for what he hoped to find out from his companion. Not yet. He asked her further about her interest in gardens and listened to her comments on the plants and trees she had found in Charlwood's grounds. Once or twice he even coaxed a smile from her. By the time they had reached the folly she was completely at her ease again, and before returning they sat for a short while on the steps. The view in the late afternoon sunshine was glorious. Charlwood lay surrounded by its grounds against the gently sloping backdrop of the Downs.

'Such beauty,' said Emily, surveying the scene. 'And such peace.'

'I am glad you think so.'

They sat in silence for a while, then Emily got to her feet. 'We must go back. Rosa will be wondering where

I am.' She smiled at him. '*Really* wondering where I am. I'm sure the hour went by some time ago.'

'You are very close to her.'

'Why shouldn't I be? Though she is very sharp-witted, she is the kindest-hearted creature in the world. It's rare to find the two in one person.'

'Didn't you find it hard when your brother married?'

Emily pulled a face. 'You've been listening to gossip, probably from Mrs Gosworth. I'm surprised at you. I love Rosa dearly, and think Philip is a very lucky man. I was delighted when they married and wouldn't change the situation for the world.'

William decided to take the plunge. 'But you were unhappy the day we met.'

She looked at him, startled. 'What…what makes you say that?'

'I've said before, you puzzle me. Every time we meet I see something new about you. And the more I think about that first meeting…'

'Really, Sir William,' she said, no longer at ease, 'I thought we had agreed to put that dreadful episode behind us. I can't go on trying to explain something I don't even understand myself…'

'Please! I don't mean to distress you, but to reassure you. I have long dismissed the notion that you are like some ladies I've met in London who seek excitement in secret affairs. The idea is absurd. The more I think about that first meeting, the more convinced I am that your behaviour that day was what you say—completely out of character. You were shaken by the escape from the bull, of course. But there was more to it than that. I think you were looking for reassurance, comfort even.'

'Why on earth should I need reassuring?'

'That is what has puzzled me. You don't appear to be suffering from an unfortunate love affair...'

'Oh, I recovered from that a long, long time ago,' she said before she could stop herself. 'And in any case I had never—' She stopped short.

'What had you never...?'

'It doesn't matter.' She paused, took a breath and said, 'You asked me to trust you. Well, I will. I love my brother and Rosa dearly, but that day I was wondering how I could tell them that I wanted my own life.'

William frowned. 'Are you not free, then?'

'Of course I am. Philip couldn't be more liberal in his attitude to what I do, and where I go. But I am no longer as *necessary* to Shearings as I once was. Rosa runs it superbly. And I...I have too much time on my hands. No, I love them both dearly, but I want to have, to create, an establishment of my own...' William started to say something, but she interrupted him. 'I know. Most women find an establishment of their own through marriage. Isn't that what you were about to say?'

'More or less,' said William. 'It's the conventional thing to do. Did you manage to tell them about your feelings?'

Emily sighed. 'When I told Rosa she was horrified. And deeply hurt. I haven't even tried to tell Philip, though I suspect Rosa has mentioned it to him. And then she set to work to find me a husband. I can't tell you how many "suitable men" she has paraded before me since then, all sizes and all ages.' She gave him a straight look. 'You are her latest.'

William laughed out loud. 'And you are refreshingly candid! How do I measure up to the others?'

Emily grinned. 'Well, you're under sixty, and you

have the use of both legs, and from what I've seen, all of your hair...'

William, still laughing, cried, 'Stop, I've heard enough! Such flattery is bad for me.'

'But don't be alarmed. I fully intend to carry out my own plans, as soon as Rosa and Philip come to terms with the thought.'

'And they are?'

'To find a suitable house with plenty of grounds, not too far away from Shearings and to settle there. Then I would run my own household and create the loveliest gardens in the county.'

'It's an intriguing idea, but not at all conventional. I can see why your sister-in-law finds it hard to understand. But does this mean you won't have time to work on plans for Charlwood?'

'I think it might be years before I manage to convince my loving brother and his wife that I could be happy living alone,' she said with a sigh. 'I don't want to hurt them. And if we don't rejoin them soon, they will surely wonder what has happened to us.'

'Then we shall walk a little faster.' They quickened their pace. '*Will* you think of plans for Charlwood's gardens?'

She threw him an amused glance. 'You know very well that I couldn't resist that. You are counting on it. Yes, I'd like to do some plans for them—such an opportunity is unlikely to come my way again.'

'Not counting on it exactly, but *hoping* you would. I am very glad you've agreed to.'

While they were still just out of earshot Emily said, 'I think I can trust you not to mention my other plans? The situation is still a delicate one.'

'Of course. You may trust me in anything, Miss

Winbolt.' She looked at him, startled, but he did not add to it.

They joined Philip and Rosa and walked back down the drive to the Dower House, where they enjoyed refreshments prepared by Mrs Lilley. Then, after thanking their host, they drove off.

William was unusually silent that evening. His mind was busy with ideas and speculation. Emily Winbolt's plans for her future were unusual to say the least. In spite of what she had said, could there perhaps be a better, more conventional solution for her problem, one which might help to solve his own?

Chapter Six

In fact, William was *so* silent that evening that Lady Deardon asked him what was wrong. 'I hope you're not feeling ill. Maria Fenton visited this afternoon and was quite disappointed that you weren't here. I invited her to call tomorrow.'

Sir Reginald grunted, 'I hope you don't expect me to be here to welcome her. I don't like her. Puts herself forward too much for my taste.'

'It isn't you she wants to see, Reggie dear,' said his wife patiently.

'I know that. It's William she's after with her invitations to dinner and her constant calls. If he goes for a walk, more often than not she's there ready to waylay him. You needn't look at me like that. William hasn't said a word to me about it, but I've noticed. You can't tell me it's accidental! If he takes my advice, he won't have anything to do with her.'

'What on earth has Mrs Fenton done to put your back up so?' asked Lady Deardon. 'Her manners are perfectly acceptable, and if she is a touch sure of herself she has every reason to be—beautiful, charming, still young…and rich. Is it such a bad thing if she is attracted to William?'

'I've told you before, I don't like her and I don't like her visitors, either.'

'You mean her brother and that friend of his?'

'He may be her brother for all I know, but he's no gentleman. Nor is the friend. They may be rich, but they're a rum lot. They hardly ever show their faces during the day, but I've caught the other one out in the middle of the night. He didn't know I'd seen him.'

'And what were you doing out in the middle of the night, my love?' asked his wife.

'Went down to the stables to see how Duchess was doing with her new pups. Saw the fellow sneaking back through the fields. I don't know what he had been up to, but I can't think it was anything good. I tell you I don't like him. Don't like any of 'em. Keep themselves to themselves too much for my taste.'

'The man's behaviour does sound a bit odd,' said Lady Deardon. 'But if the rest of the neighbourhood has your opinion of them I'm not surprised they keep themselves to themselves! You cannot say that of Mrs Fenton, however. She seems very interested in taking her place in local society. She was at Mrs Gosworth's last week and visited the Langleys the week before.'

William asked, 'When did Mrs Fenton say she would call?'

'Early afternoon. She seemed to be slightly put out when I told her you were showing Charlwood to the Winbolts today, and said she would positively insist you take her there tomorrow afternoon.'

'That's what I meant,' said Sir Reginald. coming to life again. 'Encroaching ways. You wouldn't catch

Emily Winbolt behaving like that. Good breeding, good background. Always a lady. Knows how to behave. *And* she inherited her mother's fortune. She has a lot more to offer than the Fenton woman, Will. It's the Winbolt girl you should be settling on. She's a lady of quality.'

Reggie would be shocked to the core of his conventional soul if he knew just how unladylike Emily Winbolt's behaviour could be, thought William, suppressing a smile. But Sir Reginald's instinct was sound. She was indeed a lady of quality.

Mrs Fenton called and, as predicted, demanded that William take her to Charlwood. 'For you promised you would, sir,' she said, wagging an admonitory finger. 'I have been waiting this age for you to invite me. And now I hear that you have already taken the Winbolts. It's too bad of you.'

Her playfully reproachful manner was so artificial that it put William off, but he responded with a suitably chastened air as he replied, 'Mrs Fenton, how can I expect you to forgive me? I had no idea that my poor rundown property would arouse such rivalry. In my own defence I have to say that yesterday was more in the nature of business. I invited the Winbolts to advise me on garden design—Miss Winbolt is particularly expert in the art. May I help you into the carriage?'

Mrs Fenton settled herself gracefully, her pink-lined parasol carefully shading her face. 'I wish you had consulted me first, Sir William. I, too, have always been keenly interested in gardens. They are so restful. One can forget the world in a garden, do you not think so? One is so close to nature—the scents, the colours, the play of light and shade. It is all so *uplifting*... And I am sure Charlwood's gardens are delightful.' She turned and put her hand on his arm. 'You must let me help you a little, too. I flatter myself I have an excellent eye for colour.'

They were now well on the road to Charlwood and William took time to negotiate a crossroads before he replied. He said carefully, 'I shall be happy to hear your advice when the time comes. But Miss Winbolt—'

Mrs Fenton bit her lip and said with something of a snap, 'Oh, you mustn't think I am trying to deprive Emily Winbolt of her occupation. Poor, dear Rosa Winbolt must be so *relieved* that her sister-in-law's interest is at last turning to something other than Shearings. I hear they have been at odds over running the house there ever since Rosa arrived.'

'Indeed? Where did you hear that? From what I saw yesterday, they are very good friends.'

'They were putting on company manners, I expect. Believe me, I have it on the best authority that at home they are positively at daggers drawn.'

'Whose authority is that?'

Mrs Fenton began to realise that her conversation was not having the desired effect. William's voice was decidedly frosty. She said earnestly, 'Oh, I am no gossip, Sir William. It was told me in confidence and my lips are sealed. I would not mention the Winbolt business to everyone, I assure you, but I knew I could trust *you* not to repeat it.' After a quick glance at William's face she went on, 'What delightful views there are. How much further is it to Charlwood?'

The rest of the drive was accompanied by the lady's light chatter about the scenery. As they drew in through Charlwood's gates William said, 'Tell me, Mrs Fenton, what is it about Charlwood that interests you so much? Only the garden? I'm afraid the main house is not yet ready for visitors, but I could show you the Dower House if you wish. It should soon be ready for occupation. I want a word with my caretakers so we shall have to call there.'

'Occupation? By whom? Surely you are not going to live there yourself?'

'Why not?'

'I thought you owned Charlwood.'

'I do. But renovating such a big house is a long and costly business. It will be some time before I am able to live in it, perhaps as much as a year.'

'I see.' Maria Fenton's tone was thoughtful.

William showed her the Dower House as promised, but her mind was not on the charms of what was quite a small house. She returned to the subject of Charlwood as soon as they set off up the drive. 'So Charlwood is to remain unoccupied for some time yet?'

'Unfortunately, yes.' William eyed her curiously. 'Is there something wrong with that?'

'Oh no! No, how could there be? It's just that I find it such a pity…'

'It won't be neglected. I have men working on it at the moment.'

'Yes, of course. And a caretaker, too, I dare say.' Mrs Fenton perhaps felt that she was appearing to be too curious, and she gave a little laugh and said, 'Oh, forgive me, Sir William. I always have such an affinity for houses that need our love and attention. I knew Charlwood when I was a girl and it affects me to see it in ruins.'

William laughed. 'Of course, your family comes from Stoke Harborne. Did your brother live there, too?'

'My bro—? Oh, yes, my brother. Or rather, my brother-in-law. No, he has lived in London all his life.'

'I see. And your friend? Does he also come from London?'

'My friend? I don't think... Oh, you mean Walter's friend. Yes, he does.' She smiled provocatively. 'I do believe you are jealous, Sir William! But you have no need. Walter's visitor is an old friend of the Fentons, nothing more. But we were talking about Charlwood... Is it really a ruin now?'

'Far from it. But if it is to be a home for the family, it will have to be perfectly restored. Now, do you wish to see the gardens?'

The tour William gave his companion was shorter, but followed much the same course as the day before. He enjoyed it very much less. In spite of her claims, Maria Fenton showed little interest in the garden and none at all in the views, but it was apparently true that she loved the house. She would have wandered all over the ground floor if he had let her. When they reached the salon she exclaimed at the state of the walls, and walked round examining them, picking up some of the pictures, knocking on the plaster and tapping the wood to see, she said, how much repair they would need. He found it even odder when she examined every picture in minute detail.

'If you do not need my help with the gardens, perhaps you would allow me to advise you on schemes for restoring—and especially decorating—Charlwood, sir. I am thought to be something of an expert on interiors. I cannot tell you how many of my friends have been grateful for my advice. These pictures, for example. Would you like to have them restored?'

She was becoming increasingly flirtatious, too, and William was discovering that for all her charm, Mrs

Fenton bored him. Her manner was brittle, altogether
too artificial, too contrived, and he had a strong feeling
that there was more behind her interest in Charlwood
than she had admitted. Disliking the situation, he said
drily, 'Thank you, ma'am. You are very kind. But I have
already engaged a firm from London to carry out the
restoration work. And the time to discuss schemes for
decoration can wait till I have chosen a wife.'

Still too sure of her ability to fascinate to see this as
the snub it was, she opened her eyes wide and breathed
dramatically, 'So it's true? You intend to marry? Dare
I ask who the lucky lady is?'

'Since it is not yet decided, I'm afraid I can't answer
you.'

'Really? You haven't decided? How very interesting!'
After a short silence the lady went on, 'Sir William,
you and I are such old friends by now that I feel I can
be frank with you. I so wish I could be the chatelaine
of this lovely house! I can think of no better use for
my fortune.' She sighed. 'So much money is a burden
to me, Sir William. I sometimes wish Edric had left
me less well endowed. But to use it to restore a house
like Charlwood to its former glory would be a dream
come true. You say you haven't yet chosen a wife. Then
think, my friend. Think of what we could do together...'
She leaned towards him, and he caught a breath of her
perfume.

William wondered why it was that a movement like
that from Emily Winbolt could set him alight, when the
lady in front of him evoked only a feeling of distaste.
He took a step back and said with a small bow, 'I'm
afraid I can't offer you Charlwood, Mrs Fenton. Nor
anything else. But I am sure there are other houses in

need of your care. And your money. I hope you find one to satisfy you. Shall we return to the carriage?'

This time she could not help but be aware of his rejection. The colour ran high in her cheeks and her voice was shrill as she snapped, 'My word, sir, you are very blunt!'

'I think it best to be plain when it seems necessary, ma'am.'

She turned away and with a flounce of her skirts said, 'Necessary? What do you mean, necessary? I hope you don't think my offer of help was anything more than a neighbourly gesture? You have completely misunderstood me, sir. *You* may be looking for a wife, but, I assure you, *I* have no intention of seeking another husband!'

'Of course not,' he said soothingly. 'The idea is absurd. Tell me, are you planning to go to the Harbornes' next month?'

On the way home William determinedly confined his conversation to strictly neutral topics such as conjectures about the weather or the harvest, or future events in the county, to which Mrs Fenton's responses were almost non-existent. Her attitude implied that he was unworthy of any further consideration. But when he saw her to her door and took his leave, she thanked him with a tight little smile and wished him success with his plans for house and gardens. 'Especially those involving Emily Winbolt,' she said before she went indoors.

As he drove back to his godmother's, William was coming to the conclusion that he had been much mistaken in Mrs Fenton. He had thought her the sort of society charmer with whom he had enjoyed many a light flirtation in the past. But today he had seen ugliness under that beautiful surface. Her last words had had a distinct undertone of malice in them, and the smile had been more than a touch poisonous. She was furious, of course, that he had turned down her veiled proposal. But he was sure it had been her pride, not her heart, which had suffered—she would soon recover. All he need do was avoid her as much as possible in the future. She couldn't really do him much harm, and he had at least put an end to her desire to see Charlwood.

In that he was wrong. Mrs Fenton swept into her salon and, angrily pulling off her gloves, said, 'It's no use. The place is in chaos, and I wasn't able to get near any of it except the big room at the back. And you needn't expect me to spend any more time on that conceited oaf, either.'

'Poor Sis! Turned you down, did he?' asked the gentleman sprawling in one of the armchairs. 'I told you it was a bad idea.'

'Don't call me Sis! It's vulgar. And I don't know why you think it was such a bad idea. Most men are easy enough to attract. But he has his eye on the Winbolt creature, I'll swear. I can't imagine why. She's a cold fish if ever I saw one.'

'Maybe he thinks she's richer?'

'Probably. I'll have to think of something else. Or Kidman will just have to find another way to stop them from moving into Charlwood.'

'You'd be a fool to tell him so. Kidman is not going to be pleased, Sis. And when Kidman isn't pleased he's dangerous. You haven't seen him in one of his rages.'

'Don't call me Sis! I've told you, it's vulgar. Anyway, Ashenden isn't planning to move into Charlwood for some time yet. He's putting the Dower House in order and intends to live there first.' She walked about the room, then stopped and said abruptly, 'How does Kidman know that the Valleron jewels are hidden in Charlwood?'

'I told him.'

'You! Why?' She looked at him, then shook her head. 'You're a fool!'

'If Kidman asks me a question, I answer it as best I can. That's not foolish, that's sensible. Remember that, Maria.' There was warning in his voice. 'Edric was pretty ruthless, but Kidman is worse. Edric was at least sane before he got ill. And then it was the drugs.'

Maria gave him another scornful look. 'You're a coward! I can handle Kidman. But how did you know about Charlwood? I won't believe Edric told you himself, brother or not. Edric wouldn't tell anyone.'

'I agree. But those last weeks he was so full of laudanum that he didn't know what he was saying. You know that. You were there. He rambled a lot, but he mentioned Charlwood several times when I was with him, and talked about staying there with Great-Uncle Daniel when he was a boy. That was before my time, but it wasn't difficult to work out.' There was a pause. Then his voice changed as he said, 'In fact, I wouldn't be surprised if, when Edric knew he was dying, he tried to tell someone exactly where the jewels were, but it was too late. He couldn't get the words out.' He came nearer. 'Was it you, Maria? You spent more time with him than anyone else at the end. Are you sure he didn't manage to tell you something after all?'

'Quite sure!' she said quickly. 'He couldn't say a word!'

'Then why did you move here straight after his death?'

'How can you be so cruel?' she said with a catch in her voice. 'I was unhappy in London. Edric was dead and I...I wanted to be back where I belonged—where I was brought up.'

'Which just happens to be within a few miles of Charlwood. I'm not sure I altogether believe that, and neither will Kidman. He's not what I'd call gullible. And he intends to find those jewels even if it means tearing the place down.'

'No! I...I need a little longer.'

Walter frowned. 'I suspect you're playing a dangerous game, Maria. Kidman is no fool. Take my advice and have something for him when he comes. Some little titbit to keep him occupied. Think hard. Isn't there anything?'

'I tell you, Edric was practically unconscious! He... he mumbled a bit, but I couldn't make it out. It could have been something... something about a fountain. Then I thought he had fallen asleep. And that is all!'

'Why the devil couldn't you have woken him up and asked him to try harder?'

'Even your precious Kidman couldn't have done that. Edric wasn't asleep, he was dead.'

'Leaving you a grieving widow.'

'But not as rich as I had hoped to be. Not nearly. And to think of all those jewels lying there... Tell me, how far...how far has Kidman got?'

'He and a couple of others have been searching the house ever since Edric died, and haven't found a thing. The big room at the back was the last. It's just as well it was. Some interfering neighbour saw them, and since then the place has been watched every night.'

'Well, all I can say is that it's a pity Kidman didn't

buy the place himself when he had the chance. He waited too long.'

'Who would have thought anyone would be mad enough to want a rundown ruin like Charlwood? We all thought we were safe. Kidman did his best—he made a better offer for it as soon as he heard, but it was too late. Ashenden was in possession and didn't want to sell.'

'I think it's hopeless. Better for everyone if Kidman gave up.'

'You can't know him as well as you believe! Seventy thousand pounds' worth of gold and jewels? He won't give up on a sum like that, and—listen to me carefully, Maria, because it's important—woe betide anyone who stands in his way.'

'What can he do?'

'I hope, very sincerely, that you never find out. You need to do some serious thinking. He'll be here before the end of the week, and I'll mention the fountain business. But I warn you. He doesn't like failure, and he doesn't like frustration.'

It had to be said that neither of them was looking forward to Mr Kidman's visit.

When William got back his excursion with Mrs Fenton was forgotten, driven from his mind by the news that the children would be arriving in England at the end of the month. His long-standing problem was suddenly urgent. The changes to the Dower House were nearly done, and furnishings and staff could be dealt with in a very short time after that. They could all move in not long after the children's arrival. But who would look after them there? They needed more than the impersonal care of a servant, they needed a mother.

In other words, a wife was urgently required, and
there was only one woman who would do. Emily Winbolt would not be the easiest of helpmeets, but she was
exactly what he required. He even liked her! And judging by her response at their first sensational meeting,
marriage to her could have other, more exciting, aspects.
William decided not to delay any further, but, conscious
that the lady might need considerable persuasion, he set
out for Shearings the next day without saying a word
about his intention to Lady Deardon.

He arrived at Shearings at a fortunate moment. Philip
had taken Rosa to Temperley to visit her father, and
Emily was alone. He found her in the library, the plans
for one of the gardens she and Philip had created spread
out on the desk in front of her

'Good morning,' she said with an air of abstraction.
'You're an early bird. But I'm glad you're here. Look
at this.' She pointed at a section of the drawing that
showed the supply of water to the ornamental ponds.
'It wouldn't be difficult to do something like this at
Charlwood.' She looked up. 'Is something wrong?'

'No, but I want to talk to you.'

'Please do,' she said, squinting at the drawing. He put
the drawing back in the folio and closed it. 'What are
you doing?' she asked, looking up again, astonished.

'I want your full attention,' he said. Silver-grey eyes
gave him a cool, clear look. He had seen that same look
assessing his garden just two days before.

'What about?' she said.

He took a breath, then found he was nervous. 'Is it
too cold for a walk in the garden?' he asked, delaying
the moment.

'Of course not. I'll get my shawl.'

They went out into the crisp air and walked for a while in silence as William sought an opening for his request. At last he said, 'You did me the honour of confiding in me recently. I think you said that, much as you loved your brother and sister-in-law, you felt as if you had lost the…relevance you once had to Shearings.' He looked at her, one eyebrow raised. When she nodded he went on, 'You would most of all like to have an establishment of your own, perhaps one with gardens where you could work to create the same beauty you have achieved here.'

Emily frowned. 'Are you telling me you've found something suitable? But it's too soon. I believe I told you—Philip and Rosa will take a long time to become truly reconciled to such an idea.'

'I agree with you. Moreover, I think they are right to be concerned. Have you never thought that you might feel just as lonely living by yourself as you do now at Shearings? More, even.'

She looked at him, startled. 'I would employ a companion, of course.'

'How could you be sure that a paid employee would be as congenial as your sister-in-law? That she would share your interests in the way Mrs Winbolt does? Isn't it far more likely that she would be a timid spinster, in need of a situation, too afraid of offending you to voice an honest opinion? You are too intelligent to be content with such a companion. Believe me, I think you could well be more bored, and lonelier then than ever before.' He stole a look at her. She was frowning. He went on, 'But I think I may have a solution for you.'

'And that is?'

'You could help me with a problem of my own. My brother's children, who are now my wards, are arriving in England very soon. They can stay with Lady Deardon till the end of October, but then the Deardons are going up north to visit their daughter and Thirle will be closed for months. That in itself is not a problem—I want the children to move to Charlwood as soon as possible and the Dower House will be ready for us all by then. But I haven't yet found anyone who would help me to look after them.'

'And you want me to help you to find someone?' asked Emily, puzzled.

'I mean I need a wife, Emily.'

She looked at him blankly for a moment, then understanding dawned and she said, 'You think that I... Oh, no! That would be quite out of the question!'

'Why? Why is marriage to me out of the question?'

'Because...because we don't love each other.'

He regarded her with amusement. 'I'm not asking you to love me. To be honest, love matches are something I really cannot believe in. I've seen too many marriages that began with roses and romance only to end in recrimination and regret. I suppose that's why I've never felt the slightest temptation to fall in love.'

'But that is the only reason for a woman to marry! Philip and Rosa—'

'Nonsense! Really, Miss Winbolt, to assert that a woman needs to fall in love before she will marry is flying in the face of the evidence. Your brother and his wife are very rare examples—the exception that proves the rule. Women marry for any number of reasons—to cement an alliance, to be rich, to be secure, to have a position in life, to give a child a father... Shall I go on?'

'No, I think you have made your point. But such

expediency would not suit me. I would only marry a man I loved and respected.'

'I agree that respect, and even liking, are essential for a successful marriage. But not love. Do you not like me?'

Emily paused, then said, somewhat surprised, 'I...I... Yes, I do.'

'You don't respect me, then?'

'Of course I do. But I can't marry you. Not when it sounds so cold—so like a business matter. You must find someone else to look after your children. Mrs Fenton, for example.'

He paused, looked faintly embarrassed, then frowned and said shortly, 'That is impossible.' After a moment he shook his head, and took her hands in his. 'Emily, won't you at least consider it?'

'No.'

'But why? I am offering you everything you said you wanted. You said you wanted an establishment of your own. I am offering you one. You said Charlwood should be restored. I am offering you a share in restoring it.' His hands grasped hers more firmly. 'You said you were lonely. I am offering you companionship and a real marriage, not any sort of empty business arrangement. It would have warmth and passion, I assure you—we would be lovers as well as friends. And think of the wonderful time we could have making Charlwood into a home for us all. Think of the beauty you could create in the gardens there.'

Her hands were resting in his. She could feel her heart racing. 'I...I don't know what to say.'

'Well, that's a beginning. How about saying you will?'

'What about the children? I have had no experience in dealing with young people.'

He pulled her round to face him and smiled kindly at her. 'Nor have I! We should have to learn together.'

She gazed at him doubtfully, still not sure. 'It would make Rosa and Philip happy. They like you. But...'

'Emily,' he said softly, 'stop worrying.' He took her face in his hands and held it while he kissed her. The kiss was warm, gentle, reassuring. Emily closed her eyes and was caught in its magic, its promise of a life together that would be full of friendship and laughter, comradeship working on Charlwood, the challenge of caring for two lost, young orphans. Her present life suddenly seemed so empty, so lacking in purpose... Was she being unrealistic in expecting to fall in love and be loved in return before she married? Her experiences so far had not been encouraging. Perhaps Philip and Rosa *were* a very rare exception. This proposal of William's had so much to recommend it...

'Emily? Are you going to marry me?'

She opened her eyes and looked into his. They were intensely blue, dark blue as she had first seen them all those weeks ago. She had felt happy with him then, happier than she had felt for a long time. As she looked now, the fan of wrinkles, which had so appealed to her then, slowly appeared at the corner of his eyes and he smiled. She caught her breath. It was so tempting...

He had said they would be lovers as well as friends... She had a sudden, vivid memory of that first meeting, how closely he had held her, how the feel of his body next to hers had given rise to such strange, new sensations of delight, how his caresses had filled her with a passionate desire to belong only to him. As her husband, William would have the right to take her even further into the world she had glimpsed on that evening in May. Yes, there would be much more than friendship in marriage to William. He would be her lover as well as her friend...

But not in love with her. An inner sense of caution held her back from committing herself then and there. In spite of what he said, without real love it *was* a business proposition. And whether she accepted or not should be guided by her famously cool head, not her treacherous feelings. It would be madness to say yes, simply because a man's eyes developed a fan of wrinkles when he smiled. She stared at him, in an agony of indecision.

'It's a big step,' she said eventually. 'I...I need time. I...I know it isn't what you want, but I'd like to meet the children first.'

'I see.' He thought for a moment. 'I suppose that is a risk I shall have to take.' He took her face into his hands again and looked deep into her eyes, his lips inches away from hers. 'If I agree to wait, would you give me your word that you will at least seriously consider being my wife?'

'Yes. Yes, I will, William.'

He kissed her again, this time intensely, holding her tightly in his arms, almost as if he had been afraid of losing her. Emily was deeply moved. She had found it difficult enough to refuse him a final answer before, but if he had asked her again after such a kiss as this she would have agreed to anything he suggested.

During the following weeks William called almost every day, using as his excuse that he needed to forge ahead with his plans for the house. They were seldom alone, but in the middle of practical discussions such as the decoration of the rooms at the Dower House or plans for the water conduits he would look at Emily in a way that caused the colour to rise in her cheeks, and her words to falter. Then she would pull herself together, give him a glare and act coldly for a while until he made her laugh, and they would be friends again. She discovered that she had never before been so closely attuned to another person's mind, not even Rosa's. And his sense of humour was so like her own that she found herself laughing more than ever before. He became more important to her with every day that passed, and soon there was little doubt in either of their minds that she would eventually agree to marry him.

Philip and Rosa were happy to see the friendship developing, especially Rosa, who was privately convinced that this would turn into the sort of love match she had always wanted for her beloved sister-in-law. She watched and waited, not without amusement, until the inevitable moment arrived when the two principals recognised the fact.

Of course there was gossip. William could not visit Shearings as often as he did without rousing interest among the neighbours, but on the whole the news that Miss Winbolt and Sir William Ashenden might be making a match of it met with approval. There were inevitably exceptions. Mrs Gosworth could not miss such a splendid opportunity to exercise her talents, and attacked Emily in characteristic fashion. 'I'm so glad you are taking my advice, Miss Winbolt,' she said when they met at Lady Harborne's. 'You must be congratulated on having an understanding with such a fine gentleman as Sir William. To be mistress of Charlwood is quite a step, even if it is a ruin. I suppose we have to hope that the ruin doesn't *ruin* its owner! It must be costing a fortune to restore it.' Smiling with pleasure at the idea, she went on, 'And I'm sure Mrs Winbolt is very happy at the thought that she will soon at last be free of you, and able to run Shearings without interference.'

'I assure you, Mrs Gosworth, you are premature. Sir William and I have no "understanding".'

'No understanding? Then you must use what arts you still possess to achieve one! It won't do to let him slip through your fingers. Mind you, he won't do that without thinking twice. Sir William is a very prudent man.'

'What *do* you mean by that, ma'am?'

'Why, nothing, I am sure! Only that he has so far been careful to live within his budget, and I believe that is beginning to affect his plans for Charlwood. Report has it that the work there has recently been held up for want of supplies. He clearly needs greater financial resources. Where better to find them than in a prudent marriage? I think your hopes are safe.'

Emily laughed. Getting to her feet, she said, 'It is a disappointment to me, if not a surprise, that you remain completely yourself, ma'am. You are, as usual, quite mistaken. If and when Sir William marries, I am quite certain his motives will be honourable, not mercenary.' Still laughing, she moved away.

But later when she caught up with Rosa, she muttered, 'That woman is a snake!'

Impressed with Emily's vehemence, Rosa said, 'I agree with you, but what has she said to make you so angry?' When Emily told her, Rosa said, 'That is purest malice. The poor woman is full of it. But I hope you won't pay any attention to her. Remember what happened the last time you listened. You were in

such a temper then that you forgot all about Pritchard's
bull!'

Anger was changed into amusement. Emily laughed
as she said, 'Perhaps I was luckier than I realised at the
time. The bull chased me, I climbed into a tree, and
afterwards, Rosa, I fell out of the tree into William's
arms!'

Rosa gazed at her in astonishment. 'William? William Ashenden? You sly puss! It was *William* you
kissed after you'd escaped from the bull? Of course!
I should have guessed. He was the tramp. Oh, Emily!'
She began to laugh, too. 'What a story! You'll have to
marry him, if only to tell it to your grandchildren! I
insist on knowing everything about it! Did he recognise
you when he saw you again? What did he say to you?'
A few minutes later Philip found them helpless with
laughter in the middle of a complicated tale that they
refused to explain to him. Knowing his womenfolk of
old he gave up, and, shaking his head, went in search
of other amusement.

Chapter Seven

It was early and not particularly warm when William arrived at Shearings one morning, but he found Emily already busy in a corner of one of the gardens, sketching the layout of the flower beds there. When she looked up and saw him she smiled and said, 'You mustn't think I'm suggesting we copy this plan exactly, but some of the ideas have worked very well here. They are worth considering. And if we are to be ready for next year…'

Her voice died away as she saw his expression. 'What is it?' she asked.

'I'm afraid I can't stay. Word has come that the children will arrive at Falmouth within the next few days, and I have to leave almost immediately. But I wanted to see you before I go—I shall be away for a week or more, perhaps two if the children are bad travellers.'

Emily had known that the children would arrive soon, but this was nevertheless a blow. What dismayed her most was that William would be away for anything up to two weeks! For the first time she realised just how much she had come to depend on his company. She pulled herself together with an effort and said calmly, 'I shall miss you. But I'm glad you'll see the children at last. It will be a great relief.'

'It's more than that, Emily. It's the start of a new life. And I hope more than ever that you'll join me in it.' One arm was round her, his lips were very close, the blue eyes looking deep into hers. 'Why don't you say now that you will?'

It was so very tempting. She still felt all the pull of the attraction that had caused her to lose her head completely the first time they had met. But now there was much more to it than that. They had come a long way since that first meeting and she had learned to respect him, to trust him as she had not trusted any man for a long, long time. It would be so easy now to agree, to tell him to take care on the journey, to come back safely because he was important to her, that of course she would marry him. Because she loved him...

The thought came unbidden, quite out of the blue, and it shocked her. For a moment she stared at him blankly, her mind racing. That was not the sort of thing William wished to hear from her. He had told her that love played no part in his plans for marriage, and any confession from her now would probably only embarrass them both. For her own sake she must keep a cool head. But if he kissed her at that moment, feeling as she did, there was no knowing what she might say or do. Holding her sketching block in front of her as a kind of shield, she slipped out of his reach.

'You're very persuasive, my friend,' she said, forcing a smile. 'But this isn't the moment. I still want to wait till after I have met the children. I want to be sure that I am doing the right thing, for them as well as myself.'

For a moment it looked as if he would protest, but

then he shook his head ruefully and said, 'You're a strong-minded woman, Emily Winbolt. But then I've known that from the start. I'll wait. But meanwhile...' Before she could elude him again he had taken her back in his arms and kissed her thoroughly and not at all gently. Then he went, and Emily was left dazed, half-wondering if she had after all made a mistake, if she had missed an opportunity that might not come again.

During the days that followed she found no comfort. In recent weeks she had forgotten how it felt to be lonely, but now with William away she wandered about the house and gardens like a lost spirit. However much she scolded herself for her spineless behaviour she could not settle to any activity for long. She tried to work on the plans for Charlwood's gardens, but William was not there to consult, to sound out her ideas on, not there to tease her, to make her laugh, and she put them away again.

By the beginning of the second week she decided in desperation to ride over to Charlwood, hoping to find something there that would help her forget William's absence for a while. She stopped at the Dower House and exchanged a few words with Mrs Lilley, who told her that Sam was somewhere about in the grounds, then she rode up the drive and, leaving her horse in the care of her groom, went inside the house. The workmen were busy in the bedrooms, she could hear their voices. One of them was whistling. The hall was free of debris and she made her way without too much difficulty into the salon. Some tidying up had been going on here, too, and the floor was clear to the windows at the back. She went over and looked at the gardens and the view beyond.

Up on the hill the trees were still the rich green of high summer. It would be a month or two before they started to show touches of autumn gold. But a feathery mass of silvery grey showed where the clematis climbing over the remains of the statue had gone to seed, and the roses in the fountain court were in riotously full bloom, some of them already almost ready to fall. Even as she watched a shower of petals cascaded to the ground...

A movement near the fountain caught her eye, the figure of a man...no, two men. But the afternoon sun, lower at this season, suddenly shone directly into the room and blinded her. When she managed to look again, nothing in the garden stirred. Had it been Sam Lilley? At first she had thought so. But Sam was a stocky individual and the figure had been tall. Or had the sunlight been playing tricks on her? She looked again, but there was no sign of Sam, nor of anyone else. Whoever it had been, he had vanished. Her curiosity roused, she left the salon and went out into the grounds.

In the garden she stopped, looked around her and listened. The bright sunlight was creating strong contrasts of light and shade, so that corners of the garden were almost in darkness. Voices floated out from inside the house upstairs, a few starlings were chattering in the trees, but the garden itself seemed to be deserted. There was certainly no sign of Sam Lilley. When she reached the fountain she looked round. Nothing. But on the side further away from the house the greenery that had been covering the statue had been torn away, and when she looked down she saw that the stones that had been piled up round it were scattered, and the ground was rough. She wondered if William had ordered the men to start work here. It was unlikely that he would do so without mentioning it to her, surely? She knelt down to look more closely at what had been uncovered…and jumped when a shadow fell across the stones in front of her.

'Good afternoon.'

Emily scrambled up, her heart pounding, but she was once again blinded by the sun and could only see the dark figure of a man standing a few feet away from her. She moved a few inches into the shade to have a better view of him, and saw a man in his late thirties or early forties, of average height and fashionably dressed. He was a complete stranger.

She took a deep breath and said coldly, 'Sir?'

'Did I startle you? I didn't mean to, I promise you.' His manner was gentlemanly and he spoke well, but she found the metallic flatness about his voice somehow repellent.

'May I ask what you are doing here?' she asked.

'Enjoying this garden. It is a beautiful day, is it not?'

Emily was not disarmed. Her manner was frosty as she said, 'By whose invitation?'

The stranger's smile was charming. 'No one's. But I'm not doing any harm. In fact, I'm looking for Sir William Ashenden. I'm an old friend of his.'

'And you are?'

'Charles K…Kavanagh. William and I were at school together.'

'I see.' For some reason Emily did not quite believe him, and decided not to tell him that William was away. Instead she pointed in the direction of the drive. 'Well, Mr K…Kavanagh, Sir William is not here at the moment, but if you go out that way you will pass the Dower House where you will find the caretaker. Indeed, I'm surprised you didn't see Lilley or his wife on your way in. You can leave a message there for Sir William. Good day to you.'

Mr Kavanagh stayed where he was and studied the back of the house. 'It is a beautiful building. Are you sure Sir William isn't here? He might be inside.'

'No, he is not, sir. But my groom is only a few yards away. If I call him, he will escort you to the gate. Do you wish me to?'

He regarded her thoughtfully. Then, clearly making up his mind, he said, 'Thank you, you are very kind, but there's no need. I shall find my own way. Good day, ma'am.' He gave her a polished bow and walked away.

Emily stared after him, wondering if she had been unpardonably rude to a friend of William's. There had been an air about the visitor that ought to have reassured her. His dress and manner had been that of a gentleman, and surely an ordinary intruder would not be so self-confident? But there had been something…an uncomfortable feeling that he had been laughing at her, mocking her, and she wondered how long he had been watching her before he spoke. There had been that slight hesitation when he had given her his name, too. And that last, appraising look had sent a chill down her spine. No, she was fairly sure Mr Charles K…Kavanagh was not quite what he said he was. She would wait a few minutes to give him time to speak to the Lilleys and go on his way. Then she would check with them whether he had indeed left any sort of message.

Meanwhile these stones… It was curious. In places where the stones had been displaced and the earth laid bare it looked as if a large dog or some other animal had been digging. Perhaps William had ordered the men to start looking for a water conduit? But William surely knew that this was completely the wrong place!

The afternoon was spoiled. Puzzled and uneasy, feeling as if the stranger was still watching her, Emily collected her horse and groom and rode down to the Dower House. Mr Kavanagh was nowhere to be seen, and when she questioned Sam Lilley she learned that no one had passed through the gates in the last few minutes. In fact, apart from herself and her groom, no one had come or gone all afternoon.

'I thought we'd done with them vagrants, Miss Winbolt. With all the work goin' on, the house is not as empty as it was in the old days. I thought we'd frightened 'em off.'

'This was no vagrant, Sam. He looked quite prosperous—and he behaved quite as if he had every right to be here until I pressed him.'

'Sir William never told me of any friends of his who might visit—always excepting yourselves and Lady Deardon, o'course.'

'And don't forget Mrs Fenton, too, Sam,' Mrs Lilley said. 'She was here with Sir William not long ago.' She turned to Emily and added in a confidential tone, 'Though I don't think we'll see her here again. They had words, they did. I've never seen the master look so put out.'

Sam looked annoyed. 'Be quiet, woman! That's nothing to do with us. I've warned you before not to gossip about what the master does or doesn't do.' He turned back to Emily. 'I'm sorry, ma'am. Mary means well, but it's a bit quiet for her here. She likes a chat. She'll be happier when there's more life about the place. But I don't know what to say about the fellow in the garden.

I could try to get more men to help me keep an eye on things, perhaps.'

Emily agreed with this, and then set off back to Shearings.

Once home she consulted Philip, but he had not heard of any strangers, nor did Emily's description of the man at Charlwood fit any of their neighbours' visitors.

'I'll ask around,' he said. 'He may be a genuine friend of Ashenden's, but I'm inclined to agree with you, Emmy. I don't like the sound of him. Tomorrow I'll send one of the men over to help Sam Lilley. Charlwood is a big place to look after, especially when it has to be left open for the workmen. Meanwhile, I'd advise you not to go over there again with only your groom for company. Not till Ashenden is back, at least.' He looked at his sister's face and smiled. 'Don't look so despondent. It won't be long now.'

Deprived of any further visits to Charlwood, Emily once again took to wandering disconsolately round the gardens at Shearings, but just three days later she was returning to the house when a familiar figure appeared at the end of the path.

Any remaining doubts about her feelings for William Ashenden were put to flight when she saw him. She stopped, unable to breathe, overwhelmed by a wave of pure delight. She watched as he started to walk towards her, and she had to fight to stand still, to stop herself from running to meet him and throwing herself into his arms.

Her heart turned over as he reached her. 'Emily,' he said, his eyes wrinkling as he smiled at her. He took both her hands in his and repeated more softly, 'Emily.'

It sounded almost like a caress. His voice was slightly deeper than she remembered, but it was still so familiar, so dear.

She stared at him, her mind so full of what she must not say that for several moments she found it impossible to speak. Finally she said stupidly, 'You're back.'

He grinned, then said gravely, 'Yes, I do believe I'm back.'

He was laughing at her! Emily made a huge effort and pulled herself together. 'Did you...did you have a successful journey?' she asked coolly, removing her hands from his.

William shook his head and took her hands again. 'No, no, that won't do at all, Emily. That's too cold. You mustn't sound like Miss Winbolt. Not with me. You should say something like, "I'm so glad to see you, William. I've missed you so much..." Something like that.' His arms went round her and he said softly, 'Or should I say it first? I've missed you, Emily. I've missed you abominably. Every day.'

It was an effort, but she ignored the warm happiness that flooded through her and managed to say with commendable calm, 'I missed you, too, sir. And I am very glad to see you. There's so much to talk about.' He was shaking his head again in protest at her matter-of-fact tone, but she turned to walk back along the path and went on firmly, 'You must tell me first how the children are after their long journey. When did you all arrive at Thirle?'

'Yesterday. I gave them a day to settle down before leaving them with the Deardons while I came over to see you. You shall meet them very soon. Lady Deardon hopes you could pay her a visit tomorrow, in fact.'

'That's kind of her. I'd love to meet your wards, though I confess I'm quite nervous, too.'

'There's no need.' William's voice very seldom lost its teasing note, but now he was quite serious as he said, 'They are just two lost children, Emily. They've left everything that was familiar behind in Jamaica. Just a couple of years ago they had two loving parents and a comfortable, if not particularly wealthy, home. Now all that has gone, and after months of uncertainty they have been brought to England and handed over to an uncle they hardly remember. They need security, and that is what I intend to give them.'

'They'll need more than that,' Emily said involuntarily.

'Love? Yes. That's what I want from you.' Emily's eyes flew to his, but he went on, 'Love for the children.'

'Of course.' If her words sounded somewhat flat, he made no sign that he had noticed.

The next day Emily drove over to Thirle alone. She and Rosa had discussed whether they should go as a family, but between them they had decided that too many strangers at once might be intimidating for the young Ashendens.

William had obviously been watching for her, for when the carriage came to a halt he was there at the door. He helped her out, took her hands in his and pressed them, smiling that special smile of his, which always sent a warm glow through her. He raised an eyebrow in query and she nodded. Then, taking a deep breath, she turned. The children stood at the entrance, close to each other, a boy of about eight, and a girl a couple of years younger. The boy's arm was resting protectively round the little girl's shoulders. They gazed at Emily, their eyes large with apprehension, as she advanced towards them. William said, 'Miss Winbolt, I'd like you to meet James and Laura Ashenden.'

Emily smiled at them and held out her hand. There was a pause, then James stepped forward and asked with a touch of truculence, 'Are you my uncle's friend?'

A little nonplussed, Emily nodded and said, 'Well, yes. Yes, I suppose I am.'

Laura joined her brother in front of Emily. Huge, blue eyes gazed up at her. 'Are we *really* going to be sent away to school?' she whispered.

Emily looked helplessly at William, but he remained silent, challenging her to find her own answer. She looked at the children standing in front of her, clasping hands so tightly that the knuckles showed. The boy looked ready to fight the world, his jaw set, his lower lip thrust forward belligerently. His sister's little mouth was trembling, huge eyes, the same dark blue as William's, full of apprehension. Emily's heart melted when she saw that the child was trembling. She knelt down and drew Laura to her. 'Whatever put that into your head?' she asked. 'I know for a fact that your uncle has a very pretty room at the Dower House meant just for you. And there's another for James, too. But would you prefer to go to school?'

A smile broke like sunshine through clouds. Black curls bobbed vigorously as Laura shook her head. 'No, I don't p'fer it. James doesn't, too. But she said—'

'Who is that, Laura?' asked William. 'Who is "she"?'

James answered him. 'It was Dolores. Mrs Warburton's maid. She said we were very naughty children and our uncle wouldn't want to be bothered with us. He'd send us away to school and we would never see each other again, ever.'

'Then the lady in this house here said that you were Uncle William's friend, and I thought…' Laura hesitated.

'What did you think, Laura?'

'I thought perhaps you would ask him not to, 'cos people do things for friends, don't they?'

'Yes, they do. But in this case I shan't even have to ask him. I am quite sure he wants you to live with him. You may have been very naughty with Dolores, but I wasn't there, and neither was your uncle, so we don't know. But I'm sure he wants to keep you with him, whatever she said. In any case, you will *not* be naughty in England. There's so much to do at Charlwood you won't have time. So that's settled.'

Even James was smiling by this time, but she saw that they both looked cold, so she got up and held out her hands again. 'Let's go inside. I expect you find it chilly here after the West Indies.' Laura took hold of the proffered hand without hesitation, but James hung back and looked at William. 'Are you coming, too?' he asked. Emily wondered with private amusement whether James was naturally aggressive, or just had that sort of voice. But William replied cheerfully, 'Of course I am, my boy. Come on! Let's all go inside together.' They went through the doors into the hall where Lady Deardon was waiting.

The children stayed with Lady Deardon, but spent a lot of their time with William at Charlwood. Emily frequently joined them there, and before long they were completely at ease with her. While William inspected the progress his builders were making or discussed plans with the architect, the children ran laughing and shouting through the gardens under Emily's watchful eye. On cooler days they played hide and seek inside the house, in the rooms that had been made safe. They loved what they called treasure hunting, and frequently brought her bits and pieces that had been left behind many years before by the previous occupants—anything from an old hairpin to a silver-handled walking stick, which they found under one of the floorboards. James was particularly proud of one find, and asked Emily if he might keep it to hang on the wall in his bedroom.

'What is it, James? Show me.'

James produced a small canvas and when it was dusted they saw that it was a picture of the garden. Emily exclaimed in delight when she saw it and told James he must show it to his uncle. 'Look! It's a picture of the fountain! And it's exactly as I imagined it. We can use this picture as a guide for when we rebuild it! James, you are a clever boy. May I keep it safe for the moment? Later, if your uncle agrees, of course you may put it on your wall!'

Encouraged by this discovery the children redoubled their efforts, but never again found anything so exciting.

The mysterious Mr Kavanagh did not appear again, and when Emily asked William about his 'school friend,' he said he was sure he didn't know anyone of that name. He was equally sure that no one had been asked to look at the structure of the fountain, either. He examined the soil that had been disturbed round the fountain, and James and Laura were convinced that someone had been looking for buried treasure. The children even dug up more of the ground, but the only result was two very dirty children and a bigger pile of uninformative soil. Nothing else. It all remained a mystery.

William said he didn't like mysteries, and brought forward the plans for working on the gardens, engaging extra local men to do the work. The work had already been planned as part of the general scheme for Charlwood, but the presence of the men working on it also meant that any daytime intruders would find it difficult to remain unseen for long.

Soon it was assumed that Emily was part of the Ashenden team, and when William once or twice went to London, he brought the children over to Shearings to be with her rather than leave them with Lady Deardon. In no time at all the neighbourhood was sure that an announcement of the engagement between Emily Winbolt and William Ashenden could be expected before the month was out. There were many who were genuinely glad at the prospect of happiness for Emily Winbolt, and looked forward to seeing her at last the mistress of an establishment of her own. They also wished Sir William success in his ambitions for Charlwood. There were one or two of the more hard-headed, of course, who added with a significant nod that he had chosen the right wife for such an enterprise.

But Maria Fenton was not one of the well-wishers. She arrived, ostensibly to pay a visit to Rosa, on a day when she knew William was on one of his excursions to London, but when the time came for her to leave she asked Emily to walk with her to the carriage. 'I've been told you are an expert in gardening,' she said. 'I would like to consult you about some plants I have just received.'

The excuse seemed very feeble, but, unable to think

of a reason why she should not oblige a guest, Emily reluctantly went with her.

'I intended to ask William about these plants some time ago when he was showing me the gardens at Charlwood,' Mrs Fenton began. 'But the visit ended rather awkwardly.'

'I'm sorry to hear that. But I doubt he would have been of much help. He doesn't yet know a lot about plants,' said Emily with a smile.

'I suppose it was foolish of me. And to tell the truth, I wasn't really there to see the gardens, but the house. William and I had so often discussed it and he had asked for my advice—he knows I am something of an expert in decorating. But after what happened I felt I couldn't help him any longer.'

'Oh? Why not?'

'Oh, I couldn't possibly tell you.'

Emily looked at her in surprise and didn't believe that for one moment. Though Rosa appeared to enjoy her old friend's company, she herself had never liked Mrs Fenton, and suspected that this feeling was returned in full measure. Why, she had no idea. In this instance the woman was obviously eager to tell, and hoping to be pressed, but Emily had little wish to satisfy her. Instead she said earnestly, 'In that case, my dear Mrs Fenton, I wouldn't dream of asking you to say another word.'

A brief look of annoyance flashed over Mrs Fenton's face. Then she said, 'It is only because I was taught at an early age not to boast of my conquests, especially when I have had to disappoint the gentleman in question.'

'An admirable lesson, and one with which I heartily agree. So…?'

'But I know I can rely on you, Miss Winbolt, not to spread it further. You see, Sir William was on the point of asking me to marry him some time ago, and I did not wish to encourage him. I am sure you can understand my doubts more than others would. Women like us, in possession of a fortune, learn all too soon how often we are loved not for ourselves but for what we can bring with us.'

Emily began to understand why she had been brought out for a private chat. Plants, indeed! She said coolly, 'Forgive me, but am I to understand that you seriously believe Sir William Ashenden would propose to you merely because of your fortune? You underrate your own charms, Mrs Fenton.'

'Oh, he might well have been attracted to me. Most men are. But in this case it wasn't enough to reassure me. You see, I happen to know that Charlwood is positively devouring money. I even wonder whether William's own resources are actually running out. Have you noticed that the building work has recently come to a halt? I had no wish to see my own fortune going the same way as his. It was very awkward, especially as I feel so sorry for him, saddled as he is with his pauper niece and nephew. If they really *are* his niece and nephew. The girl is very like him, is she not? But now I can forget my worries. I was so relieved when I heard that he was to be saved by...someone else.' She laughed gaily. 'At one time he told me your visits to Charlwood were just a matter of business. I thought it was the gardens he was talking about, but now...the business was more serious than that, don't you think? What a clever man he is to be sure.'

Emily found herself suddenly trembling with rage. She coldly regarded the woman before her. 'Sir William Ashenden is one of the kindest, most honourable, most scrupulous men I have ever known. Whereas you, Mrs

Fenton… Let me be more honest with you than you
have been with me. I believe your purpose in coming
here today was to destroy my friendship with a man I
trust and admire. But I don't believe you. I don't believe
Sir William was remotely tempted to ask you to marry
him, and certainly not because he wished to acquire
your fortune. I am quite *certain* that he would not ask
anyone to marry him merely for her money.'

'Not even you?'

'Me least of all. Goodbye.' Emily turned and walked
swiftly into the house.

Chapter Eight

'You were longer than I expected,' said Rosa when Emily came in. 'Were you able to help Maria with her plants…? Emily!'

Emily had been lost in her thoughts. Now she looked up. 'What was that?'

'Mrs Fenton—were you able to help her?'

'I…I think so.'

Rosa looked at her more closely. 'What's wrong?'

'I was just asking myself… Rosa, am I being a fool?'

'I shouldn't think so,' said her sister-in-law cautiously. 'You're usually very sensible. But I can't say until I know what you're talking about. Come over here, sit down, and tell me why you think you are being a fool.'

'First I must tell you that William wants me to marry him.'

'Good! Though I can't pretend I'm surprised. You and he—'

'Oh, no! Please don't think it is one of your great romances. He doesn't pretend he loves me. It would be a purely practical arrangement. As he has pointed out, he needs a wife to run Charlwood and look after the children, and I...I would have the establishment of my own that I said I wanted.'

'Really? And?'

'I have all but made up my mind to agree, but now... I'm not sure whether I would be doing the right thing! I had been starting to think I would never marry and was quite happy to look for somewhere to live independently, near you, without any sort of husband. And now...if I agree to this proposal of his, I will be putting myself, my happiness, my life even, into the hands of a man I hardly know. At the moment it seems to me this might be extremely foolish.'

Rosa smiled sympathetically, but shook her head. 'It's certainly wise to think twice before taking such a big step as marriage. But, believe me, anyone who sees you and William together wouldn't doubt for one moment that you are suited. Possibly even better than you realise. Tell me why you're so worried. Was it something Maria Fenton said?''

'I'm not sure. I don't think so. I didn't believe her, I really didn't. She tried to hint that he only wants to marry for money, because Charlwood is costing such a lot to restore.'

'Ah! I'm sorry to have to say this, Emily, but I'm sure the poor woman is jealous. She hoped to capture William for herself. She can't seriously believe such a thing of him. You must forget whatever she said—it was simple jealousy.'

'There isn't much for her to be jealous about,' said Emily unhappily. 'William has never pretended he loves me!'

Rosa smiled. 'You haven't said you love him, either. *Do* you?'

Emily got up and walked away. 'I mustn't,' she said in a stifled voice. 'This marriage was always meant to be a...a sensible arrangement, not a love match. But then Mrs Gosworth...and now the Fenton woman... And I've heard what one or two of the neighbours are saying—that they admire William for his astuteness... I'm beginning to wonder whether it isn't altogether *too* sensible.'

'Really, Emily, you *are* being foolish. Very foolish! I thought you knew William better than that. No, don't shake your head. Listen to me! No one could deny that you have a considerable fortune, or that restoring Charlwood is an expensive occupation. There will always be some who will link the two together and come up with an uncharitable answer. But I will wager anything you like that William is not marrying you for either of those reasons.' She gave a little laugh and said, 'You are so blind, both of you! However, I'll keep my ideas on the true situation between you to myself for the moment. You'll have to work it out for yourselves. But I am quite certain that William Ashenden's motives...' she put her hands on Emily's shoulders and gave her a little shake at each word '...are...not...mercenary! Put that thought right out of your mind if you don't want to risk spoiling your future happiness.' She got up and shook out her dress. 'Now, let's do something useful. Philip will be back with the children soon. They will all be looking for something to stave off starvation! Shall we see what we can do?'

She refused to say any more and Emily was forced to follow Rosa's lead and suppress her doubts for the rest of the day.

* * *

But that night she lay sleepless as her fears returned to torment her. They were not without foundation. Ever since she had been of an age to marry, she had been the target of men tempted by her fortune. At a very early stage she had been the victim of such a man, saved at the last moment from a disastrous marriage by hearing his true opinion of Emily Winbolt. 'A cool fish', he had called her to the woman he was actually in love with. 'I'd sooner go to bed with a block of ice.' Hurt and humiliated, she had since then always been ready to suspect the worst of any man who showed an interest in her.

Was she now, at this late stage, to be taken in again, deceived by the very unusual circumstances of her acquaintance with William? It had never occurred to her to question his motive until others had put the idea into her head. But now the old doubts crowded in on her like a cloud of stinging gnats. Was his plea for her to marry him just a clever ruse to gain access to a considerable fortune? Had he taken cynical advantage of her loneliness and uncertainties to finance his ambitions for Charlwood? Certainly he must be spending vast sums on its restoration—Philip had said as much. And what did she know about William's resources? Nothing. Nothing at all. In one respect Maria Fenton was right. There *had* recently been delays in the building work at Charlwood, and William had said he was going up to London 'to sort out a few financial matters'. Now, for the first time, she began to wonder exactly what he had meant.

But as the night wore on, she began to think about the man himself, and slowly the clouds of doubt dis-

persed. William was an honourable man. She had spent
a great deal of time in his company, and she felt she
knew him better than she knew anyone else—his intelli-
gence, his patience, his humour, his annoying tendency
to tease, his honesty—and his determination to keep his
promise to his brother to look after his children. These
were all William, and she liked him. He was so very
dear to her. She should back her own judgement, and
trust him. Emily went to sleep at last, looking forward
again to seeing William, hearing his voice, being in his
company...

When she was next at Charlwood, Emily saw that
work had been resumed on the house. She asked what
the problem had been, and William told her that the
builders had made a mistake in ordering some stone-
work, but that had now been put right. So much for
Maria Fenton's insinuations! What a fool she had been
to pay any attention to the woman!

Later that day they walked up to the folly; while the
children chased each other up and down the hill, they
stood looking at the view. The lush green of summer
was beginning to give way to the tints of autumn—gold,
scarlet, amber and bronze. Autumn was slowly advancing. In no time it would be winter.

Emily gazed at the clear blue sky arching over the
multicoloured landscape and gave a sigh of content-
ment. 'It is all so beautiful. I hope the children will be
happy here.' William took her hands and turned her to
face him. For once completely serious, he said, 'They
have had a rough time of it since their parents died.
Juana's family rejected them, and it proved impossible
to bring them back to England as soon as I wanted, but
they weren't happy while they waited. Now I intend

them to have a normal, loving home here at Charlwood. Will you give me your help to make it one? It's time you gave me your answer.'

Emily had made up her mind the night after her talk with Rosa and she answered him now without hesitation. 'It's yes. I *will* marry you, and I'll make the children as happy as I can.' The children were now at the foot of the hill, and they waved and started running up towards her, laughing and giggling, covered in twigs and bits of dry grass. She watched them approach. 'I'm very fond of them already, William.'

'I know. Emily, I swear you won't regret this marriage.' Cupping her face in his hands, he kissed her then, slowly and sweetly. For one moment she was back in the hollow on the hill at Shearings, drowning in the delight of a man's kiss. Then the children were upon them, Laura clasping her knees and demanding to be kissed, too. With typical bluntness James asked, 'Why were you kissing Miss Winbolt, Uncle William?'

'Because, my lad, I'm going to marry her, and we shall all live together at Charlwood.'

There was no doubt about the children's reaction. James's usually serious face broke into a huge grin, and Laura skipped around them all for joy. 'I told you she would, James, I told you she liked us,' she shouted gleefully. 'And now she's going to look after us all the time.' They were both so excited that they took off down the hill again, whooping and laughing.

'That seems to have gone down rather well,' said William, looking slightly dazed. 'It makes me wonder if my reaction when you said you would was too restrained. Should I have been more exuberant, too? Leapt in the air, perhaps? Turned a somersault?'

Emily was suddenly filled with a bubbling happiness.

'I'm glad you didn't,' she said, demurely. 'Your kiss was...more than adequate. I'm not sure I could have taken much more excitement.'

'My dear girl, you don't know the half of it,' he said softly, taking her hand and pressing a kiss into the palm. 'And teaching you the rest is one of the things I most look forward to. But I'll take care. You'll enjoy being married to me, dearest Emily, I promise you.'

He laughed and hugged her when she blushed scarlet, and his arm was round her as together they went down the hill.

Things were less happy in the Fenton household. The news that the owner of Charlwood was to marry Emily Winbolt, and that the whole family would take up residence in the Dower House very soon after, was greeted with furious disbelief.

'You told Kidman you'd break it up!' snarled Walter Fenton. 'You swore that the Winbolt woman would never marry Ashenden if she thought he was a fortune hunter! You told him you could convince her. And now what?'

Equally angry, his sister-in-law snapped back, 'I did my best, but she didn't believe me. Can I help it if the girl is a fool?

'You'll have to have a better excuse than that when Kidman comes this time, Sis! And don't tell me I'm vulgar. You're in no position to criticise anyone. Perhaps you'd better start thinking of where you'll go when he sends us packing.'

'He won't do that,' said Maria confidently. 'Not when there's a chance I might remember more of what Edric said on his death bed. You leave it to me.'

* * *

From the moment her engagement to William had been made public, Emily lived in a whirl of activity. Now officially the future mistress of the Dower House, she was consulted about the furnishings, about the staff to be engaged and a hundred and one other things. Lady Deardon seemed anxious to help, perhaps because she and Sir Reginald unfortunately had to travel up to Yorkshire three days before the wedding.

'I am so sorry, my dear,' she said to Emily, 'but my own daughter is expecting to be delivered of her first infant within the next fortnight. She's our only child and I must be with her. It's William's fault. I was always telling him to make up his mind, and now that he has it's too late for us to be at his wedding. We are leaving early the day after tomorrow for Yorkshire. William and the children will spend a last night with us, then they will have to move into the Dower House. Thirle will be completely boarded up. Most of the servants who are not going with us have left already.' She sounded annoyed as she went on, 'All such a scrambled business! It's a real blessing you are to marry, for I don't know what would happen to those children if they were left in William's hands alone. But I have to say, it's a joy to see you with them. They are so fond of you.'

'And I of them, Lady Deardon,' said Emily with a smile.

'We've arranged to take a last look at the Dower House tomorrow. Will you be there?'

'I don't think so. Philip is taking the children to Temperley for the day, and Rosa and I are planning to inspect the arrangements at the church.'

'Then I'll say goodbye now. We shall stay up in Yorkshire for some months, and after that we are to

spend time in London. You must ask William to bring
you to stay with us there. Be very happy, my dear.'

On that note Lady Deardon embraced Emily warmly
and left.

The following day Rosa decided she wanted to go
with Philip and the children to see her father, so they
agreed that inspecting the church could wait till the
evening and Emily drove over to Charlwood after all.
When she got there the Deardons' carriage was blocking part of the drive, and the grooms were laughing and
talking to Mrs Lilley, so she left the gig and her own
groom with the rest and went on foot up to the Dower
House. Lady Deardon had a good carrying contralto,
and Emily realised that William was getting a scolding.
Amused, and not at all eager to interrupt, Emily walked
quietly nearer.

'This wedding of yours should have taken place
weeks ago, William! All this scurrying and hurrying,
and no one of any importance invited. You should be
ashamed. The neighbourhood is bound to talk.'

'Let them! As long as Emily and I are satisfied, it
surely does not concern anyone else. And, apart from
yourselves, everyone who is important to me will be
there, ma'am.'

Unappeased, Lady Deardon swept on. 'I kept telling
you to make up your mind, but you wouldn't listen to
me. I did what I could. You said you wanted a rich wife
and I found you not one, but *two*—Emily Winbolt and
Maria Fenton were both young, and both respectable.
And, what is more, they both had the fortune you said
you needed for Charlwood. Perhaps that was a mistake.
One would have been enough. You would have made

your mind up sooner and there would have been time for a decent celebration.'

Unable to move, Emily was forced to listen as Sir Reginald interrupted. 'Well, I have to say, Sarah, I think he's chosen the right one.' He gave a rich chuckle. 'Though if I remember rightly, Will, the Fenton woman was your first choice. You weren't at all keen on Emily Winbolt.' The chuckle grew louder. 'What was it you called her? A plain, strong-minded woman! That was it.'

'She still is,' said William curtly.

Several minutes—or was it hours?—later, Emily was driving at a breakneck pace back to Shearings. In her fever to get away she had forgotten her groom and was alone in the gig, rattling through the lanes, deaf to the noise as she scraped its sides on the turns, and blind to anything else on the road. Her headlong rush stopped just short of Shearings. Philip and Rosa were out for the day, but the servants would be there, with curious eyes and sidelong glances. She sat for a while, trying to think where she could go. It was hard to think at all. The pain was making it difficult to get her breath, and the cruel words were hammering in her head: *Plain, strong-minded…. She still is. She still is. She still is…* Emily bent her head and put her hands to her ears, but the voice, William's voice, curt, dismissive, did not go away: *Still is, still is, still is…*

'Miss Emily! Are you all right, miss?'

She looked up. Will Darby was standing in front of the gig, an expression of concern on his homely face.

'Yes. Yes, I'm all right, W-Will. But I…was just trying to…to decide what to do about the gig. I want to walk…to walk back to Shearings, you see.'

'I could take it for you, miss. But are you sure you're all right?'

Emily straightened up and made herself talk in her usual decisive manner. 'Of course I am. But I need a touch of exercise. Thank you.' She got out, handed the reins over, and waited till Will Darby touched his cap and drove off.

She watched him go and then took the path that ran alongside the stream. She was like a sleepwalker, making for her goal without consciously knowing where it was. But after a few minutes she had reached it, and sat down in the hollow on the hillside below the oak tree. She looked round. When she had last been here the ground had been a refuge after her fall, soft and welcoming, and overhead she had seen a canopy of bright green leaves. Now the trees were nearly bare, and their dead leaves lay on the ground, crackling harshly when she trod on them. She had become a different person here with a stranger who had comforted her, made her feel cherished, and then had aroused such a storm of passion in her... Why had she not seen then that this was just one of fate's cruel tricks? She had been off her guard when she met him again, more afraid of discovery than suspicious of a possible fortune hunter. Later, still blind, she had been amused by him, had learned to like him, to trust him. For a short while she had even allowed herself to fall in love with him.

And now it was all over. William Ashenden was just another fortune hunter, and she was not going to marry him, after all. Why had she not seen at the beginning that he was actually just like all the others? Why had she forgotten the harsh lessons she had learned when young? Philip was a beautiful child; Emily was plain. Philip was charming, attractive to all; Emily was too

independent, too stubborn. What was the word again?
Strong-minded. A plain, strong-minded woman. *She
still is She still is. She still is...* She took a sharp breath
as the pain hit her again like a knife thrust. Then she
smiled bitterly. At least, unlike her first betrothed, William Ashenden could hardly call her *'a cold fish'*! He
knew better than that. That was something he had found
here in this very place. Had it amused him to find out
how vulnerable she really was?

She sat lost in her thoughts for some time, till an
awareness of her surroundings began to return. The sun
had gone in, and she was cold. Philip and Rosa had
promised to deliver the children back to Thirle, but they
would soon be home. If she wasn't there, they would
start to wonder where she was. She must face the world
again. She got up, dusted down her clothes and set off
for Shearings.

On the way she discovered that there was one thing
at least she was sure about. Rosa and Philip would have
to wait till tomorrow before she told them anything. In
her present state she would find it impossible to face
their consternation, the inevitable questions her decision
not to marry William Ashenden would provoke. Above
all, they would want to know what would happen to the
children, and she wasn't ready even to think about that.
This awful sense of betrayal left no room for anything
else. She would avoid it all by pleading a sick headache
and retiring to her room as soon as she got in.

Rosa was sympathetic, but gave in to Emily's request
to be left in peace, and Emily spent a sleepless night
struggling to regain something of her former calm
good sense, berating herself for her weakness when

she failed. William Ashenden had broken through the coolly detached approach to life with which she had protected herself. Today, with a few short words, he had destroyed years of patiently regained self-esteem. Now she had to learn all over again that Emily Winbolt was plain. And not only plain, but quite pathetically stupid, too! Stupid enough to have believed that in one man's eyes at least she *was* beautiful—because he cared for her.

She lay awake, trying to plan how she could tell Rosa and Philip that her marriage would not take place. They would want to know why, but how could she tell them about William Ashenden? How could she bear to say the words, when it felt as if each syllable was twisting a knife in her heart. And then there was William himself. What was she to say to him? If only she could forget her heart and use her head!

As dawn was breaking she came to a decision. William was bringing James and Laura round to Shearings some time during the morning. Before they came, she would break the news to Rosa and Philip, and ask them to look after the children, while she spoke to their uncle. Her mind balked at trying to imagine what she would say, and how he would reply. But however it went, they would have to sort out what was to happen afterwards. With the Deardons gone, and Thirle closed up for the winter, the only place where the three Ashendens could stay was the Dower House. But someone else, not her, would have to look after the children. Perhaps Rosa could find a suitable woman in the village to be a stopgap until a governess or nurse could be appointed. Emily herself would go to stay with her grandfather in London for a while.

* * *

Telling Rosa and Philip was every bit as hard as she had foreseen. Rosa kept saying that she didn't believe it, that there must be a mistake, until Emily spoke more angrily than ever before to her gentle sister-in-law. 'Why do you always want to believe the best of everyone? I tell you, he had asked Lady Deardon to find him a rich wife! Not just any wife, Rosa. A rich one, to help him with Charlwood.'

'But, Emily, he hadn't met you then. Perhaps he did ask Lady Deardon, but that's the sort of thing one says without meaning very much by it. I've watched him with you. He likes you, really likes and admires you, I'll swear he does.'

Rosa's defence merely fuelled Emily's anger. 'Does he?' she demanded. 'Must I tell you what he said? Do I have to give you the words, Rosa? He thinks I *am* plain. Of course, we both know that I am plain, but I believed him when he said he thought I was beautif…beautiful. He called me strong-minded and I *am* strong-minded. But, fool that I was, I thought he l-liked me for it. And all the time…all the time…' She stopped, unable to continue. After a moment she said bitterly, 'I suppose it's not so surprising what a lot of plainness, what a lot of strong-mindedness, can be tolerated when gilded over with the prospect of a fortune.'

Philip said sharply, 'Emily! My dearest Emily, don't!' He came over and held his sister in his arms, stroking her hair in an effort to comfort her.

Rosa was restless, torn between sympathy for Emily, and her anxiety for the children. As soon as Emily was calmer she could keep silent no longer. 'I'm sorry, Emily, but I have to ask this. What is going to happen to the children?' When Emily shook her head and turned away, she said, 'You *can't* abandon them! They are so attached to you. What can you possibly say to them?'

Emily had steeled herself in the night to face William Ashenden, but had given up when faced with the problem of telling James and Laura. She still had no idea how to deal with it, and was relieved not to have to answer Rosa when one of the servants came in. She was less happy when he told them that Sir William Ashenden had called and was asking to see them urgently. 'Bring him in,' said Philip, and, turning to Emily, he said, ' He's earlier than I expected. Does he know about this?'

She shook her head, now no longer so sure that she could face William calmly. The temptation to flee was strong, but before she took one step William was inside the room, James and Laura holding his hands. He began without ceremony.

'Forgive me for bursting in on you like this, but I'd like to leave the children here earlier than we arranged. I couldn't leave them at Thirle—the Deardons are already on their way to Yorkshire. I had a message this morning, and must ride over to Charlwood without delay. There's been a fire in the night and the Dower House is badly damaged. Barnaby Drewitt, my man, is already on his way over, but I must follow him there as soon as I can. May I leave them with you?'

Rosa came forward. 'What a shock! Of course you may!' She turned to the children and said with her gentle calm, 'It's lovely to see you. Did you sleep well? Tell me, have you had breakfast this morning?' They shook their heads. 'Then we shall see about it immediately before you starve. What about you, sir?'

Emily had remained frozen in the corner of the room and William was looking at her with a puzzled frown, but he turned at this and bowed. 'Thank you, but I must hurry to Charlwood. I don't yet know how bad it is.' Turning back to Emily, he said, 'You're looking pale. Aren't you well, Emily?'

'She has a bad head,' said Rosa. 'She shouldn't really be downstairs. But a…a day's rest and she will be…will be herself again. Come, James, don't look so unhappy. You'll feel better after you've had something to eat. Emily, will you bring Laura? And we'll find you a tisane for your poor head at the same time. Goodbye, Sir William. I do hope things at Charlwood aren't as bad as you fear.'

Correctly interpreting a look from his wife, Philip said slowly, 'I'll come with you, Ashenden. You might be glad of company.'

'It may not be as bad as it sounded, and Barnaby Drewitt will be there, but I'd be grateful if you would. Thanks.'

But when they got to Charlwood, the damage was if anything worse than William had feared. More than half of the Dower House was a smoking shell, and Sam Lilley had been injured. His second-in-command was surveying it in despair. 'I don't understand it,' he said. 'I didn't hear or see a thing, sir, neither did any of the rest of us. It's a complete mystery.'

William walked round, inspecting the damage. His face was grim. 'Where is Sam Lilley now?' he asked.

'In the lodge, sir! He's not all that fit. He was asking for you.'

'Why the devil didn't you say so before, man?' William left Philip and Barnaby Drewitt to see if anything could be done at the site, and strode off to the lodge. A red-eyed Mrs Lilley met him at the door, twisting her hands in her apron. She took him through to the kitchen, where Sam was sitting at the table with a bruise on his face and a bandage on his arm. He was very pale.

'This is a bad business, Sam.'

Sam Lilley said nothing, but sat with his head bowed, avoiding William's eye. Mrs Lilley hovered anxiously nearby. 'Will you sit down, sir?' she said.

William sat down opposite his foreman and gazed at him, wondering what was wrong with the man. Sam Lilley had once farmed a small plot of land up the valley. He had been independent, till a series of disasters had ruined him and he had been forced to sell up and look for employment. When William had been looking for a caretaker and foreman for Charlwood, Sam had applied. His manner held a certain honest independence that pleased William, and he gave him the job. Mrs Lilley, too, had been respectful, but dignified. She had certainly never been servile. Today Sam looked like a dog who expected to be given a beating, and his wife was nervously anxious to please. Something more than Sam's bruises and burns was wrong with the Lilleys.

'Tell me what happened,' William said. 'You didn't get that bang on your head trying to put a fire out!'

Sam looked up for the first time, but he still couldn't quite meet William's eyes. He turned his head away. 'I tried to stop them,' he said. 'But they laughed at me.' A quick glance at William. 'I swear, I tried to stop them, sir.'

'Who are "they"?'

Sam put his head in his hands. 'I...I don't know,' he said. 'I can't tell you.'

'He's not well, sir,' said Mrs Lilley, looking at her husband's bowed head. 'They left him lying there on the ground and he wasn't found for hours. Perhaps he'll remember in a little while.'

'I hope so,' said William sombrely. 'I'll be back later.' He got up and left the Lilleys and went back to the ruins of the Dower House. He was met by Barnaby Drewitt.

'Been talking to the men,' said Barnaby. 'Queer go. If they're to be believed, they were all fast asleep when it happened. Don't remember a thing. Want me to see if I can persuade them to remember?'

'No, I don't. We're not in Brazil now. Find the man who has taken over from Lilley and let me talk to him. George Fowler, I think his name is.'

Fowler was ashamed and puzzled. He kept shaking his head as he said, 'We was all down at the stables, master—that's where we sleep when we're supposed to be on watch, see. Except for Sam Lilley. He sleeps at the lodge. Well, the house was ready, and you was goin' to move in the next night. Tonight, that is, now. And we had a bit of a celebration. The men who'd been keeping a watch on the house were all there, and we all had a drink, but we didn't skimp on our watch. Not at first. We took turns to make a round or two each. Then Sam comes down to the stables wi' a cask of ale. Drinks for everyone, 'e says. Courtesy of the master. Well, we were all pleased, o'course, and we all drank your very good health. And then after that I couldn't seem to keep my eyes open. Not nohow. And the others felt the same. I can tell you, we had a terrible shock when we woke up this morning and saw what had happened. Ask anyone.'

'But that fire must have been burning for a good while to do so much damage. Surely someone among you must have seen it, smelt it, heard it, even?'

Fowler shook his head. 'That ale you left us was surely powerful stuff.'

'I didn't leave any ale for you! Sam must have found it, and thought it was from me.'

Fowler looked uncomfortable. 'I don't know about that. He didn't say.'

Looking grimmer than ever, William joined Philip and Barnaby, who had been examining the smoking embers. Philip said quietly, 'What do you make of this, Ashenden?' He turned something over with the toe of his boot.

William squatted down. 'I'd say this was a remnant of an oil-soaked rag,' he said slowly. 'And there's another.' The two men stood up and looked down at the rags. Then William stood up and shouted, 'I want to see all the men who were here last night. Now!'

In a few minutes, a line of unhappy men were doing their best to look William in the eye. He regarded them silently, but with such an air of menace that they shuffled their feet and shivered. 'Someone, possibly one of you, destroyed my home last night,' he said with steel in his voice. 'I don't believe you all slept through everything. Which of you saw it burning and did nothing? One of you must know more than he's saying, and I intend to find out who—one way or another. You! Did you set fire to my house? Or you? Or you?' He pointed at each of them in turn, but they all shook their heads and stammered out their innocence. William turned away in disgust. 'Lock them all up. And send for the constable.'

One man shouted, 'That's not right! It ain't us, master! You ask Sam Lilley!'

'What?'

'That's right! It wasn't any of us who set fire to your house. But Sam Lilley could tell you who did!'

'What do you mean by that?'

'Strangers, that's what! Sam's been seen talking to strangers. Ask him!'

Mary Lilley met William at the door of the lodge again in real distress. 'Don't be too hard on him, sir! It's hit him real bad.' When he didn't reply, she twisted her hands in her apron and moaned, 'I knew it would come to no good. I told Sam he shouldn't listen. The money won't do us no good, I said. But he was that set on having a place of his own again...'

'Don't! Don't say another word, Mrs Lilley. Not for the moment. You're too distressed to think of what you're saying. I should like to talk to Sam. Now.'

She nodded and he went through to the kitchen. Sam was sitting where he had left him. He seemed more willing to talk. 'Don't blame Mary, sir,' he said. 'She had nothing to do with this.'

'Nothing to do with what, Sam?'

'The fire. But I never thought they would set it on fire, you see? They told me they just wanted to look over the place. Not burn it down. I swear I wouldn't have listened to them if I'd thought...' He shut his eyes and turned his head away. 'I wanted the money. All they wanted me to do was to make sure that nobody else saw them. And I didn't think you'd be any the wiser, y'see. I didn't mean to hurt you. And then he...he...'

'Who, Sam?'

'There were two of them. I recognised one of them, but I couldn't put a name to him. The other one always stayed out of sight except the once. But I knew him. He was in the garden once when Miss Winbolt was here.

He told her his name was Kavanagh, but that wasn't his real name.' He stopped for breath.

'What was it?

Sam gave a shuddering sigh, and said, 'I think it was Kidman. That was what the other one called him. Kidman.'

There was a silence. Lilley put his hand on William's arm. 'I know I've done wrong, Sir William, and I'll be punished for it. But don't make Mary suffer. She's had enough to bear. Please, sir!'

'You should have thought of that before.' William got up. 'I trusted you, Sam Lilley. There was a good job for you here, a very good one once Charlwood was working. Whether you meant to hurt me or not, you've certainly succeeded. I don't yet know what will happen to you, but I will see that your wife doesn't starve. You'd better stay here for the moment.'

Apart from setting the men to work on clearing up the mess, there was little more William or anyone could do at the Dower House. He had the information he needed from Sam Lilley, and could guess the rest. As they walked round for a final look at the devastated house, he told Philip the story and then gave vent to his frustration.

'Damn it, what's to happen now? We're in a fine mess, Winbolt. It will be months before the house is fit to live in again, and what are we all to do meanwhile? If this had happened two days ago, the Deardons might have helped, but as it is… They are gone, and by now Thirle House will be thoroughly boarded up and the rest of the servants back home or on their way to London. It's a damnable affair! Just when everything seemed to be working out so well. What will it do to Emily and the children?'

Chapter Nine

Philip hesitated, but decided not to say anything of Emily's present state of mind. Ashenden had enough to contend with for the moment. Instead he said, 'It's Lilley I don't understand. What took possession of him? He had so much to lose!'

'I don't know. It shakes my confidence in my own judgement. I would have sworn he was honest. Those two arsonists certainly fooled him.'

'What are you going to do about him?' asked Philip.

'He needs to recover. That was a hard knock on the head, and I wouldn't be surprised if his cheekbone was cracked. I've left Barnaby to keep an eye on him. He won't run away.'

'Can you trust your man to hold him?'

'Who? Barnaby Drewitt? I'd trust him with my life. In fact, it has more than once come to that. And don't be deceived by his size. He's small, but more than capable of keeping any number of wrongdoers under control.'

The work on clearing up the Dower House had

already begun. William gave one or two further instructions to George Fowler, then said, 'We must get back. Emily will be wondering what has happened. But I'd like to have a quick look at the main house first.' He and Philip walked on up the drive and turned off into the garden. Staring at the back of Charlwood, William asked, 'Why?'

Philip did not need to ask what he meant. 'I can't imagine. Either you have an enemy looking for revenge, or...'

'Or what?'

'Someone wants you out of Charlwood.'

'I don't think I have an enemy who hates me enough to burn my house down. But why should someone want me out of Charlwood?'

'That's something I can't tell you. But I've heard that you've had one or two costly delays...?'

'Stupid, unaccountable mistakes. There've been one or two unexplained accidents, too.'

'There you are then. Delays and accidents haven't put you off. You were about to move in to the Dower House, and it looks as if whoever it is got desperate. This will stop you taking possession for months. He might have hoped it would even put you off for good. I suppose you know that the house has a reputation for ruining its owners?'

William's smile was cynical. 'Does it, indeed? Well, *I* shan't be put off, Winbolt.' He regarded Philip for a moment. 'Are you afraid Charlwood will ruin *me*? Do you still believe I have only my naval pension to support me?'

'No, I assumed you must have a little more than that. You couldn't even begin to take on an enterprise such as Charlwood with just a pension.'

William nodded and said, 'Shall we collect the horses and go back? We can talk on the way.'

As they walked slowly down the drive William said, 'In point of fact, I've been expecting you to quiz me on my prospects. Isn't it usual for the bride's family to make sure the bridegroom can support her? To make enquiries?'

'What makes you think I haven't?'

William stopped and looked at Philip in some amusement. 'And there I was, thinking you were being quite flatteringly trusting!'

'Not where my sister's well-being is concerned.'

'Dare I ask what the outcome was?'

Philip smiled and contrived to look apologetic. 'My friends in the city seemed to think you were sound enough.'

William nodded. 'So they should.' They walked on. 'I take it, therefore, that you aren't among those who think I aim to fund my ambition with Emily's money?'

'Should I be?' asked Philip cautiously.

'A number of your neighbours think so.'

'Well, I don't, though…'

'Good! I'm relieved. Let me tell you something. I suppose as Emily's brother you should have been told this before, but I have a curious reluctance to publish it abroad.' He stopped again and turned to Philip. 'So keep it to yourself, if you don't mind. As it happens, Winbolt, I have no need of anyone's fortune. I have more than enough of my own to rebuild the Dower House—three times over if necessary. There's probably enough to buy and restore another Charlwood as well, *and* to leave something to live on. Comfortably.'

Philip gazed at him in astonishment. 'Good God,

Ashenden, what did you do? Rob the exchequer? You've kept it remarkably quiet!'

'After I left the Navy, I spent a year or two in South America and was lucky with ventures into mining there. But don't worry. The profits are all now safely and respectably invested. The children's future is secure, and so is Emily's.'

'Yes, well…' Philip felt he ought to say something to prepare William for Emily's present state of mind, but once again he stayed silent. Emily had not been herself this morning, and, after what he had just been told, he was sure there must be some mistake in what she had overheard. He hoped there was. He liked William Ashenden and it looked as if this disastrous fire could be something of a blessing in disguise. The necessary postponement of the wedding would give his sister time to avoid taking a step she might regret for the rest of her life. She could be a touch pig-headed, but if she discovered how very unlikely it was that Ashenden was a fortune hunter, she might be persuaded she had made a mistake. But one crucial question remained. 'When will you tell Emily what you have just told me?' he asked.

'Very soon. This fire changes everything. She needs to know about the delay in our plans, but perhaps it will cheer her up a little to know that there's no shortage of funds to put it right. I'll speak to her as soon as we get back.'

Philip took a breath and said, 'Good! But I should tread carefully if I were you, Ashenden. Emily was not…was not herself this morning. And she sometimes needs to be handled a little diplomatically. She can be… can be…'

William laughed. 'What are you trying to tell me?

That she's a woman who knows her own mind? I know that, Winbolt. And I wouldn't have her any other way.'

They arrived to find Emily and Rosa playing a game of battledore and shuttlecock with the children in the garden. But the game was abandoned as soon as the children saw their uncle and ran to greet him. Philip shook his head in answer to Rosa's enquiring glance.

'I'm afraid...'

'There has been a lot of damage, Mrs Winbolt, but nothing that can't be put right,' said William. 'But I'd like a word with Emily, if you don't mind. Perhaps she and I could take a walk in the garden while your husband tells you about it.'

'I'm not sure...' Rosa began with a worried look.

'I think that's an excellent idea,' said Philip firmly. 'Sir William has things to say to Emily, Rosa. It will clear the air a little.' He swept Rosa and the children up in a comprehensive wave of his arm and led them into the house.

'Before you say a word, Sir William, I have to tell you that I have decided I cannot possibly marry you,' Emily said abruptly.

William's reaction astonished her. He even smiled, a touch wryly. 'We seem to be even more in tune than I had realised, my love. I agree with you completely!'

'I beg your pardon?'

'The Dower House is so severely damaged that we couldn't possibly move into it for weeks, if not months. I'm relieved to hear that you have already seen that our wedding will have to be postponed.' He took her hands in his. 'It's a blow, I agree, and I'm sorry, Emily. But I do have something more to tell you…'

She snatched them away. 'You are mistaken. We are not at all in tune, and you cannot possibly have anything to say that I wish to hear! The wedding will not be post-poned. It will not take place at all! The whole affair is cancelled, finished. I am not going to marry you, not ever!' Emily heard her voice rising and stopped. This was not the way she had planned it. She took a breath and said coldly, 'That is all I have to say.' She turned away.

William pulled her back and said, 'What do you mean, "not ever going to marry me"? Is this a joke? If it is, I'm not sure it's very amusing.'

'It's no joke. I meant every syllable.' Emily looked away from the dark blue eyes gazing so confidently into hers and found it impossible to keep the bitterness out of her voice as she said, 'I'm afraid you'll have to charm some other gullible heiress into sharing her fortune with you! You might even be lucky enough to find one who is not so *plain*. Nor so *strong-minded*.'

'What the *devil* are you talking about?'

She braced herself. She hadn't seriously imagined that he would let her dismiss him without an explana-tion. But it had seemed so easy, lying awake the night before, to decide what she would say when she told him. He had never known that she loved him. She would tell him coolly, dispassionately, in a manner quite in keep-ing with their relationship, that she wished to break off their engagement. But she *had* loved him, and the hurt was deep. Cracks were appearing in her composure as she went on,

'I must congratulate you! You were very clever. I had learned to watch out for fortune hunters and thought I could see them coming. But *you*…! I didn't see *you*. *You* almost succeeded. What a pity you failed at what was very nearly the last fence!'

'Emily, what is this all about? Are you ill? I'm no fortune hunter! I have more than enough—'

Emily wasn't listening to him. She swept on, 'They all warned me—Mrs Gosworth, the gossips, even Maria Fenton. She was your other choice, wasn't she? What happened? Did she turn you down, William? Is that why you decided to make do with *plain, strong-minded* Emily Winbolt?' She took a breath which was suspiciously like a sob. 'But I'm not strong-minded, William. I'm weak-minded. Weak-minded enough to have been gulled by someone I trusted—'

'Will you calm down and listen to me! I never thought of your fortune. I didn't need to—'

'Stop lying to me, William!' she cried. 'I've found you out. You were after my fortune from the beginning! I heard you say so Why won't you admit it?'

'That is enough!' William's face was stern. He put his hands on her shoulders and held her so firmly that it hurt. 'You can't possibly have heard me say anything of the kind. I have never even thought it. What's all this about, Emily?'

'Not even to Lady Deardon? I suppose you'll try to tell me you didn't say I was plain and strong-minded, either.'

William frowned. Then his face lit up in relief. 'My God! You little fool! You must have overheard yesterday's conversation! That's something I can easily explain. But what were you doing there? Why didn't you join us?'

Emily pulled away from him and started to walk towards the house. 'Don't bother to explain anything,' she said over her shoulder. 'I wouldn't listen to you if my life depended on it!'

William caught up with her and pulled her round to face him. 'Oh, no, you don't!' he said. He kissed her then, hard. 'If words won't serve, then this might', and he kissed her again. At first she struggled to free herself and his hold tightened until their bodies were pressed so close that she could feel every inch of that long lithe figure. For a moment she was swept up in the old magic as he kissed her a third time, so gently, so sweetly... until it was suddenly no longer slow or gentle but urgent, passionate, betraying the deep need they had of each other. William was the first to break the kiss. He took a long breath, then slowly loosened his grasp until he could look at her again, and smiled into her eyes.

'Well?' he asked.

Furious that she had allowed herself to be seduced into his arms so easily, Emily tore herself away and cried, 'No! No! I won't be made a fool of again! I don't want your kisses. Keep them for the next heiress!'

William looked astounded. Shaking his head in disbelief, he said, 'Emily, what has *happened* to you? You're behaving like an idiot. This is all a complete misunderstanding! What if I told you that I have more than enough money for both of us? You could throw your damned fortune away if you wished, it would make no difference to me. I am a very wealthy man, Emily. Don't do this to us, I beg you!'

There was conviction in his voice. She stood a few feet from him, still trembling with reaction. 'Are you?' She put her hand to her head. 'How can I tell? How can I tell anything?' After a moment she shook her head and said, 'I really don't know any more what is true and what is a lie. But it doesn't change the rest. When

the Deardons said I was plain and strong-minded, you
agreed. Didn't you?'

'But damn it, they were quoting something I'd said
before I even knew you! Before I knew who you were,
at least. This is ridiculous. Emily, believe me, as soon
as I had linked the Miss Winbolt they talked about, to
that wonderful girl on the hill, I have thought you the
most intriguing, the most attractive woman I have ever
met.'

She shook her head. 'That is not what I heard yesterday. This wasn't months ago. This was yesterday. Yesterday you didn't argue when they called me plain. *"She
still is,"* you said. I heard you, William. You sounded
as if it annoyed you that I was plain, you spoke so...so
impatiently. *"She still is."*'

'Heaven give me patience! If I sounded impatient,
it was because I was annoyed with the Deardons for
reminding me how wrong I had been. But aren't you
forgetting what followed?'

'I didn't stop to listen. I had heard enough.'

'What? You mean all this nonsense is based on those
few words? You didn't stop to listen to the rest!' William controlled himself with a visible effort. 'Well, you
should have, Emily Winbolt. It would have spared us
both this idiotic melodrama. Why didn't you come out
of your hiding place and confront us? Why didn't you
have faith in me?'

'I don't think I will ever have faith in anyone again.
And...and I'm sorry, but I...don't wish to discuss it any
more. I have made up my mind. I really...cannot...
marry...you!'

Normally a most moderate man, William lost his
temper. 'I can't believe what I'm hearing, I really can't!
One stupid misunderstanding and suddenly, for no good

reason, you're acting like a tragedy queen, refusing to listen to reason, and ready to abandon everything we've planned. So much for your promises! So much for your so-called concern for my children, your declared intention to give them love, a home, to make them happy.' He glared at her. 'I make no claims for myself, Emily Winbolt. You seem to have written me off, though I'm not sure why. Or is all this just an excuse? Perhaps when it comes down to it, you really are the cold fish someone once called you. You can't face the prospect of giving up your independence, of living with a man in marriage and the intimacy that comes with it.' He shook his head. 'I wouldn't have believed it. I thought I had found a warm, living, passionate woman, the very woman for me, one I could grow to love, but now... Well, I suppose I could live with a cold fish if I had to.' He took her by the shoulders, and for a moment she was afraid when she saw how angry he was. 'But you! What sort of a woman are you to win the love, yes, the *love* of two small children, to raise their hopes of happiness, and then to throw it away without a second thought? Tell me how you can live with that?'

Emily put her hands to her face. 'Stop it, stop it!' she cried. 'Of course I care about the children, of course I don't want to disappoint them. But how can I marry someone I don't trust any more?'

William thrust her from him and walked away. 'I can't believe it,' he said. 'First the destruction of the Dower House, and now this...the annihilation of all our plans... James and Laura will be devastated.' He stood with his back to her for a moment in silence, obviously fighting to regain his control. After a minute he said with decision, 'I can't let it happen. Not to them.' He turned round and she saw he was calm again. He gave

her a coolly speculative look. 'Very well. I will accept
the situation and make no further claims on you. But in
return you will agree to put off telling the children that
our relationship is at an end. They must have time to
cope with one disaster before we tell them of another.
We have a perfectly reasonable excuse for postponing
the wedding—the children will understand that we can't
marry when we haven't a home to go to. And, by the
time the Dower House is fit to live in, I'll have found
an opportunity to break it to them gently.'

Emily slowly nodded. 'I'd agree to that,' she said.
'And William, I'm sor—'

'Spare me your apologies,' he said harshly. 'It would
have been better for both of us if I had found a suitable
nurse, a governess, a tutor for the children. Anything
but this stupid idea of finding a wife.' He stared at her,
and for a moment the anger in his eyes died and was
replaced with regret. Then he straightened himself and
said brusquely, 'And now you must excuse me. I have a
mountain of things to do, including looking for a place
to live. One of the men I thought *I* could trust, my own
employee, took part in setting fire to my house last
night. I intend to find the men who were behind him.'
He strode away towards the house.

Emily watched him go. Her heart was aching, and
after a moment she was surprised to realise that it was
not for herself, but for William. There was something
about his walk, a look of dogged determination, a lack
of his usual confident lithe grace, which gave her a
pang. For a moment she had a mad impulse to run after
him, to say she would take the risk and marry him,
whatever he thought of her. But instead she turned and
slowly walked away from the house in the direction of

the maze. Once inside she sat down, deep in thought.
Till now her acute sense of betrayal had blinded her to
the wider-reaching consequences of her decision. She
had thought about the children, but she had not given a
moment's consideration to the effect it would have on
William's life. During the night she would even have
been glad to hear he was suffering.

But things had changed this morning. He had come
back from Charlwood, knowing that the Dower House
was lost, deliberately destroyed by an unknown enemy.
Far from getting the comfort he could have expected
from her, he had been faced instead with a sudden, cruel
reversal of the rest of his plans. A lesser man would
have been crushed by two such devastating blows. But,
hurt and angry though he was, William's first thought
had been to protect the children, and he had gone on
from there. Emily wasn't proud of what she had done.
The sharp edge of her initial pain and fury had begun
to fade, and, though she was still far from feeling that
she could forgive him, she knew she must help him as
far as she could with his present dilemma.

When she entered the house again she found that
Rosa was in the salon sewing, Philip was out somewhere
on the estate and the children had been fed and, tired
by their early start, were now having a sleep under the
watchful eye of Mrs Hopkins. Rosa looked up as Emily
came in.

'How are you?' she asked.

'I'm well enough, thank you.' Emily said. She looked
round.

'William isn't here,' Rosa said quietly. 'He has gone
back to Charlwood to see if he can find out anything

more. Philip offered to go with him, but he seemed to want his own company. Emily, what have you done?'

'I've told him I can't marry him.'

'I see. Have you told him why?' Emily nodded and Rosa went on, 'He looked so weary when he left. I can't believe he's the villain you say he is. Nor can Philip.'

'You might be right. At all events he isn't a fortune hunter. If what he says is true, he's richer than I am. But I still don't want to marry him.'

Rosa snipped a thread with some force. 'Philip and your grandfather have both told me you were stubborn as a child, and I'm sorry to see that you haven't changed. You're a fool, Emily. You have rejected a good man, and hurt him deeply in the process.' She looked up and waited a moment, then, when Emily stayed silent, she went on, 'But I don't believe you're completely heartless. Tell me what you intend to do about James and Laura? What is to happen to them?'

Somewhat disconcerted by the note of condemnation in Rosa's voice, Emily said stiffly, 'William has asked me not to tell them yet and I have agreed. We both care about the children, Rosa. I care very much about them, and while I was outside I was considering what I could do. They urgently need somewhere to live. Could they stay here for a while?'

'Of course. As soon as Philip told me about the state of the Dower House, we decided that they should. The east wing will easily accommodate all three Ashendens. But now I'm not so sure…'

'What do you mean?'

'That was before we knew that you were persisting with this idiotic idea that William isn't good enough for you.'

'What difference does that make?'

'How on earth are you to avoid meeting him if he and his children are living here at Shearings? Or do you plan to run away to London, leaving some other woman to take your place? I suppose in that case you would expect their guardian to engage a nurse or governess for them?'

Since this was what Emily had planned during the dark reaches of the night, she rejected it now with surprising force. 'Of course not! That's a stupid idea!'

'Or…perhaps it would best for the children if he found someone else to marry. Do you know if he has anyone in mind?'

'Rosa, don't! Why are you being so hard, so…so unsympathetic? I want what is best for the children, of course I do. But I don't believe they could switch their affections to someone else as easily or as quickly as you're suggesting.'

'I am not suggesting anything of the sort! I am quite sure they won't. James and Laura have given you their unquestioning love. At my father's yesterday all their talk was of you and the life you would all lead together. Oh, no, Emily, they will not transfer their affections without considerable heartbreak first. But I assume you took that into account when you made your decision.'

Emily got up and walked round the room. Rosa and she had always been good friends. She had never known her like this before. She stopped and stared at her sister-in-law. 'Any one would think I had done wrong,' she said defensively. 'Am I supposed to welcome a fortune hunter with open arms, marry him, beg him to make what use he wishes of my money? Am I not to feel hurt when he says I am plain, strong-minded—'

'Emily, listen to yourself! Even you must find it difficult now to believe that William is any kind of fortune hunter! That's something I could have told you months ago, long before we knew he was almost a millionaire. If you remember, I did warn you not to listen to the gossips. As for the rest, I am certain there is an explanation. I only hope you come to your senses before it is too late. If it isn't already too late.'

'What…what do you mean?'

'William is very like Philip. They appear to be so easy, so charming in their manner, that those who don't know them are deceived. But when necessary they can be quite hard. I'm not sure the man who went out of this house a while ago will forgive you very easily.'

'Forgive *me*? What has William to forgive *me* for?'

'For being stubborn—strong-minded was the word he apparently used. For being fickle—'

'Fickle?'

'Good heavens, girl, you trusted him enough to agree to marry him just a short time ago. And now for the sake of a few words, probably misinterpreted, you turn his life upside down. As well as deserting him when he most needs support. I call that fickle.'

Emily sat in silence, making an effort to understand this new perspective. Rosa carried on sewing, with an occasional glance in her direction. Eventually she said, 'Well, Emily?'

'I…I need time to think.'

Hearing the slight tremor in Emily's voice, Rosa folded up her needlework and came over to where she sat. Smiling sympathetically, she said, 'The children will be down soon. Shall I tell them you're still not quite well?'

'No. No, I haven't seen a great deal of them. I'd like

to play outside with them for a little while, before it gets too dark. The air will do us all good.'

Emily and the children were still in the garden when William arrived back at Shearings. He heard their voices as he rode up the drive and his face twisted in a wry smile. They sounded so carefree. He dismounted and went into the garden. At the entrance he hesitated, not quite sure how to approach them. But the children saw him and ran towards him, as they always did, begging for a hug. He scooped them both up and looked at Emily over their heads. 'A truce?' he asked 'For them?'

'What's a truce, Uncle William?' asked James.

Emily came up and lifted Laura out of her uncle's arms. 'It means that your uncle and I have…have made an agreement not to quarrel.'

'That's funny!' said Laura going into a flurry of giggles. She gave Emily a kiss. 'You never do!'

'Shall we go into the house? I've something to tell you,' said William, shifting James on to his shoulders. Laura shouted, 'Me too, me too!'

Emily tried to do the same for Laura, but was having difficulty till William came over and lifted the child on to Emily's back. 'Put your arms round like this,' he said placing Laura's arms round Emily's neck. For a moment Emily felt his hands on her and shivered. He removed them instantly, saying, 'That's it! Now off inside!'

Once inside, he made the children sit down quietly and then told them about the Dower House. When they heard they were not going to move in for some time James looked solemn, and Laura's little face started to crumple. Emily said quickly, 'You mustn't worry. We've found somewhere else for you to stay until the Dower House is ready again.'

William frowned, but she ignored him and went on calmly, 'It has a maze, and a swing, and a garden with a battledore and shuttl—'

'Here, here!' the two children shouted. 'With you and Mr and Mrs Winbolt.' Their tears were forgotten as Rosa held out her arms and they ran to her.

'Is this true?' asked William under cover of the children's noise.

Philip had joined them and said, 'Of course. We're glad to help. And there's what amounts to an independent apartment for you all in the East Wing. You could come and go as you please. If you agree, you and the children could move into it tomorrow, once the furniture has been rearranged a little. Welcome, Ashenden. Meanwhile, there's a room for you upstairs for tonight.'

William glanced briefly and coolly at Emily, then turned to Philip. 'You are very generous. If you really mean it, I should be very pleased to move into your East Wing. It will take one of the heavier loads off my mind. But I can only accept the offer if you agree to my hiring someone to look after James and Laura when I'm not here. They should in any case be starting some kind of tuition.'

'I rather thought Emily—'

'Emily can see them as often as she wishes. Indeed, if we are to keep up the fiction that we are still planning to marry, I should like her to. But the ultimate responsibility for my children is not now her concern.'

'Emily?' Philip was puzzled. 'This is a little unexpected. I thought you had settled your differences.'

Emily looked down. 'I'm afraid not. But for the children's sake we are keeping up the pretence of an engagement until the Dower House is ready for...for occupation.'

Philip shook his head and looked grave. 'It's your business, not mine, Emily. But I hope you know what you're doing.'

'It is no longer a one-sided decision, Winbolt. Your sister and I are in complete agreement that we should not suit,' William said decisively. He sounded very definite, thought Emily, and wondered why she wasn't feeling more relieved.

Chapter Ten

Over dinner that night they discussed what they were
to do. The children were in bed, and the four adults
were sitting round a table in the warm glow of the
candles, cutlery and glasses gleaming in the light. It
might have been any ordinary family gathering. As it
could have been, thought Emily with a pang, if only
I had not gone to Charlwood yesterday. The glass of
wine she was holding to her lips shook and she put it
down. Where did that thought come from? she asked
herself. I'm *glad* I went. Surely it is better to know
what he really thinks of me? I might have married him
and been bitterly unhappy if I hadn't overheard what
he said. Her mouth twisted. As unhappy as I am now?
When she looked up William's eyes were on her, so
she sat straight in her chair, lifted her chin and, picking
her wine glass up again, took a large sip from it. For a
moment his face softened with a hint of rueful admiration, before he turned to Philip.

'I have to go to London for a few days,' he said.
'There are one or two people I need to see. And if I am

to find a governess for the children, the sooner I set about it the better. I could arrange to take the children with me, but it would help a great deal if I could leave them here?'

'Of course you may!' said Rosa. 'It would be horrible for them in London! And how could you interview governesses and the like with two children on your hands? No, they must stay here.'

'Thank you, Mrs Winbolt.'

'I think you should call me by my given name, William. I regard you as almost one of the family.'

Philip gave a little cough, and Emily dropped her fork. But William gave Rosa one of his most charming smiles and nodded. 'Thank you, Rosa' he said. 'I am honoured.'

'What is more,' Rosa continued, 'I agree that the children need a governess. But may I make a suggestion?'

'Of course!'

'The lady would naturally live with us here for the immediate future. It would be so much more comfortable if we could find someone who was…compatible. I think Emily should be involved in choosing her.'

'Oh, no! I couldn't possibly—' Emily began in some agitation.

'Of course you could go to London,' said Rosa firmly. 'The children know us now and will be quite happy here for a day or two. Just think, Emily. You would want them to be taught by someone you approved of, wouldn't you?'

William had been watching Rosa with a gleam in his eye, but now he leant back in his chair and said, toying with his glass, 'I think it's an excellent idea. I'm sure

Emily's notions of a suitable governess would be better than mine. But where would she stay?'

'With her grandfather,' said Rosa promptly. She gave Emily a mischievous look as she said, 'I believe she was intending to pay Lord Winbolt a visit.'

'But not with—' said Emily. And stopped. She threw an appealing glance at Philip, but her brother's eyes were on his wife and they were full of amused appreciation.

'I'm sure my grandfather would be delighted to see her,' he said slowly. 'And the governess idea is a good one.'

'But why can't you see how impossible it is?' asked Emily in desperation. 'You both know that William and I...that William and I...'

'Have a truce?' asked William coolly. 'For the sake of the children? Surely you haven't forgotten, my dear? After all, we shouldn't have to spend very much time in each other's company. I have other things to do in London. Apart from escorting you to Lord Winbolt's residence, then seeing that you arrive safely at the agencies' premises and back again, I shan't be there to bother you. We needn't exchange a word, if you don't wish to.'

Emily gave up. With all three ranged against her, she was bound to lose. She was not even sure that she minded if it meant she would have a say in the choice of someone who was to be in charge of William's children. But whatever he had said, the thought of going to London and back with William himself was daunting.

'When do you wish to go?' she asked finally. 'The agencies would need a little notice.'

'Shall we say in three days' time? I have one or two matters to sort out at Charlwood, but after that...'

'Three days it shall be,' said Emily rather grimly.

One of the grooms was immediately dispatched with a message to Lord Winbolt's residence in Arlington Street, and a letter to two of the best educational employment agencies in London. During the intervening days Emily spent a lot of her time with the children, and spent most of the rest trying on dress after dress before deciding what to take to London with her—much to Rosa's quiet enjoyment. Emily's sister-in-law thought she knew the man Emily was trying to impress, and it wasn't her grandfather!

William came and went, but Emily hardly saw him except at dinner. He seldom addressed any remarks directly to her and when he did his manner was businesslike, very different from the warmth she had been used to. In return she avoided speaking to him whenever possible, but listened attentively all the same to what he was saying. The damage to the Dower House had been assessed and estimates for repairing it were being drawn up, but he had no idea how long it would take. Rosa and Philip sympathised and advised, and carried on a normal conversation with him. The armed neutrality of their two dinner companions seemed to amuse rather than disconcert them.

But on the third evening things were different. William told them that he had been talking to Sam Lilley. He glanced at Philip as he said, 'You probably don't approve, officially, at least, but I've decided not to take action against Lilley. I believe what he says. He may have been stupid and he was certainly gullible, but I don't think he deserves the sort of punishment meted out to arsonists.'

'Hanging, or at best transportation,' said Philip.

'Exactly. So I'm letting him go. I've written to a former naval friend of mine who lives in the West Country. I've told him the whole story, and I'm almost sure he will agree to take Sam and his wife on.'

Philip was doubtful. 'Dangerous. Once an arsonist…'

'But that's just it! Sam never was an arsonist. He was trying to save the Dower House when he was injured. Quite badly, too.'

'I think you're right, William.' The smile that accompanied these words from Emily was entirely involuntary.

He turned to her, and addressed her directly for the first time. 'Emily, do you remember meeting a Mr Kavanagh in the garden at Charlwood?'

'Of course I do. But I don't think that was his real name. I told you at the time.'

'I think his name is Kidman. Could you describe him again to us?'

'He was tall, between thirty and forty. He had rather curiously pale light blue eyes, I remember.'

'Can you remember how he was dressed, or any other details of his appearance?'

Emily shut her eyes and tried to call to her mind a picture of the stranger. 'He was dressed for riding—quite ordinary clothes, buff breeches, brown coat, I think. And, yes, he wore a signet ring on his left hand. A snake coiled round the letter "K".'

'Clever girl!' William exclaimed. His voice was full of approval, full of warmth and so like his former manner to her that Emily had to look down at her plate to hide a treacherous threat of tears. After a pause William continued in a much cooler tone, 'Barnaby Drewitt has done some ferreting about the last two days. Sam Lilley was right. His name *is* Kidman, and he lives in London.'

'Barnaby has been in London?' asked Emily, amazed.

'Hadn't you noticed that he wasn't here? He wasn't really needed—even if it were necessary to keep an eye on Sam Lilley, George Fowler is perfectly capable of it. Barnaby has just returned from London. He can move quite quickly when he chooses and has made a number of discoveries about Mr Kidman. But I still don't know what Kidman's game is, or why he wants me out of Charlwood.'

'Kidman... Kidman... Where have I heard that name before?' said Philip slowly. 'You didn't mention it at the Dower House!' He sat searching his memory while Rosa carried on with the conversation. But after a while he exclaimed, 'I remember! It was Sir Reginald! He was complaining about someone called Kidman. I don't think you were there at the time, William. Er...' He hesitated, looked at Emily, then went on, 'The man was apparently staying at Maria Fenton's place?'

The name brought their conversation to a sudden halt. 'Maria Fenton?' Rosa asked after a pause.

William was frowning. 'I find that most intriguing,' he said. 'That lady has always seemed excessively interested in Charlwood. I wonder what the connection is.'

Emily spoke before she could stop herself. 'I understood that Charlwood's chief attraction for Mrs Fenton lay with its owner,' she said tartly.

'Indeed?' said William, raising one eyebrow. 'You must agree she would have had something to offer him,

Emily. She is said to have inherited a considerable fortune from her late husband.' He returned Emily's glare with a look of bland indifference.

Philip coughed and said, 'Actually, William, I'm not altogether sure in this case that rumour has it correct. I haven't had much to do with the lady, and she certainly appears to be wealthy. However, I do know that Edric Fenton's affairs were…mixed, shall we say?' He met William's eye and said apologetically, 'Something I found out recently from my friends in the city—while I was making other enquiries. Fenton had dealings with some shady characters.'

'Really? This gets more and more interesting—so many lines leading in the direction of Charlwood. Is it coincidence? That's something more I'll look into when I'm in London.'

'Talking of which,' said Rosa, 'if you are to make an early start tomorrow, then Emily should think of retiring to bed.' She rose, and, after bidding them goodnight, she ushered Emily out.

But a few minutes later she was back again, alone. 'William, you'll have to pardon me. Philip will say that I ought not to interfere, but I love Emily too much to listen to him. Please don't be too hard on Emily during this visit to London. I…I am still convinced that you are made for each other, and I can't bear to think that a stupid misunderstanding will keep you apart. Given time, I am sure she will come about. I am hoping that this visit to London might be a turning point for both of you.'

William smiled. 'Is that why you arranged it?' He took her hand and kissed it. 'Rosa, let me pay homage to your gentle, caring heart. If I could make you happier, I would. But Emily seems to have made up her mind, and if she will not change it for the children, then she is most unlikely to change it for me. And at the moment I have no desire to try to persuade her.' He looked at her downcast face. 'But I promise not to quarrel with her for the next few days. Will that do?'

Rosa shook her head. 'I want more than that. I'd like you to promise to be kind. She's hurting so much inside!'

'And you think I am not?' The question came out involuntarily, and he went on, 'I rather think I shall be too busy to see much of Emily in London, to be kind or otherwise.' At the sight of Rosa's worried face his tone softened. 'Very well, I'll do my best.'

Philip came over and took Rosa's arm. 'Come, sweetheart. You've done what you could. It's up to William and Emily now.' He turned to William. 'I think you've been remarkably patient, Ashenden. Good luck with your efforts in London. Let us know if there is anything we can do. You might think of talking to my grandfather. He may be old, but he is still very much in touch with affairs, particularly in the city. Meanwhile, you can be sure that Rosa will keep those children happy. She will probably ruin them!'

The first stage of Rosa's plan had already failed by the time the carriage left the following morning. There would be no opportunity for any dialogue, kind or otherwise, on the journey. Emily and her maid were travelling inside, but William had chosen to ride alongside it with Barnaby Drewitt. Apart from one or two stops on the way, they had no contact with each other.

They arrived at Lord Winbolt's residence in Arlington Street in the late afternoon. If Emily had promised herself to escape from William without inviting him in to meet her grandfather, she was frustrated. Maynard, her grandfather's stately butler, met her at the door, and before she could do anything about it one of the footmen had taken William's outer garments and Maynard himself was ushering them both into the library. Her grandfather was sitting in a chair on one side of a fireplace in which burned a huge fire.

'Come in, come in!' he shouted. 'Don't stand by the door. Let me see you!'

Lord Winbolt might not have the robust good health he had once enjoyed, but he still had all of his considerable faculties. He accepted a curtsy and a kiss from his granddaughter, then told William to come nearer. 'I want to see Emily's beau for myself,' he said. He examined William with an eagle eye. 'So you're William Ashenden,' he said. 'The one Emily thinks is after her fortune.'

William stiffened. 'I am Ashenden, Lord Winbolt,' he said. 'But you are mistaken, sir, if you think I am at all interested in Miss Winbolt's fortune.'

'I don't think that at all, young man. It's not what I said! I know you aren't. You've no need of anyone's fortune—you're as rich as a nabob yourself. So why aren't you marrying her?'

'Grandfather, please,' begged Emily, scarlet with embarrassment. 'Sir William and I have agreed that we do not suit.'

'Your granddaughter has refused to marry me, Lord Winbolt, because she has decided that she cannot trust me. Much as I regret it, there's not a great deal I can do about it. So, I hope you won't think me discourteous if I say I should like to move on. I am sure Miss Winbolt would like to rest and refresh herself after her journey, and I have more to do in London then I have time for.'

Lord Winbolt frowned. 'Hmm... Well, go on, then. You have to do what you're here for, I suppose.'

William's lips twitched in an involuntary smile. 'Am I to infer you know what that is? You seem to be as well informed as your grandson.'

'Better, I hope! But you're right—it was he who mentioned this business to me. And I've had one or two enquiries made. There's a Kidman with lodgings in Bond Street. He might be the man you're looking for. But I'll be disappointed if your affairs prevent you from dining with us tomorrow—I was looking forward to some sensible conversation for a change. I don't get out much nowadays.'

'It doesn't seem to stop you from keeping your finger on every pulse in London,' said Emily with a fond smile. She grew serious. 'But I don't think Sir William has a desire to be quizzed any further about his personal affairs, Grandfather. And nor have I. I wouldn't blame him if he made his excuses for tomorrow evening.'

'Why don't you let the man answer for himself, miss? If Ashenden is about to escort you round London for half the day, I'd like to know a little more about him. And whether you trust him or not, you surely wouldn't grudge him a good dinner at the end of it? Will you come or not, Ashenden?'

William bowed and said, ' I shall be delighted. And I'll do my best to acquire some sensible conversation beforehand. Now I must go. Miss Winbolt, at what time do you wish to be collected tomorrow?'

'There really isn't a need for you—'

'You are doing me a great favour in interviewing these ladies. The least I can do is to see that you go and come back safely. I shall call at eleven. Will that do?'

'Yes. And thank you.' She went with him to the door,

and, keeping her voice low, she said, 'My grandfather is very outspoken, but I hope you won't be put off by it. Whatever we think of each other, I should like you to come tomorrow. He so enjoys company.' She looked back affectionately at the figure by the fire. He was leaning back in his chair and appeared to be falling asleep.

William said, 'You are very fond of him?'

'I love him dearly.'

He eyed her curiously. 'You are such a mixture, Emily, so all or nothing. On the one hand, you can be so devoted, so passionately loyal to those close to you. On the other, you are so cool, so suspicious of the rest of the world.' He took her hand to bid her goodnight, then added, 'But I think there would be no place in that heart of yours for doubt or lack of faith in a man you really loved. You would have absolute confidence in him. And I would envy him. Goodnight.'

He called for her the next morning so promptly that she was not quite ready. It had taken three different changes of dress before she had decided what to wear. In the end she chose a walking dress, in French grey Circassian cloth, its pelisse trimmed with bands of grey velvet, finished off with a small ruff of white silk at her neck. She decided the effect was exactly right—businesslike, but very feminine.

However she was a little dashed when her grandfather said with typical vigour, 'Good God, girl, what sort of outfit is that? Looking like a nun is no way to attract a red-blooded male like William Ashenden!'

'Attracting William Ashenden was not my aim, sir,' she replied acidly. She was disconcerted when Maynard announced that Sir William Ashenden had called for her and was waiting in the hall. She was not sure whether he had heard her or not, and his greeting gave no indication.

'Good morning, Emily,' he said courteously. 'I hope you slept well and are rested after your journey.'

Pink with embarrassment, she replied in kind. 'Thank you, sir, I am feeling…I am feeling…much refreshed. And…and I hope that you are…you are…too.' The unholy amusement in his eyes as she stammered out these words convinced her that he had indeed overheard her. She put up her chin and led the way out of the house.

In the carriage Emily showed him the replies that had been waiting for her at Arlington Street, and they proceeded to the first agency. It was not far away, and the second was within walking distance of the first.

'Thank you, sir,' Emily said as William helped her out of the carriage. 'I know you have a great deal to do. It really isn't necessary for you to—'

'Save your breath, Emily. I am not about to abandon you here and leave you to walk to Mrs Timpson's with only your maid for escort.' He smiled at her. 'The nun-like air is very becoming. A Quaker girl with style. No Piccadilly beau could resist such a tempting morsel. Even I am attracted.'

Emily removed her hand and said coldly, 'Please, don't waste time on empty compliments, sir. We both know that a plain girl like me is unlikely to attract any attention of the sort. So you really need not concern yourself about my safety.'

His expression hardened. He said, 'Still harbouring your grudges, Emily? Isn't it time you shed them?' Then he took a breath, shrugged and went on, 'As you wish. But I shall accompany you all the same. My time is not so short that I can't spare an hour or two. Besides, I would prefer to have a say in the choice of this governess.'

'But you said—'

'I did indeed. But I have changed my mind. Lead the way!'

They interviewed two ladies at the first agency and three at the second, but not one of the applicants met with Emily's approval. One was too young, the other too unimaginative. At the second agency two were definitely not up to her standard, and the last too...too... middle-aged.

As he handed her into the carriage after they left the second agency, William said, 'If I did not know better, Emily, I would say that your heart is not in this work. I think you want to teach the children yourself.'

'No, that's not true! I know I can't, not really. Even if...things were different...'

'You mean, if you and I were still going to be married?'

'Yes. Even then the children would have to have some sort of tutor or governess. But those women were not what I want for James and Laura. They were too dull! Your children are so lively, and so young...'

'Younger children than James and Laura have governesses. Some are even sent to school.'

'William, you wouldn't!' Emily turned a shocked face to him.

'I've already told them they will stay with us—' He stopped. 'That is to say, they will stay with me, Emily, however difficult it may be. *I* honour my promises.'

The slight emphasis on the pronoun silenced Emily. Her tone of voice was restricted as she said after a while, 'I have hopes of hearing something from friends of

Rosa's, who are staying at the Pulteney Hotel. They have asked me to meet them there tomorrow. But I shall not require your help. The hotel is only a step from Arlington Street and one of my grandfather's footmen will escort me. Now I should like to go back there, if you please.'

He nodded and they completed the journey in silence.

At dinner that night Emily learned more about William than ever before. Up to the present their talk had always been centred on the design for the gardens at Charlwood, on the children and on their plans for the future. But tonight she was fascinated, as was Lord Winbolt, by William's account of his life in the Caribbean and South America. He was a good conversationalist, too, never dominating the talk for too long, always returning to topics of general interest, and, when he discovered that his host had interests in property in London, quizzing him on living conditions in the capital. But eventually Lord Winbolt asked him if he had discovered anything of significance during his day's searches.

'I think I have, sir. In fact, I'd like to ask you if the name Valleron means anything to you? Was he an associate of Kidman's?'

'No, no, no, my boy! Far from it! The Marquis de Valleron was a French aristocrat, an *émigré* and owner of a collection of jewels and antique gold coins. The collection was an important part of Valleron family history—some of the items in it went back to Charlemagne. But it was stolen three or four years ago, and has never been seen since. I expect you were abroad, otherwise

you would have remembered it. It was a ruthless affair.
There was a lot of fuss at the time.'

'How was it stolen?' asked Emily.

'The Marquis was travelling to London from Bath
when his coach was attacked by an armed gang. The
coachman and two guards were quite deliberately shot
dead, and the Marquis himself was badly wounded. The
thieves got clean away, but one of them was later found
stabbed to death in a copse about half a mile further
along the road.'

'A quarrel among thieves,' said Emily.

'No, I think it was rather worse than that. Listen to
the rest. The strongbox that had held the collection was
nearby, but it had been forced open and the gold and
jewels removed.'

'Efficient!' said William.

'But why on earth was the Marquis carrying such a
valuable cargo along the Bath Road?' Emily asked. 'He
must have known it was dangerous.'

'He was taking the collection back to France with
him. The Vallerons had been living in Bath, but once
the war was over they decided to return, and where
they went the collection went, too. Twenty years after
smuggling it out of Paris and bringing it to England, he
was taking it back home again.'

'And it has never been found, or even heard of since?'
asked William, leaning forward attentively.

'Not as far as I know. Why do you ask?'

'Because Barnaby Drewitt has been talking to one
or two past associates in London—not the sort you're
likely to know, Lord Winbolt. And he has heard that
name linked with our friend Kidman.'

'I call that very interesting,' said Lord Winbolt. 'The

robbery took place, in fact, at a spot on the Bath Road not very far from your house, Ashenden.'

'William! He hid the jewels in Charlwood, don't you agree? That's why he wants to get rid of you. He wants to be free to search wherever he wishes.' Emily stopped and looked puzzled. 'But I don't understand. If Kidman hid the jewels, why does he have to search for them? Why doesn't he know where they are now? And why has he left it so long before looking for them?'

'It's obvious,' said William. 'There was too much commotion at the time to get rid of the things very easily, so he left the jewels where they were. But it wasn't Kidman who hid them. It can't have been.'

Lord Winbolt had been listening attentively. Now he said, 'Kidman was a younger associate of Edric Fenton, who was strongly suspected afterwards of having had a hand in the business.'

'Fenton!' exclaimed Emily. 'But—'

'You knew him?' asked her grandfather, surprised.

'No, but I know his widow. She lives not far from Charlwood. She moved in about a year ago…' As the significance of this slowly penetrated, Emily stared at William and her grandfather in turn.

Lord Winbolt said, 'Just after Fenton died, perhaps? If we are right, he was a thief and a murderer, but he came to a miserable end. He had some sort of an apoplectic fit and eventually died, but for months before he was hardly able to move at all, or speak more than a few words.'

William said slowly, 'If he was the thief and murderer, he was well served. He died unable to fetch the jewels himself, or to tell anyone else where he had hidden them. And now his friends are frantically searching for them. What a shock it must have been when Charlwood was sold.'

'They must have thought they had all the time in the world to look for those jewels,' said Emily thoughtfully. 'Until you bought the place, William, Charlwood had been a haunted ruin for years No one in their right mind would have taken it on.'

'Thank you,' said William. 'You must remember I was desperate.'

'First for a house, then for a wife. Wasn't that it?' Emily's tone was suddenly bitter again.

'I wasn't in search of a rich one, Emily,' William said impatiently. 'But you know that now. Why can't you put your prejudices aside for once?' He held her eyes for a moment, then went on, 'I still think I was lucky to find Charlwood. One day it will be a beautiful home. And for a while I thought I had been lucky enough to find the ideal mistress for it, too.'

'And now?' asked Lord Winbolt.

William had been regarding Emily sombrely. But now he turned to Lord Winbolt and said with decision, 'And now I must wait. This Valleron affair is dangerous. It hangs over Charlwood like a cloud. When that has cleared, then I can start to plan my life again, but not before. Early tomorrow I shall see a few more people and find out if Barnaby Drewitt has any more news for me, and then I think I must return to Berkshire. Kidman and his crew will not give up on seventy thousand pounds' worth of gold and jewels. They will be back—and heaven knows what they will do next.'

'These men are dangerous, Ashenden,' said Lord Winbolt.

'So am I,' said William. 'When what is mine is threatened.' Turning to Emily, he said calmly, 'I assume you

will wish to stay on in London? I could send Barnaby
Drewitt to escort you home later in the week, if you
wish.'

'If my grandfather doesn't object, I should prefer to
go back to Shearings with you.'

'But what about your search for a governess?'

Emily avoided his eyes as she said, 'You were quite
right this morning when you said that my heart wasn't
in it. I didn't think any of those women I saw today
suitable. I certainly couldn't imagine them fitting in at
Shearings.' She looked up now and went on, 'But…but
I've been thinking. The Rector at Stoke Shearings has a
daughter who would make a very suitable governess, if
she would agree to come. They are a large family, so she
is used to small children. I don't expect she would want
to live in, but James and Laura don't yet need full-time
tuition. I will tell Rosa's friends we have found someone
suitable.' She leaned forward and asked with pleading
in her eyes, 'Would you…would you agree?'

William looked at her. Emily's eyes were dark in
the candlelight. Her dress, fashionably low cut for the
evening, revealed a slender neck, and enticingly rounded
curves below. The light enhanced the delicate line of her
cheekbones and the line of her jaw. Her face had determination and strength, but he found himself thinking
that they had both been wrong. Emily Winbolt was far
from plain. She could look beautiful. For a moment he
was filled with a sudden desire to beg her there and then
to give them both another chance, not to throw away
something precious. But then he hardened his heart. If
their relationship was to have any real future, Emily
must come to him of her own free will to give him back
the trust she had taken away without any real cause. He

had begged enough. But it was difficult to refuse this request.

'If that is your wish,' he said slowly. 'For the moment. But we shall have to sort out their future sooner or later.'

Lord Winbolt had been observing them closely. Now he said, 'There's time for that, Ashenden. I completely agree with you—you must deal with this business at Charlwood before you do anything else. I won't have my granddaughter living in a house haunted by thieves and murderers.'

'Grandfather! Haven't you been listening? Sir William has already explained. He and I are not going to be married!'

'Really?' asked Lord Winbolt. 'That's that, then… But don't forget to invite me to the wedding.'

William held up his hands. He laughed as he got up from the table and said, 'I can see that nothing we can say has an effect, sir. You have your own ideas on the matter. But if I am to be ready to go back to Berkshire, I haven't time to argue with you. I must take my leave.' And, after thanking his host for a most enjoyable evening and arranging when to call for Emily the next day, he bade both Winbolts goodnight and left.

After he had gone Lord Winbolt sat in silence, then said, 'You always were your own worst enemy, Emily.'

'Why on earth do you say that? It's a little harsh, surely?'

'You're such a fool. You are letting that fribble, that good-for-nothing, destroy your whole life.'

'*William?* A fribble? You can't mean it!'

'Of course I don't mean William Ashenden, damn it! I meant the Colesworth fellow.'

'But I haven't thought about him in years—' Emily stopped short. She had. She had forgotten the man, but had remembered the hurt. She had judged and condemned William because of him.

'Exactly!' said Lord Winbolt. 'You've dismissed a man, a real man, because of what a characterless weakling did to you years ago. You say you can't trust him! You're a fool. And now, if you want him back, you'll have to work hard to convince him you're worth bothering with.'

'What if I don't want him back? He thinks I'm plain, too strong-minded.'

'Judging by the look in his eyes, that's not what he was thinking just now, girl!' He leaned forward. 'Emily, you've been a granddaughter any man would be proud of. But you have two major faults. One is that you're stubborn.'

'Why do people keep telling me that?'

'Perhaps because at the moment you are being quite remarkably so.'

'And the other?'

Her grandfather paused and put a gnarled hand on top of hers. 'William Ashenden is an honourable man. I know it, Philip and Rosa know it—and you know it too. It must be obvious, even to you, that he never wanted your fortune. Yet you still say you don't trust him. Why? Is it only this famous stubbornness of yours? Or is it something else? Emily, my dear, for some reason which I have never been able to fathom, you've convinced yourself that happiness will never come your way. And now when it looks as if you might be wrong, you are doing your best to make sure it

doesn't. He's an honourable man and a generous one,
but he's proud. He won't wait for ever for you to come
round. No man of character would. So what are you
going to do about it?'

Chapter Eleven

After such a conversation with her much-respected grandfather it was inevitable that Emily would ponder over her relationship with William during the night, and by the small hours of the morning she had acknowledged something she had known, but never openly admitted, even to herself. The others had been right and she had been wrong. William was no fortune hunter. Moreover, it was even possible that she had somehow misunderstood the rest of his words to Lady Deardon on that fateful day, too. She fell asleep at last, determined to make some amends to him during their journey home.

As a result, when William called the next morning, he found her waiting for him with the request that he keep her company inside the carriage. When he looked surprised, she stammered, 'My...my maid w-wishes to travel outside on the box. She suffers from queasiness when travelling inside. And...and I...I was very interested in what we were talking about last night, and would like to carry on with the discussion,' she added, trying to sound as if it was a perfectly reasonable suggestion.

William took it calmly, without reminding her that she had originally said she wanted as little as possible to do with him, and went out again to have a word with Barnaby Drewitt, who was in the street with the horses. By the time he came back, Maynard was waiting to escort him to Lord Winbolt's bedchamber. Emily was already there, talking to her grandfather, who resembled nothing so much as the Grand Turk, propped as he was against a mountain of pillows, and dressed in a magnificent brocade dressing gown and nightcap. The effect was only marginally diminished by his spectacles and the books and papers covering the bed.

'I've enjoyed meeting you, Ashenden,' said Lord Winbolt. 'If you're in town again, call on me—I'd like to hear more about the Americas. I've been reading about them here—a very interesting part of the world.'

'Thank you, sir. I'll certainly do that.'

'Let me know if you need help with any further investigation. I'm quite confident that you will soon sort out this Valleron business, and then you can settle down at Charlwood and be a good neighbour for my grandson and his wife. I won't go further than that. You and Emily will have to sort out the rest of the story. I'm past the age of meddling.' Emily uttered a most unladylike snort, which she managed to turn into a cough. He gave her a glare over the top of his spectacles and went on, 'But I'd like to see this girl of mine suitably established—without any of this nonsense of living alone!' This was accompanied by another glare.

Emily bent over and kissed him. 'I think you will meddle until the day you die, sir—it's in the nature of the beast! But I love you. Philip and Rosa will be delighted to hear that you haven't lost any of your touch. I'll give them your love, shall I?'

'Yes, yes. That's enough now. You'd better be off if you're to reach Shearings before nightfall. Goodbye, Ashenden. Look after my granddaughter—if she'll let you.'

They set off soon after, and after turning into Piccadilly and passing Green Park on their left, they made for Hyde Park Corner and the Bath Road. William seemed disinclined to talk and, after giving him one or two quick glances, Emily sat gazing out at the lively scene as they drove through Kensington, and along the road to Hammersmith. Stage coaches, post-chaises, market carts, horsemen and other travellers jostled for space and the dust rose in clouds as they pressed on along the busy thoroughfare.

After a while Emily decided she had waited long enough for William to open the conversation. She would have to break the ice. So she took a breath and said, 'It's so noisy. So many people…'

'London is spreading fast,' he agreed. If she hoped this would encourage him, she was doomed to disappointment. Silence fell again. After a while Emily tried once more.

'It's not far to Brentford now,' she said brightly. 'And after that there's the Grand Junction Canal.' Even to Emily herself the remarks sounded like the empty chatter of an idiot.

William was polite, if not enthusiastic. 'A splendid piece of engineering. It was there the last time I passed this way. And ten years ago, too,' he added drily. Emily bit her lip and fell silent.

They passed through Brentford and crossed the Canal without comment. I'll try one more time, she told herself and then I'll give up. 'The road to Syon House is just off to the left,' she announced. 'I once visited the house with my grandfather.'

'Did you indeed?' he said. After a pause he yawned and asked, 'Was his Grace at home?'

Emily's patience snapped. 'Yes. And, no, I don't remember very much about it, though it's kind of you to be so interested,' she said crossly. 'I have been to Osterley, too, though I don't suppose you wish to know that either.'

He looked at her with a hint of challenge in his eyes. 'Emily, why are you so annoyed?'

'Because I am trying to start some sort of conversation with you, but it's a very uphill affair!'

'I thought you didn't want to talk to me except when we were in company.'

'Things have changed. I am trying, William, to be more… more friendly.'

'Why?' The indifference might have gone, but his tone was still not particularly warm. The expression on his face as he looked at her was difficult to read.

'I…I…' she began hesitantly, but then in a rush, 'I…I think I may have been overhasty.'

'In what respect?'

'In my judgement of you.'

'Overhasty? It was rather more than that, surely?' She had his full attention now. His eyes were on her, but the expression in them was still not encouraging.

'Wrong, then!' she exclaimed and went on doggedly, 'I was wrong to think that you…that you wanted to marry me for my fortune. Will that satisfy you?'

'Well, I can't say that it's a very handsome admission, considering that it has been proved to you quite conclusively, and more than once, that I had no need of your fortune in the first place. Still, I suppose it's a beginning.'

Surely the old William would have accepted her apology more graciously than this? She began to realise that it was not going to be as easy as she had thought to make amends. She said, 'You are really making this very difficult, William.'

'Why should I make it easy?'

'Because I'm truly sorry, and…and would like us at least to be friends.'

He smiled then, but his smile had a touch of cynicism about it, which was not reassuring. 'Has Lord Winbolt been talking to you, Emily? Is that the reason for this sudden change of heart? Perhaps you have now realised what a very desirable match I am? By desirable I mean rich, of course. Is that the reason for this tête-à-tête on the journey home, why you wish us to be "friends" again?'

'William!' Emily was really shocked. She looked at him briefly, then turned away, unwilling to let him see how much he had hurt her. There was silence again in the carriage.

After a moment William said in quite a different voice, 'I'm sorry. That was unnecessary.'

'It was a dreadful thing to say!'

'I know. I ought not to have said it.'

Emily turned, tears sparkling on her lashes. 'You ought not even to have thought it! Neither of me, nor of my grandfather!' She brushed away a tear that had spilled over on to her cheek with an impatient gesture.

He took hold of her hand. 'I am really very sorry,' he said, 'I had no intention of making you cry.' He carefully put the hand back in her lap. 'I should have remembered how it feels to have one's motives so badly misinterpreted.'

She forgot her tears and stared at him, saying eventually, 'Were you by any chance trying to make a point, William?'

'Not deliberately, no. I'm sorry.' She looked at him suspiciously. The blue eyes were sincere, but not particularly warm.

Emily had a sudden picture of William in the garden at Shearings after she had told him she was not going to marry him, his air of dogged courage, how he had walked back to the house without any of his usual lithe grace. The loss of his house and the destruction of his plans—two blows coming one after the other—had almost defeated him. He had picked up the pieces and gone on with all his previous energy and determination, but he had not yet forgotten the occasion.

She nodded sadly. 'Even if you weren't trying to make a point, I suppose you had every right to. I've been a fool.' She paused. 'If I were to ask you now what you said…to the Deardons…that…that day, after I had gone, would you tell me?'

'Does it matter? Now?'

'It matters a lot to me.'

'But *why* does it? Are you *still* looking for proof that I was honest with you? That whatever I may or may not have said in the past, when I said I admired you I really meant it? No, Emily. It's done with.'

'What do you mean? That you have no wish to be friends?'

'Friends! You and I could never be just friends, Emily Winbolt. There are too many other feelings in the way. Too much enchantment, too much disillusion, too much hope and too much disappointment.' He paused. After a moment he turned and looked at her again. 'But if you mean that you'd like to rebuild something, less than what we had, but still something, then, yes, I would be willing to try. It won't be easy, but I am willing to try, if only for the sake of the children.'

Emily swallowed. Rosa had said, despite William Ashenden's easy manner, he could be hard when the occasion arose. Now for the first time she was seeing it.

Looking at Emily's profile as she gazed out of the carriage window, William felt a pang of remorse. Had he been too hard on her? Then he remembered how her obstinate refusal to be convinced had enraged him, how her lack of trust in him had hurt him, how readily she had abandoned their plans, knowing how much the children loved her, needed her... He glanced at her again. She looked so unhappy. Knowing her as he did, proud, strong-minded, slightly arrogant, but so vulnerable, he could guess what an effort it must have taken her to admit she had been wrong. And he *had* promised Rosa...

'Emily, I have a suggestion,' he said at last.

She turned her head and he saw that she had been crying again. The urge to take her in his arms and comfort her was so strong that it took all his self-discipline to hold back. But, sorry as he felt, he wasn't prepared to go down that particular road again. Instead, he held out his handkerchief and said, 'You needn't fear to use it. It's clean.' After she had mopped her face, he went on, 'They have told me that it will be several months at least before there's any question of the Dower House being fit for habitation. With that in mind, I've even considered abandoning the whole notion of using it, and instead making a push to finish Charlwood itself. But before anyone can move in anywhere I have to rid the house of the curse of Kidman and his gang. The best way to do that would be somehow or other to locate the Valleron collection, and announce publicly that we have returned it to its owners.'

Emily was clearly still uncertain of what he was proposing. She said, 'The children would think that wonderful. A real treasure hunt! They would regard it as an exciting game.'

'I'm not so sure about that—it could be a very dangerous one. I think it would be better not to tell them. But my point is that a busy time lies ahead, and I would appreciate your help. You know so much of the background, and I still value your ideas. For the time being, at least, let's deal with the work, and leave the rest in the past. Could you do that?'

The brilliance of her smile surprised him. She was so obviously pleased at the idea of them working together again. When she nodded he went on, 'Good! Then we shall talk about the Kidman-Fenton connection. Or is any mention of the name Fenton unwelcome?'

'No, William, it is not. When I repent, I repent with a full heart. Carry on! Did you discover anything new this morning?'

'After I had bought Charlwood, someone made an offer for it. A better one, but I refused it. According to the agent, the man who made the offer was Kidman. A small point, but significant. He told me something else that you won't like very much. He told me that a badly decomposed body was discovered in Charlwood's grounds some years ago. At the time it was assumed it belonged to a vagrant, so the body was removed and

buried without much fuss or enquiry. But from what
the agent said, I think it must have been found not long
after the attack on the Valleron coach. It's possible it
was a member of that same gang.'

Emily was shocked. 'You mean Fenton killed his last
accomplice, too?'

'If it was Fenton who was the leader.'

'I'm sure of it. William, he was completely ruthless!
He got rid of everyone else concerned in that robbery.
Just look at it. There were four of them. One was killed
during the attack. That left Fenton and two others. He
killed one of the two in the copse, possibly with the con-
nivance of the other, and he and the other man went to
Charlwood to hide the jewels. Once there, he killed the
second of the two and left the body in the grounds to be
found weeks later. After that, Fenton was the only one
who knew exactly what had happened to the Valleron
collection. All the rest were dead.'

'And that is why, now that Fenton himself is dead,
no one can find it! We know that Kidman is looking for
it. I already have someone keeping track of him. The
question is, how far are Maria Fenton and her brother-
in-law involved?'

'That's something we shall have to find out.'

They discussed other plans for a while, and then
stopped for a meal. As they entered the Crown at
Slough, Emily caught sight of Barnaby Drewitt hover-
ing nearby. With him was another, equally unprepos-
sessing, figure. When William gave them a nod the two
men disappeared into the back rooms of the inn. He
saw her looking, and said briefly, 'You know Barnaby
already. The other one is a friend of his, an extra pair
of eyes, ears, and, if need be, fists. You needn't concern
yourself with him.'

* * *

Emily had more appetite than she would have expected and they made a good meal before getting in the carriage again. There was a limit to the amount they could usefully plan before they arrived at Shearings and heard the latest developments there, so after a while they fell silent again. Then William leaned back, stretched his legs out and said lazily, 'Now, what were you saying about Syon House and the Duke of Northumberland? I had no idea you moved in such elevated circles.'

Emily looked blankly at him, then realised what he was talking about and, for the first time in days, she laughed. 'I was four at the time, William. And I said that we visited the *house*, not the Duke!'

The journey continued in this amiable mood till they reached Shearings in the late afternoon.

They were both a little disappointed not to be greeted by the children when they went in, but Mrs Hopkins told them that Rosa and Philip had taken them into the garden for some fresh air. So, still dressed for travelling, they went out and walked down towards the maze. At the end of the path were two small figures skipping ahead of two taller ones, but as soon as they saw William and Emily they raced towards them, nearly knocking them over as they reached them. Laughing, William swung James high up in the air while Emily caught Laura in her arms and hugged her. A babble of greetings, questions and news ensued as all, adults and children alike, made their way back into the house. The servants had carried their luggage in and at Emily's request had left sundry small parcels in the hall. Once they were all settled in the salon and the talk was slightly less confused, Emily asked James and Laura to fetch them in.

She handed Laura an elegantly tied packet to give to Rosa, and James was asked to take one, more plainly wrapped, to Philip. While Rosa was exclaiming over a very pretty silk shawl, and Philip was leafing through a folio of pictures from Hatchard's, the children were cautiously eyeing the two remaining parcels.

Amused, Emily said, 'There are two parcels left, I see. What *shall* I do with them?'

'Are they for us?' asked Laura, her eyes huge with longing. 'I'd like the funny knobbly one... I think it might be a doll!'

'I don't want a doll,' said James. 'I'd like the other one. It feels like a book.'

'You'd better open them and see.'

The children needed no further encouragement. Impatiently tearing the paper off their presents, they exclaimed in delight over a china doll with blonde hair and blue eyes, and a handsomely illustrated book on treasure trove. William looked at Emily over their heads. 'When did you find the time for all this?' he asked.

Rosa laughed. 'Once Emily is in London, she becomes a dedicated shopper,' she said. 'I know from experience that she will always make time to visit the shops, however difficult it is.'

'There was nothing difficult about it,' said Emily. 'I had a free afternoon, so I used it.'

'I thought you were supposed to be seeing the ladies at the Pulteney Hotel?'

'And I did, William. But I didn't spend long with them.' She turned to Rosa. 'I'm sorry, Rosa, but I told your friends that I've found what we were looking for.' She hesitated, then with a look at the children who were still absorbed in their presents, she said, 'I'll explain later.'

Then Philip wanted to know how Lord Winbolt was, and the talk became general. But it was interrupted by one of James's blunt questions. Still holding his book he asked, 'Uncle William, are you and Miss Winbolt married now? Can we call her Aunt Emily?'

After a startled silence, William said, 'No, James. You know we said we couldn't get married yet because of what happened to the Dower House. That…that hasn't changed. What made you think we would be?'

'Will Darby said you'd most likely gone to London to get married in Westminster Abbey.'

'Good Lord! Nothing so grand, James! No, we aren't married.'

'I knew you wouldn't be,' said Laura, busy with her doll. 'I told James he was silly. How could you get married without a bridesmaid? I wasn't there! But I'm very, very glad you're back!' She got up and hugged Emily. 'And even if you aren't married to Uncle William, you nearly are! Can't we call you Aunt Emily, anyway?'

William met Emily's look of enquiry with a rueful smile. 'It's up to you,' he said.

She hesitated, looked at the expression in Laura's eyes, which were dark blue and so like William's, and made up her mind. 'That would be wonderful!' she said. 'There's nothing I'd like better.'

Rosa was enthusiastic about Emily's wish to employ the Rector's daughter as a governess for the children, and even went with her to the Rectory, the next morning to speak to Mr Anstey. After carefully enquiring about the children, their uncle and the conditions of his daughter's employment, Reverend Anstey thought

Charity would be interested. Unfortunately, the young lady was out with her mother, but he promised to let them know her answer very soon.

As they walked back to Shearings, well pleased with their mission, Emily said, 'All the same, Rosa, you were stretching the point a little when you said William and I were shortly to be married.'

'Oh, dear! Should I have said within the year instead? But Mr Anstey seemed rather reluctant to accept a bachelor as a proper employer for his daughter, didn't you think? To my mind the prospect of an imminent marriage was the only thing that made William acceptable to him.'

'That is ridiculous! The girl is not going to live in, she will spend her time in the library at Shearings, chaperoned by Philip, who is a local magistrate, by you, his wife, by me, his sister, not to mention half a dozen servants and a highly respectable housekeeper! You are just making that up, Rosa.'

'These reverend gentlemen are only too aware of the temptations of the flesh, Emily,' said Rosa with a mischievous look. 'They preach about them every Sunday morning. In their minds, any bachelor as handsome as William represents a threat to every girl he comes across. They are only safe when they have been married off. Don't you agree?'

But she instantly became serious when Emily said in tones of despair, 'I seem to have made such a mess of things, Rosa. I don't believe that William and I will ever marry. You were right to warn me about him. As you said, he's just like Philip—so easy and charming on the surface, that you don't see the rock underneath. And at the moment he can't overlook the way I treated him. I doubt he ever will.'

'You seemed to be on quite good terms when you came back from London. Am I wrong?'

'He's asked me to help him, that's all.'

'That's something. What are you to help him with? Only the children? Or is there more than that?'

'There's more. We haven't yet had time to tell you about Charlwood and the Valleron mystery. Or about the Fentons. I'm sorry if it distresses you, but your friend Maria Fenton is not as innocent as she appears!'

'I never thought her innocent, exactly,' said Rosa. 'Not from the way she has always behaved. And I shan't be upset if she turns out to be someone I wouldn't wish to know. Her lies to you about William have already put me off her.'

'Well…'

'Well, what?'

'William and I were wondering… No, I'd prefer to wait until tonight when we can talk to both of you together. William and I have a story to tell, and some plans to lay before you. There wasn't time to talk about them last night. We were too busy hearing about the children.'

Rosa nodded and they talked of the children until they were home again.

That night over dinner William told Rosa and Philip the story of the Valleron robbery and what happened after. In listening to William, Emily realised how very busy he had been during his time in London. His account of the people he had spoken to, the places he had visited, was impressive, and it was clear that Barnaby Drewitt had played an active part in it all, too.

'William, who is Barnaby? Where does he come from?' asked Rosa.

'He was born in Portsmouth and ran away to sea to get away from a monster of a father when he was twelve. I came across him when he was stranded in South America, tied to labour in a silver mine without much hope of escape. You could say I rescued him, but that was after he had saved my life. We've been together ever since. I've even trained him to be a gentleman's gentleman!'

'That can't have been easy.' Philip grinned. 'He doesn't exactly look like one.'

'Don't be deceived by his looks! He's astonishingly good at it. But he has a large number of other talents, picked up, I fancy, during his earlier days in an effort to survive. And one of them is a gift for picking up bits of information in the most unlikely places. I have found it very useful in the past.'

'What are you planning to do about Kidman and the rest?' asked Philip.

'Thanks to Fenton's wholesale murder of anyone who knew where that treasure is, we are all, every one of us, in the dark, so to speak. He hid it somewhere in Charlwood or its grounds, but that's all anyone knows.'

'This Edric Fenton...he was Maria's husband?' asked Rosa. William nodded and she went on, 'Was she with him when he died? She should have been.'

They all looked at one another. 'Of course!' said Emily. 'She would be. And what about that brother—Walter Fenton? Where was he at the time?'

'I think,' said Rosa, 'that we should cultivate the Fentons.'

'That won't be too easy, considering that I more or less turned down her offer of marriage—'

'William! You mean *she* actually asked *you*...?'

Emily's voice failed her. 'What a…a…prevaricator the woman is!'

'Why don't you say what you think, Emily? The woman is a liar! But strictly speaking, no, she didn't ask me in so many words. She just gave me to understand she was very willing.' He looked at the expression on her face. 'Why are you so outraged? Did you believe that *I* had asked *her?* I thought you knew me better than that, Emily.' His face changed. 'But, no, of course you didn't.'

'I could ask Maria to call,' said Rosa hastily. 'She doesn't know what I think of her—not yet, anyway.'

Philip frowned. 'I am very willing to help all I can myself,' he said. 'But I don't think Rosa ought to get involved in this. Not at the moment.'

'Philip, you promised before we were married that you wouldn't stop me again from doing what I think is right—even if it does mean going into danger!' said Rosa with unusual force. 'Have you forgotten?'

'No, I haven't. But surely I have a right to ask you not to do anything remotely dangerous at the moment. Not when you are possibly carrying my son and heir!' Rosa looked indignant and opened her mouth, but before she could say a word Philip added, 'Or a lovely daughter— as beautiful as her mother.'

Emily looked from one to the other with her mouth open in amazement. Then she recovered, jumped up and, laughing with tears in her eyes, embraced Rosa. 'Darling Rosa! What wonderful, wonderful news! Philip, I'm so happy for you!'

William waited until the Winbolt family's excitement had subsided a little, then said, 'My congratulations, Winbolt. And of course Rosa mustn't do a thing.'

Rosa said firmly, 'I have no wish to argue with you,

William, but I intend to carry on living a perfectly normal life for the next four or five months! And I fail to see how talking to Maria Fenton could do me much harm! Even Philip couldn't object to that.'

There was some argument, but Rosa had her way in the end. It was decided that Maria Fenton should have an invitation to Shearings as soon as it could be arranged. Rosa's behaviour towards her would be perfectly normal, but she would have a pretty good idea beforehand of what they would talk about. And, in view of what she was planning to say, it would be better if Emily and William were nowhere near her. They would probably take the children to Charlwood on that afternoon. Philip refused to go with them, but insisted on remaining within call, probably in the library.

'Really, Philip, what could the woman do?' Rosa protested.

'If Maria Fenton is still working with her late husband's associates, she is a very dangerous woman. I'm taking no risks, Rosa,' Philip said with finality in his voice.

Chapter Twelve

Charity Anstey called on them the next day and was an instant success with the children. With seven younger brothers and sisters at home she was well used to handling children, and she also proved to have a talent for teaching. The old schoolroom at Shearings was brought back into use, and James and Laura quite happily spent two or three hours in it every morning with Miss Anstey. And when Emily was otherwise occupied they were perfectly content to go for walks with her in the afternoon, too.

But, on the afternoon when Mrs Fenton was due to call, Miss Anstey was not required. William, Emily and the children had left Shearings and set off for Charlwood well before two o'clock.

It had rained during the morning, but by the time they reached Charlwood the sun was shining. The children demanded to see the Dower House, and, in spite of some doubt on Emily's part, William wanted them to see for themselves how hopeless it was to think of living there.

So they stopped to call on George Fowler, who now occupied the lodge, and to visit the ruins. The Dower House was a pathetic sight, its ravages cruelly exposed in the bright sunshine. When they got nearer they saw that a team of men was still carefully sifting through the ashes as they were being cleared away.

Laura wept when she saw the exposed walls of what would have been her room. 'The pretty wallpaper,' she sobbed. 'You chose it specially for me and now it's all dirty!'

'Wait till you see the room meant for you up at the big house,' said William, picking her up to console her. 'It has an arch over the bed! And I'm sure if you asked her, Aunt Emily would help you to choose an even prettier wallpaper.'

James was more interested in what the men were doing, and William explained they were looking for anything that might give them a clue about the fire. James's eyes brightened. 'Like treasure trove?' he asked. 'I like looking for treasure trove. I've found some splendid things—a walking stick with a silver handle, Uncle William! And there's my picture, too.'

'What picture is that?' William asked.

'The picture I found in the big house. I thought you'd seen it, Uncle William! I'm glad I took it to Shearings, I can tell you. Laura wanted me to hang it up in this house here, but I wouldn't. I'd have lost it in the fire if we had.'

'It's a painting,' Emily said. 'Of the fountain court before it all fell into ruins. I shouldn't think it's very valuable—'

'It is, Aunt Emily! It's a…an historic record! Mr Winbolt said so.'

William smiled. 'I'd like to see it. And in a minute or

two...' he paused and looked mysterious '...in a minute or two, if it's a picture of the fountain and the garden, you can tell me if you think it's accurate.'

Ignoring the puzzled look on all three faces, he helped them back into the carriage and drove them up a much improved drive to the back of the house.

The children clambered out unaided and ran into the garden. Here they stopped short. The brambles, weeds and all the broken stones had been removed from the fountain. A track of bare earth leading to the centre suggested the presence of a new channel for water underneath, and recently cut stones lay nearby waiting to be put into position. The basin in the middle had been repaired and the statue in its centre restored. The rest of the fountain court had been cleared of weeds too, and the urns round the edge had all been set straight and repaired or replaced.

While James and Laura ran excitedly round and round the fountain and in and out between the urns, William sought Emily's eye. 'I promised to do it,' he said. 'Is it right?'

Emily nodded, unable to speak. It was exactly as she had planned it. The beds were already prepared for roses and climbing plants, and the stones would soon be put in place. By the following summer the view from the window would be as lovely as she had imagined it would be. She smiled tremulously. 'It's exactly right, William!'

For a moment it seemed as if he would respond. He even put his hand out to her. But then the children called out, his expression changed and the warmth in his eyes had gone. By the time the children reached them he had already moved away.

'It's all right, Uncle William,' said Laura kindly. 'You

can hug Aunt Emily if you want to. People can hug as much as they like when they're married—and you are as good as.'

In spite of her bitter disappointment, Emily pulled herself together and even managed to laugh. 'But not in public, sweetheart. Come, what else has been done?'

'That's all there is outside,' said William in the impersonal tone he used to her nowadays. 'Would you like to see inside?'

The children once again raced ahead, heedless of Emily's warnings to take care. William said in the same cool tone, 'I think it's safe enough now. I've had an army working here in the last week. They've not only made the hall and stairs secure, they've been keeping an eye out for strangers, too. Incidentally, the workmen thoroughly excavated that fountain and found nothing at all unusual. Kidman must have made a mistake.'

They went inside. Here the hall was clear of the debris that had been blocking it and it was possible to see the marble floor and the lovely curve of the staircase. Laura was already halfway up. 'I want to see the arch!' she said.

To please her, they first looked into the room that was to be hers and admired the arch. William had even hung a few pictures of scenes in Jamaica around the room, which delighted her, and there were more in James's room, too. But when Laura began to skip along the landing towards a suite of rooms at the end, William stopped her. 'No, Laura,' he said with decision. 'That part of the house isn't ready yet. We'll go downstairs.' Emily stared at him as, surprised at his peremptory tone, the children went obediently towards the stairs. They were already on their way down when William came to a halt at the top stair and turned to Emily. He said abruptly, 'The men have stopped working on those rooms for the moment, until I decide what is to happen to them,' he said. 'Till recently I was planning to share them with you, of course. They have the sort of view you enjoy.'

William might be keeping his feelings well hidden, and his tone was measured, but this time Emily saw through the barrier he was trying to keep between them. In those few words, uttered almost in spite of himself, she had caught a glimpse of all the plans he had made for this house, his thought for her happiness, his desire to please her. She wanted to say how sorry she was, how much she regretted what she had said and done, but the lump in her throat made it impossible to speak. They gazed wordlessly at each other and the attraction between them sprang to life again, so strong that it was almost tangible, so powerful that she found herself moving towards him, not doubting for a moment that this time he would take her in his arms...

He kissed her with longing and passion, holding her against the taut length of his body, his hands caressing her, pulling her even closer. She responded instantly and as passionately, murmuring his name as they kissed and kissed again. For a moment everything about the world outside was forgotten, lost as they were in this tempest of feeling. Only this place, this time, existed...

But it was only for a moment. Suddenly and quite deliberately he put her from him. His hands were trembling and his voice shook as he said, 'This won't do, Emily. It was a mistake. You... you have this power over me. I have never known anything like it. But until this business is finished I must keep my mind clear, and my feelings under control. I must! I have made too many mistakes.' He stopped, then went on more calmly, 'And

later, when we are finished with this business, I shall
think again about marriage and what it means. I was
wrong to assume that all I needed was a house and a
suitable wife to look after the children. There's more
to marriage than that—much more.' He had still been
holding her hand. Now he let it go and added briskly.
'But those are questions for later. First we must sort out
what I am to do about Kidman and friends.'

Emily grew cold at this return to his former businesslike tone. How could he put aside that storm of feeling
so coolly, almost as if it had never happened? She tried
to be calm, not to plead, as she said, 'Don't shut me
out, William. I can understand about this house, and
Kidman. But don't shut me out completely.'

He smiled wryly. 'I doubt I could.' He shook his
head, then, as a shout came from down below, he said
in a different tone of voice, 'We must go downstairs and
see what the children are doing.'

They went into the salon and found James and Laura
at the window, engaged in a lively argument. Looking
round, Emily saw that William's men had performed
miracles. The room had been transformed. Walls and
ceiling had been plastered and painted, the woodwork
painted white or polished, the delicate carvings restored.
Light, airy, beautifully proportioned, Charlwood's salon
would be the perfect place to sit, to talk, to receive visitors. And the views were still outstanding, even at this
late season. Emily joined the children at the window,
where they were arguing about the number of urns they
could see in the fountain court. She looked out, remembering when she had first seen this view. The colours
of the landscape had changed with the season, but the
underlying shape was the same. The avenue of trees had
been restored, but it still led up to the folly. The same

hills rose in the background. It was she who was different. Older, wiser, more aware. And so, she thought, was William. Some things were the same about them both—below the surface there was still a strong link of physical attraction between them, which had sprung into instant life at their first meeting and continued to run like a powerful stream, in spite of anything they did. But there was something more—a tenuous feeling of something she felt might become even stronger, even more important than passion alone. She would call it love. But would he ever acknowledge its existence? She could only hope that when the time came she would be able to convince him.

Movement behind her brought her back to the present. The children had lost interest in their argument and were wandering out into the hall. Emily followed them, and saw James walking purposefully towards the door at the end, which led to the servants' quarters.

'James, wait!' William joined him. 'This part of the house is still being worked on. The kitchens are down there. It could be dangerous.'

Emily looked through the open door. It opened into a long passage, wide but dimly lit. 'It's quite a different house down there,' William said. 'Dark. Older. It reminds me of Temperley.'

'Rosa says her father's house dates from the fifteenth century, and you're right. This looks the same.'

'I think the old manor house was built about then, too. About a hundred years ago the owner of the time started to modernise the building, but he couldn't finish the work. Along with a good many others he lost all his money in a rash piece of speculation.'

'I can see why Charlwood has a reputation for ruining its owners!'

'Not this one, Emily! Not this one! I'll finish it, you'll see! But until it's all done... Come back, James!'

'It's all right, Uncle William. I've been down here before. I want to show you where I found the picture. It's quite safe.' James was some way ahead by now, and Laura was pushing past Emily to follow him.

Emily caught hold of her and took her firmly by the hand. She said to William, 'Could we perhaps have a short look? He's so proud of that picture! I seem to remember looking for him once before, and finding him beyond this door.'

William looked resigned. 'Very well,' he said. 'I suppose it's better we know what there is down there. Keep hold of Laura and go slowly!' He took off down the passage to catch up with James, and Emily and Laura followed. Their footsteps echoed as they went. The walls were made of heavy stone, and the only light came from a small window at the far end.

They passed a massive oak door. Laura eyed it nervously. 'I don't like it here,' she said in a small voice. 'It's too scary. Where does that door go?'

'I don't know, Laura. It's probably just a broom cupboard.' Emily said, her voice carefully matter of fact. She tried the handle, but the door wouldn't open. 'We'll ask your uncle in a minute.' William and James were by a flight of steps that led downwards. Emily eyed it with distaste. 'If those steps lead to the kitchens, I'm glad I've never had to dine at Charlwood,' she said with decision.

'Those steps lead to the cellars,' said William, amused. 'The kitchens are further on, but they are, I admit, a mile or two from the dining room. Don't worry. New kitchens are being installed at this very moment just down there on the other side. The new dining room for the family will be here, so that we shall all be able to enjoy moderately warm food.'

He opened a door on the other side of the passage and they went through. The room had been some sort of parlour in the old manor house, and it had been left very much in its original style. It would be a cosy room in winter, for a large fireplace with a stone surround filled at least a third of one wall, and the rest of the room was box panelled in oak, with shutters for the diamond-paned windows. On the wall opposite the fireplace alternate panels were filled at head height with small paintings.

William pointed to them. 'We've just hung these up again. They're not in a very good condition and the quality is dubious, but they're obviously designed to fit the panels. A couple of them were still hanging on the wall when I first saw the room, but the rest were lying scattered over the floor, as if a child had thrown them down in a temper. Do you think they're worth keeping?'

'Uncle William! I found *my* picture here! It was on the floor, too. It's just like these. But mine's the best.'

Laura was busy counting the pictures. 'Seven, eight, nine, ten, *eleven!*' she said triumphantly.

Emily took a closer look at the pictures. 'Do you know, I think there should be twelve,' she said. 'Your picture might well belong here, James. These are all pictures of the garden, and so is yours. They're all by the same artist, and Uncle William is right—not a very skilled one! Yes, I would say quite definitely that there ought to be twelve, and yours is the one that's missing.'

'I think so too,' said Laura. 'Because look! There's an extra space at the end.'

'We'll have a look when we get back. But don't worry, James. I regard the picture as yours,' said William.

They went out into the passage and made for the door to the hall. As they passed the oak door, Emily said in response to a nudge from Laura, 'Would you tell us, please, where that door leads to? It's locked.'

'The key is hanging high up on a hook just next to it. I keep it locked because it leads to a watch tower that was part of the old manor house, and I don't want the children to open it when we're not there. Do you want to see it?'

'Please,' said Emily, holding on to Laura's hand. William reached up, took the massive key from its hook and turned it in the lock. The door swung open with a ghostly groan and a draught of cold air came out and hit them. Laura gave a frightened gasp and hid her face in Emily's skirt. Emily picked her up. 'It's all right, sweetheart. Look, it's just a tower with a spiral staircase inside.'

'There's an open platform at the top which is why the wind whistles in,' William said. 'It's just as well that this door is completely draught proof, otherwise we should all freeze in winter. I don't advise you to try the staircase—it's not in good repair.'

'Have no fear! Neither of us will try anything of the sort,' said Emily. 'Not even you, James, my lad. Thank you. You may lock it again now.'

'I don't like that staircase, Aunt Emily. I'm cold.'

'So am I, Laura. I think we should all go back to Shearings soon. We could remind ourselves of James's picture.'

William was frowning as they came back through the door and into the hall. 'I'd like a look at some papers I collected from the lawyers in London when we get back.

They have bits about the old manor house and some of its history. I could probably tell you more about the place after I've studied them. Come, James! We'll go back. Lead the way, Laura!'

They blinked in the sunlight as they came out. The two sides of the door belonged to different centuries, thought Emily. The fifteenth, heavy, dark and mysterious, and the eighteenth, all light and air.

'We'll call at the Dower House again on our way,' said William as they got into the carriage. 'I'd like a last word with George Fowler.'

When they met George, he had something in his hand which he held out for William to inspect. It was a brass button, dirty and distorted, but quite unmistakable. 'One of the men found it in the ashes, sir,' he said. 'I thought you ought to see it.'

William examined it. 'I've seen one like this,' he said, frowning thoughtfully. 'With the same design. But where?'

'It doesn't belong to any of the men. I've checked.'

'I'll take it with me. It may help me to remember. Thank you, Fowler. Give this to the man who found it, will you?'

A few minutes later they were on the way back to Shearings.

While Emily, William and the children had been making discoveries at Charlwood Rosa, well briefed, had been making discoveries of her own.

She rang for tea and sherry wine as soon as Mrs Fenton arrived, and the two ladies sat in the salon discussing a variety of topics, none of them significant, for a while. Rosa pressed some wine on her guest, saying without a blink that she always took a glass or two of wine at this hour of the day. When she judged that her friend Maria would be ready to talk more freely, Rosa sighed and said, 'In fact, I am so glad to have this opportunity, Maria, to have a word about Emily with you. I'm afraid she was somewhat rude to you when you were last here. Is that why we haven't seen you since?'

Mrs Fenton gave Rosa a look, but there was only a slightly worried innocence in her hostess's blue eyes—nothing to suggest that Emily had reported anything untoward. She smiled graciously and said, 'I was surprised at your sister-in-law's manner, I must confess. I was only speaking to her for her own good. I shall overlook it, of course!'

Rosa shook her head. 'You are generous. I love Emily dearly, but she can be very obstinate. As I fear Sir William is now finding.'

Mrs Fenton looked pleased. 'Really?' she said.

'Yes.' Rosa sighed. 'She is so convinced that he is merely after her fortune that she says she is tempted to call off the engagement. Neither he nor I can persuade her to change her mind. And yet I know she would be devastated if he were to carry out his threat to look elsewhere. Oh!' Rosa put a hand to her mouth in a pretty gesture of confusion. 'It must be the wine. I really shouldn't be saying this—to you, of all people! Pray do forget I said a word.' Mrs Fenton, looking like a cat with the proverbial saucer of cream, assured her hostess of her complete discretion, and Rosa went on earnestly, 'I wouldn't like to lose your friendship. As a girl I always admired you, but you probably know that. Of course, that was before your marriage to Mr Fenton. Had you...had you known him long before you married? I do so want to catch up on what you've been doing all these years.'

In the long afternoon that followed, the two ladies exchanged gossip about their lives before they had met each other again at the Langleys' ball. Several items of interest emerged, and later, when the council of four were at dinner, Rosa reported them with a precision that would have amazed Maria Fenton.

Anyone who knew the circumstances of Rosa's first marriage would have been astonished at the extent to which she had talked of her husband that afternoon, and had referred to her life as a widow, all with the aim of extracting information from her visitor. Perhaps only Philip really appreciated what it cost her. But by talking of her presence at Stephen's bedside in the last days of his life, she had established that Maria Fenton had indeed been with her husband, Edric Fenton, during his last illness. She had also learned that he had been able to talk, though not at all distinctly.

When she paused, Philip came over and, putting his arms round her, said, 'Rosa, I never cease to marvel at you! You are so courageous.'

'Clever, too!' said Emily. 'But then I always knew she was!'

'I haven't quite finished,' said Rosa, 'and this was interesting. As a boy Edric Fenton stayed occasionally with his uncle.'

Her three companions looked blank. 'And?' asked Emily.

'His uncle,' Rosa said with a small air of triumph, 'was a tenant at Charlwood at the time.'

'Rosa!'

'So he knew the house,' said William. 'And that

means that he probably knew exactly where he was going to hide those jewels even before he stole them. And then, in spite of all those murders, all the careful planning, he wasn't able to retrieve them after all. The thought must have driven him mad. He *must* have tried to tell someone! Rosa, did Maria Fenton really try to persuade you that Edric Fenton hadn't said anything at all of significance?'

'It was odd. The scene she described was most affecting, but there was something false about it. It sounded… like a well-rehearsed story, which she had told before. I think he probably did say something, which she did understand, but if so she's keeping it to herself.'

'Then I'll have to see what I can do,' said William, a touch grimly. 'When I seek her out again, having fallen out with Emily. My congratulations on your excellent groundwork *vis-à-vis* my shaky relationship with my betrothed, by the way. That will help.' He looked at Emily. 'Of course, it *is* in fact shaky, but will it stand the strain of what we planned? Will you fly into a rage again if I approach Maria Fenton, or are you strong enough to believe me when I say that the lady does not, and never will, attract me, whatever I may say to her in the next week or two?'

There was a short silence, then Emily said, 'Yes, I believe you. And you can be as convincing as you like. I don't believe she has a heart to break. I shan't get annoyed, I promise.'

'Good!' Sitting back, William took out of his pocket the button Sam Lilley had given him. 'Does anyone recognise this?'

They examined it and shook their heads. Rosa said, 'It's a man's coat button, isn't it? The buttons on

Maria's pelisse had the same design, but they were much smaller...'

'That's it!' exclaimed William. 'It's one of the buttons off Walter Fenton's riding coat—I remember now. When I saw them I thought the design was far too ornate for a man's coat. Certainly not a riding jacket. Well, well, well!'

'You mean...it was Walter Fenton who was the other man with Kidman when he set fire to the Dower House?' asked Emily.

'Unless someone else was wearing his coat, he was certainly there when it happened. I can see that my visit to the Fentons will be even more interesting than I had thought—'

He broke off and turned round as a small figure in a white nightgown peered round the door and approached the table. He was being chased by a harassed-looking nursemaid, who took hold of his arm and tried to lead him away. But James shook her off and said very firmly, 'I told you! I'm not being naughty, I'm being extremely helpful! I'll go back to bed in a minute, but I want to give this to Uncle William first. I promised him!' He held out his picture. William tried to look stern, but failed. He nodded reassuringly at the nursemaid who was stammering her excuses, and took the picture from James's outstretched hands. 'So you did,' he said, 'and I forgot to collect it. Thank you, James. I'll take care of it.'

'And I wasn't being naughty, was I?'

'No, not this time. But you had better go back to bed now. So...would you like me to take you upstairs?'

James gave his uncle a huge grin. He knew this was no tame offer. It meant sitting on Uncle William's shoulders, being quacked at as a reminder to duck his head

as they went through any of the doors, and then riding
a growling bear up the stairs. Best of all, he would be
tossed into the air and then dropped like a parcel on to
his bed when he got there. 'I should say so!' he said.

When William returned, the three Winbolts were
already studying the picture. Like the rest of the set
it was not particularly well painted, but the fountain
and the garden with its surrounding urns were clearly
recognisable. Philip looked up with a puzzled frown. 'I
don't understand. It's no work of art. And if the rest are
anything like this one, I wouldn't give them wall space.
I can't see anything significant about it, William.' He
turned it over. 'There's a number on the back—nine. Is
that significant?'

'I don't think so. The rest were all numbered, too.
It's as we thought, though. This is the missing one of
the set in the small parlour at Charlwood.'

'What else have you got?'

William had been holding a solicitor's box and he
now put it down and opened it. It was so full that the
papers inside spilled out on to the table. 'Work,' he said
briefly. 'Lots of it. They're all the papers the agent had
connected to Charlwood. Would anyone be willing to
help?'

All four went into the library where they worked
with such a will that by the time William left Shearings to call on the Fentons the next day, the papers were
all sorted into neat bundles, ready for inspection after
dinner that evening.

When the manservant came to tell Maria Fenton that
Sir William Ashenden had called she was not completely surprised. Rosa's 'indiscretions' had prepared

her to believe that Sir William, having failed with Emily Winbolt, might seek out other, more sympathetic, company. He came in, as charming as ever with his athletic stride and easy grace, and she found it quite hard to be as cool towards him as she had intended. After exchanging greetings she invited him to sit down, then waited, one eyebrow raised, for him to speak.

'I have been taking a look at Thirle on behalf of Lady Deardon,' he said. 'And as I was in the neighbourhood, I decided to call. I...I've been away in London, otherwise I would have been here sooner.'

'Really?' said Maria, not yet prepared to be helpful.

'Yes. I...I want to say...' William stopped. Looking embarrassed, he went on, 'You were kind enough to offer me your help with Charlwood some time ago, and I'm afraid I took it amiss, and was somewhat ungracious. I can see now that I was as mistaken in your motives as I have since been in those of...of others.'

'How is Miss Winbolt?' asked Maria sweetly.

William frowned. 'Forgive me, ma'am, but it wouldn't be right for me to discuss my...my betrothed. With you of all people. But I do wish to ask your pardon.'

'I see.' Maria got up and walked round the room. She turned and said, 'I will be honest with you, Sir William. I was hurt. Deeply hurt, that you should be so suspicious of an offer that I made sincerely as a friend. But I am not one to bear grudges. I accept your apology.'

'Thank you,' said William meekly. 'You are very generous. How can I regain your favour?'

She studied him thoughtfully, obviously weighing what she was going to say, then gave him a delightful smile, which didn't quite reach her eyes. 'I still have this stupid desire to see Charlwood,' she said. 'Our last visit was…well, cut rather short, shall we say? I know there's so much more to see.'

William hid his satisfaction. There was nothing he would have preferred. 'But won't it perhaps bring back unfortunate memories?' he asked doubtfully. 'Perhaps we could go somewhere else? Windsor, perhaps?'

'No, Charlwood will be very pleasant.'

'In that case, I should be delighted to take you. In fact, there are aspects of the house on which I still need a feminine point of view, but I find it difficult at the moment to discuss them with…with Miss Winbolt. Indeed, until certain matters are…are resolved between us, I do not know what will happen. So, dare I ask if you would be good enough to give me your advice? Or is that too much to expect?'

William could see that Maria Fenton was finding it difficult to hide her eagerness. True, she hesitated, but before long she said graciously, 'As I have said, I am not one to bear a grudge, Sir William. And you know how much Charlwood fascinates me. Yes, I think I could help you. When do you suggest we go?'

'There are still some hours of daylight left. What is wrong with today?' asked William boldly.

Chapter Thirteen

Not a great deal was said on the journey to Charlwood. William's mind was busy with what advice he could possibly want from Maria Fenton, and his passenger, too, seemed to be occupied with her own thoughts. But as they drove past the ruins of the Dower House she roused herself to utter an exclamation of horror, put a hand on William's arm and say with an appearance of sympathy, 'My poor friend! What a loss! A truly dreadful affair. But why would anyone do such a thing?'

Since William had every reason to believe that the lady knew full well who had started the fire and why, this piece of arrant hypocrisy put to flight any scruples he might have had about deceiving her. But he nodded and said heavily, 'It is indeed a loss, and I fear they might never catch the arsonist who planned it. But it has had one compensation.'

'What is that?'

'It has given me the chance to rethink my plans for the future. Perhaps you understand?' He smiled at her. She laughed prettily and wagged her finger. 'No, nor

will I ask what you mean by it, sir. You are too bold!
But I shall be pleased to give you my advice about the
house. And this time you must show me all of it!'

'May I first show you the salon again?'

He took her into the salon where she exclaimed over
the changes, but after a cursory glance at the walls she
quickly seemed to lose interest. She stopped at the
window and spent some time looking out at the fountain court. 'Someone has been doing a lot of digging,'
she said complacently. The look of malicious enjoyment
on her face confirmed something William had already
suspected. Maria Fenton knew all about the Valleron
jewels and was playing her own game in the matter. She
knew who was looking for them and had quite possibly
pointed them in the wrong direction herself. She *knew*
that the fountain outside had been a false trail.

'Do you mean the work we've been doing recently?' he asked, deliberately misunderstanding her. 'You
should have seen it before we started, ma'am. The fountain had been wilfully damaged and the area round it
thoroughly churned up. I can only think it was the work
of vandals. Who else would do such a thing?'

And perhaps only because he was listening for it did
William hear the note of mockery in her voice as she
said, 'Some people are idiotic enough to do anything,
Sir William. And for the most absurd reasons.' With
a small secret smile, she turned and asked, 'But what
other renovations have you been working on?'

With his new insight William took her round the
house, now quite sure that her enthusiasm to see Charlwood had a specific purpose. But to one set of rooms
he did not take her. The master suite was left out of the
tour. The thought of Maria Fenton walking through
rooms he had pictured Emily in was intolerable. Instead

he gave her a brief excuse to the effect that they were completely bare and in a state of renovation, and took her into Laura's room, where he had already hung up a few pictures. She looked at every one of them, and, as he had half-guessed she would, she examined one in particular with great care.

'You are interested in pictures, ma'am?' he asked eventually.

'What? Oh, no! No, I was just admiring this water colour. Is it of the garden here?'

'I'm afraid I brought that back from South America. My niece particularly likes it, which is why I put it in this room. If you are interested in watercolours, I have one of Kingston Harbour in my nephew's room. Or…does the subject interest you more? In which case there is a collection of paintings of Charlwood's garden downstairs, but they are of a very poor quality. I hardly like to show them to anyone, particularly to a connoisseur such as yourself.'

He had her undivided interest. 'You flatter me, Sir William! I should love to see them.'

William gave way to his weakness for teasing. He was now pretty sure he knew exactly what she was looking for, and if he was right, the lady was due for a disappointment, for she wouldn't find it anywhere in Charlwood. But he had no wish to enlighten her. On the contrary, he was helpfully innocent. 'Are you sure?' he said hesitantly. 'It's getting rather late and the light is fading. Would it be better to come back another day?'

'Certainly not!' she said impatiently. 'I would *love* to see pictures of your garden. I think you know already that I am quite passionate about gardens. Where did you say they were?'

Right again! William was enjoying himself. 'They're

in the small parlour. As a matter of fact, the parlour is exactly what I wanted to consult you about. I plan to turn it into a dining room and would like to know...' As they went downstairs, he expounded his ideas at tedious length, undeterred by the marked lack of interest on the part of his companion. She stopped even pretending to listen once they were in the room, but he kept firm hold of her elbow and guided her very slowly round each wall in turn. By the time they ended up at the pictures, he could tell that she was very nearly screaming with impatience. He regarded her blandly and said, 'So what do you think, ma'am?'

Maria Fenton's eyes were fixed on the line of pictures, straining to see them more clearly. 'What?' she said.

'What should I do about this fireplace? Should I leave it as it is?'

'The fireplace... Oh, the fireplace! I really don't know, Sir William.' She disengaged her elbow and walked along the wall, looking at the paintings. 'But what did you mean when you said these pictures were poor? I think they are delightful.'

The light coming through the small leaded windows was very dim. William contemplated the pictures. It was not at all obvious that one of the set was missing. If Laura had not counted them, he would never have noticed it himself. Not, that is, until Emily had pointed out that James's treasured picture of the fountain must be the twelfth of the set.

Maria Fenton was still moving along the row, peering at them in the dim light.

'Mrs Fenton...ma'am! They are really not worth so much of your attention,' said William, grasping her arm as if to take her away. She pulled herself free with a jerk and carried on with her search.

'Oh, but they are! Such.. such an exhilaratingly primitive sense of colour, and…and line. I find them absolutely fascinating!'

I'll wager you do, thought William, but not for their merit as works of art.

'Are they *all* here?' she asked, sounding very disappointed as she reached the end of the line.

'I'm not sure,' said William, his fertile imagination at work. 'You see, we found all but two scattered over the floor and some were damaged, as you can see. The workmen probably threw the worst ones on the dust heap without even consulting me. They would think they were rubbish.' He gave a jolly laugh. 'And they are!'

'Oh, no!' Her cry of horrified dismay was the first perfectly genuine sign of emotion of the afternoon. 'They can't have thrown it away! They mustn't!'

'What?'

'The picture—' She stopped and looked at him. 'I mean…any of them. I think they are lovely. Let me look at them once more…' She went back to the beginning of the row and peered frantically at each one again. But it was hardly surprising that she came to the end without success. The picture she wanted was safely in James's room at Shearings. William decided he had had enough. It was time to end the charade.

'Mrs Fenton, would you mind telling me what you are really looking for in my house?' he asked in a very different tone from the one he had been using all afternoon.

She was startled. 'I…I'm not sure what you mean,' she said.

'You offered to help me, but you don't seem to be as interested in my plans as I had hoped.' She looked at him blankly without speaking, but he guessed that her mind was racing behind those china-blue eyes.

'Shall we...shall we go outside?' she said at last. He held the door open for her in silence. They went along the hall and out into the drive, where they stopped. She faced him boldly enough, and he wondered what she had decided to say. It was a little late for an innocent denial, so what would be her excuse?

She began with a little laugh, a charming gesture with the hands and a delightful shrug of her shoulders. 'I see you are not to be deceived, Sir William. I was foolish to try. But I value your good opinion, you see, and I was afraid you would think me a sentimental idiot.'

'I assure you, Mrs Fenton, that I would never think anything of the sort. Not of you,' said William.

She looked at him uncertainly, not sure what to make of that, but then began, 'The fact is, I was looking for something.'

'And that was?'

'A picture. A very precious picture.' She shook her head and gave a small sigh. 'I was very fond of Edric, my late husband, you know, and in his last hours he talked to me a great deal about the past. I think that is what we do when we are in pain and perhaps drugged, don't you agree? We remember the happy days of our childhood. Poor Edric. Poor, poor Edric!' She took out a wisp of lace handkerchief and held it briefly to her eyes.

'And?' asked William, doing his best to sound sympathetic rather than sceptical.

She went on, 'He talked about a summer he spent

at Charlwood. Did you know that many years ago his uncle lived here?'

'I have recently heard so, yes.'

'Apparently, his uncle had a series of views of the gardens at Charlwood, and one in particular, a picture of the fountain court, was Edric's favourite. Remembering it so many years later, sick and in pain, he described it to me. I can hear his poor, weak voice in my ears, as I speak. He told me that the figure in the middle of the fountain looked just like me. He called it the spirit of Charlwood. It meant so very much to him, that he even talked of it in his dying moments. I wanted to own it in his memory. If I had seen it today, I was going to ask you to sell it to me.' She gave him a misty smile, but perhaps something in his face suggested that he was less than completely convinced. She put her lace handkerchief to her eyes again. 'I should have told you all this at the beginning. I'm so sorry.'

Not bad at all, William thought. She thought all that up in three or four minutes, and if I didn't know better, I'd be taken in by it. His voice was full of regret as he said, 'Now I understand, of course. And, believe me, I feel for you. Are you sure your picture isn't in that room? If it isn't there, or in one of the other rooms you've been through today, then I'm afraid it has gone. There is nothing else of the kind in the rest of the house, I assure you.'

She bit her lip in vexation, but, after a moment's debate, evidently decided he was telling her the truth, for she put her handkerchief away, and asked him to take her home. She was as silent on the journey back from Charlwood as she had been on the way there. Whatever she was thinking of, it was not pleasant, for she sat frowning and biting her lip.

William used the time to think out his strategy. At present Maria and her friends had no idea that he knew anything about the Valleron business, and he wanted them to continue in ignorance. So, though he had originally planned to see Walter Fenton when they got back, to question him about the coat button, he decided he would leave it to some future time. At the moment, he had no wish to do anything to disturb the Fentons' peace of mind. So, when they arrived at Maria Fenton's house and she made no attempt to invite him in he merely looked disappointed and turned to go. 'Goodbye, ma'am,' he said. 'I was impressed by your sad story. If I do find a picture like the one you described, I shall certainly not forget you.'

When William arrived back at Shearings he found Emily alone in the library. 'Miss Anstey has taken the children to the Rectory for tea,' she said. 'It seemed a good idea to let them go—there are children of their own age there to play with. And it meant I could spend the afternoon reading these papers.' She hesitated, then asked coolly, 'You look pleased with yourself. Did you enjoy your afternoon with Mrs Fenton?'

'Very much indeed! She's a fine woman.'

Emily bent over the papers again, turning them over rapidly one after the other. 'She is certainly not at all plain,' she agreed. 'And takes pains to appear very willing to please. I dare say gentlemen think her not at all strong-minded.'

William came over to the table and looked at her with amusement in his eyes. He shook his head and said, 'Emily, Emily! I thought you promised us.'

'Promised? Promised what? What did I promise? I am not in the slightest jealous of Mrs Fenton, if that is what you mean. Though what you found to discuss for four or five hours…'

'I took her to Charlwood.' He held her chin and made her look up at him as he said, 'Emily, Maria Fenton has a hard line to her exquisite lips, calculation in those china-blue eyes, and a mind like an iron trap. I would rather have spent the afternoon with a tarantula spider. Or with you.'

Emily turned her head to remove her chin out of his grasp. She tried to stare coldly at him, but he carried on looking at her with such a quizzical look in his eye that her lips started to twitch and then she laughed. 'What a choice! I'm not sure whether to feel flattered or insulted.'

'But it was worth it.'

'All those hours?'

'No. To hear you laugh. But, yes, the afternoon was certainly worth it. Rosa said she thought her friend Maria wasn't telling all she knew about Edric Fenton's last words—remember? She was quite right. I think Maria Fenton has been leading her friends by the nose. There's at least one small detail she forgot to mention.'

'Which was?'

'The word "picture", or possibly "painting". But isn't that the children returning? There isn't time to tell you any more, and besides, I'd like to tell Rosa and Philip at the same time. I assume they're out?'

'They've gone to Temperley.'

'We'll see them tonight. But for now I'd like to spend some time with the children before they go to bed. Will you help me? I want to convey to James, without worrying him, that he shouldn't talk of his "treasure trove" outside this house. And for the moment I think we should take the picture into care, too.'

'Take all of his treasures into care,' Emily suggested. 'Don't single out the picture as anything special. We could do what you want by reading him some of the treasure trove book I brought from London for him. I'm sure you could think of a way of getting him to let you take care of his prizes.'

'Excellent!'

They had a happy time with the children, ending with a rollicking time in the nursery before bed. And Emily was right. The book, *Treasure Trove and Treasure Seekers*, was just the thing to persuade James not only to keep his own treasure trove secret, but to leave it all with his uncle for safe keeping.

That night over dinner William gave them all an account of his visit to Charlwood with Maria Fenton. He ended by saying, 'It seems obvious that James's picture is connected in some way with Edric Fenton's hiding place for the jewels. And I'm fairly sure Maria knows that fact, but has been keeping it from her associates.'

'You think she wants to find them for herself?' asked Emily.

'I wouldn't be surprised. As Edric Fenton's widow, she quite possibly believes she has a right to them.'

'Apart from the Vallerons, perhaps,' said Philip drily.

'Our Maria wouldn't let a little thing like that worry her,' said William.

'But, William, why has Maria only recently started looking for them herself? It's over a year since Edric Fenton died,' asked Rosa.

Philip broke in. 'I can guess why. Kidman and the

others somehow learned about Charlwood and she had to wait until they had finished searching the house. When they didn't find anything, they came back to her and wanted to know if Fenton had said anything else.'

'And she fended them off by telling them that he had mentioned the fountain.'

'That's why K…Kavanagh, or Kidman as we now know him to be, was there that day!' Emily exclaimed. 'But it isn't the real fountain, but the picture—William, do you mean to tell us that James's picture is the key to it all?'

'I think so. And so does Maria Fenton, judging by the rigmarole she told me today.'

'But how?'

'That's what we're going to find out.'

'You make it sound so easy,' said Emily, doubtfully. 'But it isn't. Not with Maria Fenton and Kidman both on our trail.'

'Emily, look at it! We have so much on our side. We now know the picture is significant. Maria may know that, but I'm not at all sure that Kidman does. That means we have a very good idea of where the Valleron jewels are hidden—or at least which room they're hidden in. We have the picture, the key you could call it, in our possession. Not one of the others, not even Maria, has any idea where that picture is at the moment. And, possibly most important, they haven't the slightest idea that we know anything at all about Charlwood's connection with the Valleron robbery, and certainly not that we are looking for the jewellery ourselves.'

Emily pulled a face. 'I was wrong,' she said. 'It will be as easy as falling off a log.'

'Or out of a tree?' She gave him an exasperated look, but then spoilt it with a smile she tried to suppress but couldn't. He nodded and went on, 'Perhaps not quite as easy as that, but I do believe we have a good chance of success. Shall we have a look at the picture?'

They put the picture on the table and examined it. It was painted just as badly as the others, and like them it had no frame, but consisted simply of a canvas on a stretcher. A large nine had been scribbled on the back.

Rosa had been feeling round the edge but she suddenly exclaimed, 'Ouch! That hurt!' She examined her fingers. 'But it hasn't broken the skin. What is it?'

William was already examining the edge of the stretcher, and passing his finger to and fro over something underneath. 'It's a very small piece of metal like a flat hook. You must have pinched your finger on it. It's very firmly fixed.' They crowded round to look.

'That must be some sort of mechanism,' Emily exclaimed. 'It will act as a key, I know it will! I can't wait to take it to Charlwood to try it.'

Philip's handsome face had a look of concern on it. 'Emmy, aren't you forgetting how dangerous these people are?'

'No, but they won't suspect what we're doing, will they? William, let's go tomorrow. Let's all go!'

William looked at her. Recently Emily had been subdued in his presence, had spoken to him always with a touch of reserve. They had both been at fault, he knew. But tonight she was as eager as she had been months ago when he had first shown her Charlwood and its gardens. The memory of her eagerness, her openness then, was very sweet. On the other hand, Philip was right. With people like Kidman there was always a risk. He knew that Philip would never let Rosa anywhere near the place at the moment, whatever Rosa felt, and he had no wish to start an argument between them. He said slowly, 'I think you and I could go, Emily. It would be quite natural for us to have a look at what is being done there. But if we go tomorrow, I'd like to leave the children behind in the care of Philip and Rosa.'

Philip was by no means happy with the idea of Emily going to Charlwood but, after a certain amount of discussion, he eventually agreed. The trip would ostensibly be to inspect the house and the fountain court, where Emily would plant a few bulbs. She would have with her a basket of small gardening tools and bulbs, which William would carry for her.

'There's just one thing,' he said, somewhat hesitantly. 'I...I may have given our Maria the impression that you and I...'

'That we had fallen out? How unlikely!' said Emily.

He nodded. 'She thinks you still regard me as a fortune hunter. She doesn't know about the money.' He regarded her sardonically and said, 'So, if we meet her, it would be better if you managed not to regard me too affectionately, and even bring yourself to address a few sharp words to me—I know how difficult this will be for you, but you must try, for the sake of verisimilitude.'

'I think I shall be able to manage that,' Emily said with a slight edge. 'Easily.'

The next day they set off in the gig. They were both dressed suitably in old clothes and stout boots, the perfect picture of a couple interested in doing some gardening. After she was seated, William handed Emily a large basket and climbed in beside her. He said, 'I apologise if it spoils your dignity to keep hold of the basket. I've wrapped the picture up and put it under that sack of bulbs. And if all goes well, on our return we might be carrying it and seventy thousand pounds' worth of extras. One wouldn't wish to leave such a load lying in the back of the gig.'

'You really think we shall find the jewels, then?'

'Do you know, Emily, when I look at you now in those dreadful boots, with your hair scraped back and your dress so drab, looking so like the girl who tried to pull the wool over my eyes, and compare that with how lovely you can look—inspecting my gardens in an apricot dress, talking over dinner in the candlelight at your grandfather's, or, most of all, enchanting me on a hillside in May—I am encouraged to believe that anything is possible.'

'William! Please, you mustn't tease me. I know what you think of me.'

He stopped the gig and turned to face her. The road was deserted, and Emily was just about to ask what was wrong when he pulled her to him and kissed her hard. 'Believe me, Emily,' he said as he released her, 'you have no idea what I think of you! But I have no intention of telling you at the moment, either. Walk on!' And, before Emily had recovered her breath, the gig set off again.

'What do you mean by that? This is not what I came with you for, sir! How dare you kiss me so roughly and then…and then… What do you *mean*?'

'Not at the moment. We have business on our hands.'

Emily was incensed. 'Let me tell you, William, I don't need any encouragement at all to speak sharply to you. It comes quite naturally. You are the most disagreeable man I ever met, the most insufferable…'

He only laughed. 'Excellent! Keep it up!'

* * *

When they arrived at Charlwood, Emily jumped nimbly down from the gig without waiting for William's help and walked off, back straight, and chin in the air, not even turning round when William called to tell her she had forgotten her basket. This amused him so much that he had difficulty in keeping a frown on his face, as he picked up the basket and strode in pursuit. No one watching their manner could doubt that there was something very wrong with their relationship. Once inside, Emily turned to him. 'William, someone was waiting at the top of the drive! I saw him as I got down.'

'Two, in fact. Barnaby Drewitt and friend. Don't worry about them. They're here in case of trouble. Where is that picture?'

They went into the parlour and, after William had put the basket on the floor, Emily carefully took out James's picture. William was examining the ones still on the wall, and re-hanging them according to the numbers on the back. When he reached number eight he found Emily waiting for him with the ninth in her hands. 'Now!' he said, and hung the picture of the fountain in its square. Nothing happened.

'It's not fully inside its panel,' said Emily. 'Press it in harder.'

He pressed, and with the slightest of whispers the panel slid back. They looked at one another in awe. 'It worked!' said William. 'Emily, it worked!'

'I can't believe it could be so simple. Is there…is there anything inside?'

William put a long arm inside the hole, and, not without difficulty, drew out a canvas bag. 'It's devilishly heavy,' he said. 'No, I'll put it down. You couldn't hold it.'

When the bag was out on the floor beside the basket, William undid a knot or two and, when it was open, held it out to Emily. 'You look,' he said. Emily peered into the bag, and drew out a chain. It was of heavily worked gold links, set with diamonds, rubies, emeralds and sapphires. Even in the dimly lit parlour, the stones were dazzling, sending out sparks of fire. Emily whispered, 'How incredibly beautiful!'

'There's a lot more here, too. I think we may safely say we've found the Valleron jewels, don't you?'

Emily was still gazing at the chain. 'William, I'm frightened. I hadn't realised… This alone must be worth hundreds, if not thousands, of pounds. What are you going to do with it?'

'Pack it up as quickly as we can before anyone else sees it. Get it back to Shearings safely. I shall take it to a bank in London as soon as possible—perhaps even tomorrow. Then I shall see it is eventually returned to the Valleron family. Don't you agree?'

'Yes, yes. I want it out of our hands as soon as possible—it frightens me. It has cost too many lives already. Let's go, quickly.'

'Not yet. First we have to put things back as they were. Put the jewellery and money into this sack.' He emptied out the sack of bulbs, which, to Emily's surprise, also contained quite a number of pebbles. 'Then put the bulbs and stones into the canvas bag and tie it up as it was.' As she looked at him, amazed, he said, 'Don't waste time, but do as I say! Right! Hand me the bag.' He put the bag, now heavy with bulbs and pebbles, back into its hiding place, and carefully pulled the picture, together with its piece of panelling, back into position. When he heard the click he took the picture away and handed it to her.

'Back in the basket with this and the sack, and then we put the tools on top. Don't worry—I'll carry it. We mustn't let it appear to be heavier than it was before, and you would find that difficult. Seventy thousand pounds' worth of gold and jewels is quite literally a heavy responsibility.'

On the way down the drive Emily said, 'I'm impressed with the way you planned this. Do you always think it all out beforehand—the stones, the sack, all the rest? And I notice that we now have protection in the form of Barnaby Drewitt not far behind.'

'It's just a habit. Sometimes in South America my life depended on it. In the past I've enjoyed adventure.'

Emily sighed. 'And now, I suppose, this adventure is all over. The jewels are found and will soon be back with their rightful owners.'

'It isn't over yet. There's still Kidman and his gang. And look over there at the Dower House. Someone has to pay for that. No, it isn't over yet, Emily.' Suddenly he put his hand on her arm and said very quietly, 'Maria Fenton! She's over there at the Lodge, and she's seen us. Remember to act up!'

As they got nearer, he added, 'Act, damn it!'

Emily took a breath and launched into an attack. 'Must I tell you again, sir, that I will not have you speak to me like that! You may have no money, but you could at least have some manners! The sooner you find someone else to put up with your insults and look after your brats, the better! I cannot imagine why you insisted on bringing me here today at all. The garden is very well as it is. What are you doing now?'

William pulled up at the Lodge and got down. 'Why,

good morning, Mrs Fenton!' He bowed and raised his eyebrows. 'May I help you?'

'Good morning,' Maria said. 'I...I think I may have lost something yesterday. A...a button. I was asking the man here, but he's new and doesn't know anything about it. I suppose it doesn't really matter, but its design was unique.' She looked pale and worried—quite unlike herself.

'Why would you think you had lost a button here of all places, Mrs Fenton?' asked Emily coldly.

For a moment Maria Fenton looked blank, then, with a flash of her old spirit, she said, 'Why, when dear William showed me round the house before it was burnt down, of course! Did you not know?' She turned to William. 'Have you heard any more about my picture? I can't believe it is lost for ever.'

'William, Rosa has been looking after your children for long enough. We must hurry back,' Emily said impatiently.

William frowned, shrugged his shoulders and, with an apologetic bow, said, 'I'm sorry, but I can't help you.' With a glance at Emily, he went on, 'You must excuse me. Emily is right, we must go back. But you must feel free to look for your button here if you wish.' He called one of the men over and said, 'Give Mrs Fenton as much help as she needs.'

'William!' called Emily sharply.

As they drove off Emily looked back to see Maria in conversation with William's man. 'It's Walter's button, of course, but he can't look for it himself in case someone recognises him,' she said.

'I wonder why she's so *very* worried,' said William thoughtfully. 'She isn't a woman to panic lightly.'

'Don't tell me you're sorry for her!'

'Not in the slightest. Congratulations on your playacting ability, by the way. I'd be sorry for myself, if the way you spoke to me in front of Maria Fenton was a sample of the way you would speak after we're married,' said William. 'If I thought it was real, I'd call off the engagement tomorrow.'

After a silence Emily said carefully, 'What engagement?'

Chapter Fourteen

'What engagement?'

William shook his head ruefully. 'I'm sorry. I forgot. It isn't a real engagement at all, is it?' Emily held her breath. He waited then asked again, 'Is it, Emily?'

'I...I suppose not. You...you said we should not suit. You said it was done with.'

'Well, if that isn't just like a woman! You were the one who broke it off, not I! I thought we had an agreement, you and I. I realise now it wasn't ideal, but it was what I would call a gentleman's agreement. A reasonable, rational contract. You promised to marry me and look after the children, and in return I offered you an establishment of your own and independence to run it. Then suddenly for no real reason you tell me in the unkindest possible terms that you won't marry me! Is it any wonder that I told your brother we should not suit?'

'I've said I'm sorry that I misjudged you!'

'So you should be.'

They drove in silence for a while. Then, in a small voice, Emily said, 'Are you going to forgive me?'

'I already have,' he said curtly. He looked at her. 'I've come to understand why you acted the way you did.'

'I'd still like to hear the rest of what you said that day. Will you tell me now?'

He didn't pretend not to know what she was talking about. 'If you must know, I was angry with both the Deardons for reminding me of the stupid remarks I made before I knew you. Strong-minded you were. Plain you could never be. I told them so. I said I was proud of you, and very proud that you had agreed to marry me. That you were the most intriguing woman I had ever known. That I couldn't imagine anyone else as my wife.'

'Oh, William, did you really?' She stopped to swallow a lump in her throat. 'What a fool I was! I lost so much by running away too soon.'

The distress in her voice touched him. He said more gently, 'Not everything. In spite of it all, we've managed to work together. And I'm hoping that, when this business is all over, we might begin again, differently this time.' Till now he had been serious, but William never allowed himself to stay serious for too long. He looked at her sideways and smiled irrepressibly. 'But I'd like to begin again with the oak tree. And the hollow. I liked that girl, Emily.'

As soon as they were back at Shearings, William spoke to Philip and Rosa and spent a short time with the children. Then he gathered his things together, put the Valleron treasure in a more fitting container and, after collecting Barnaby Drewitt, left for London. He

planned to put the Valleron treasure safely under lock
and key, but had decided not to return it to its owners
immediately. That was bound to be a long and complicated business, and, in the present circumstances,
would keep him away from Shearings for too long for
his peace of mind. Even so, it meant that he would have
to spend two nights in London and could not hope to be
back before late afternoon of the second day.

After his departure Emily took the children riding.
Philip had recently offered a pony to each of the children and they were very eager to exercise them. They
had a good ride, but she kept them inside Shearings's
fences. James's picture of the fountain had brought the
deaths and dangers of the Valleron robbery too close to
home, and until Kidman and his friends had somehow
been disposed of, she didn't feel like straying too far,
especially as William was not available to call on for
help.

Meanwhile Maria Fenton had continued to search the
ruins of the Dower House for the button her brother-in-
law had lost. Her mind was not fully on the search. She
was far more seriously worried about the disappearance
of the picture of the fountain. Since the day before that
had become a very serious matter indeed. It occurred
to her that some of the men now at work on the Dower
House might have worked on the main house too, and
might have seen the picture there. She decided to ask
them, but without letting them suspect how desperate
she really was. 'I seem to be having such bad luck at
present,' she said lightly. 'First I lose a button off my
pelisse, and then a picture I particularly wanted, and
which Sir William was ready to sell me, seems to have

disappeared. He tells me it might be on a rubbish heap somewhere. Could you ask if anyone has seen it? It was a picture of the fountain in the garden. I was so disappointed when he told me it had gone.'

She shuddered inwardly as she said this. Disappointment was hardly the issue. She was very afraid it might be more a question of life or death. Why on earth had she not realised that Kidman was in the house when she had come back from her excursion to Charlwood with William Ashenden? Now, as she watched the men, a picture of the scene from the day before was vivid in her mind. She had arrived home and Walter had asked her where she had been...

'To Charlwood with William Ashenden. If you must know, I was looking once again for the Valleron jewels, though he didn't know that, of course.'

'I thought you had given him up? As I remember it, you called him a conceited oaf.'

'Yes, well, he came here today while you were out and started making up to me again. He still doesn't know I'm not as rich as I pretend, and he's fallen out with Emily Winbolt.'

'Sis, it's time you stopped thinking about Ashenden and concentrated on the Valleron stuff instead.'

'If you were to ask me, Walter, I'd say that Ashenden might be a better future prospect for me than the "Valleron stuff", as you call it. That won't be found for years. If ever.'

'What the devil do you mean by that? Why not?'

Her angry frustration had caused her to be less cautious than usual. 'Because the key to it has probably been thrown on the rubbish heap, that's why!'

A different voice, and one to be dreaded, asked softly, 'What's this about a key, Maria?'

She whirled round in shock. Kidman stood in the doorway. Staring at him, Maria was not deceived by his dispassionate look of enquiry. She had once seen him, with just the same look on his face, using his own methods to question a man until he was screaming for mercy.

'Kidman!' she exclaimed nervously. 'How…how wonderful to see you! I…I was just about to say I wished you were here. We need your help.'

'What key?' He took a step closer, and this time his voice was even softer. 'Tell me.'

Maria did the best she could in spite of the shivers running up and down her spine. 'I…I've been thinking and thinking about those last hours with Edric. It… it was all so confused, and I…I was distressed. Very distressed. It's not surprising I didn't remember it all at once. It was so…so p-painful that p-perhaps my mind didn't want to remember. You can understand that, can't you?' He stared at her in silence and she tried not to stammer as she went on. 'I t-told you he had mentioned the fountain.'

'You did. As I remember, Maria, you told me that after a touch of prompting. But not before.'

'Yes, yes. I know. That was…was b-because I…I didn't think it was important. I thought Edric was just muttering nonsense. B-but when I really thought about it afterwards, it…it became c-clear to me that it might have been *fountain*. Silly of me, wasn't it? And then just… just recently it came back to me that it hadn't been just the fountain. He had said *picture* as well. *Picture* of the fountain. S-so I went to look for…for a p-picture of the fountain.' She tried to give him a flattering smile. 'You always thought the jewels were inside the house, didn't you? I think you must have been right—as usual.'

Kidman listened in silence, but it was clear that he was not taken in by this tale. She added, 'I was hoping to surprise you, Kidman, I swear!'

'Do you know, Maria, if I didn't know you better, I'd say you were lying to me. That you were looking for those jewels—my jewels—for yourself. But you wouldn't do that, would you? I think *you* know *me* better than that.' He came closer still and caught her wrist. 'I don't like liars, Maria. Especially when they're trying to cheat me.'

'I wasn't! You're hurting me, Kidman, and I don't deserve it,' cried Maria with a sob in her voice. He threw her away from him so that she stumbled and fell.

'Find the picture,' he said. 'If that is the key, I want it. Find it.'

Still on the floor, she cried, 'But I can't! I've searched the house for the damned picture, but I couldn't find it. And then Ashenden said it had probably been thrown on the rubbish heap.'

'Then get in to the rubbish heap and turn it over until you find it, Maria. Otherwise...' He paused. 'Otherwise I might think you're playing with me. I might even suspect you know where my jewels are already, and have a...dangerous ambition to keep them yourself.' She scrambled to get up, and he made no attempt to help her. He waited for her to stand, then pulled her to him and caressed her throat with long fingers. 'Don't, Maria. The jewels wouldn't look pretty on a corpse.'

'I don't know where they are! I swear I don't. Walter, why don't you tell him?' But Walter was silent.

Kidman went to the door. 'I'll be back tomorrow or the next day,' he said. 'Find the picture.'

* * *

He had gone again, taking Walter with him. She didn't know where. Kidman had always come and gone like a ghost. And she had been left alone and afraid. She had even considered flight, but where would she go? He or one of the others was sure to hunt her down, and the end would be the same. Now, after a sleepless night, she was here at the Dower House. Maria looked round her. What was she doing here now, looking for a button that might or might not incriminate Walter, when Kidman might appear again at any moment? She was lost!

'Mrs Fenton! Ma'am!' It was William's man. 'We haven't found no button, ma'am, but one of the men says he thinks he knows where your picture might be.'

'*What?*'

'Your picture, ma'am. One of the men heard young Master James talking about it when he was here after the fire. He's got it.'

'Master James? You mean Sir William's nephew?'

'That's the one. He's got it at Mr Winbolt's house. He calls it his treasure trove, or some such nonsense.'

The relief was so enormous that Maria felt a moment's dizziness. This was such a totally unexpected reprieve. At first she was quite unable to speak, then, as the man stared, she recovered enough to thank him before hurrying back home to consider how she could get hold of this all-important picture...

Maria's luck seemed to have turned. The next day, after a little judicious questioning in the village, two facts emerged that would make her plan much easier to carry out than she had feared. One was that Sir William Ashenden was in London on business and would not be back till the following day, and the other was that the Winbolts were to visit Lady Langley that very afternoon. Armed with this information, she set out for Shearings, fully intending to arrive after the Winbolts had left.

Nevertheless, she said at the door how disappointed she was to have missed *dear* Mrs Winbolt, especially as she had brought some little sweets for the *darling* children. She was afraid for a moment that the stupid man at the door was not going to react as she had hoped. She said charmingly, 'Perhaps I could just see Master James and his sister?' To her relief he said after a pause,

'Well, ma'am, the children are out in the park for a walk with Miss Anstey. You could meet them there, if you wish.'

Better and better! Maria walked gracefully along the path towards the park, and when she saw Miss Anstey and the children she greeted them warmly and asked if she might join them on their walk. Charity Anstey had not met Mrs Fenton, but she knew of her, and was impressed by her air of fashion. The children seemed to know the lady too, and had responded naturally to her greeting, so Charity was quite ready to agree. So they all set off again along the avenue of trees, and soon Maria had them talking about Charlwood. James might have been told not to mention his picture outside the house, but the boy was no match for one of the most skilled manipulators in London. Mrs Fenton had the right credentials in his eyes to be an exception. She had visited Shearings more than once, and obviously knew Charlwood very well. What was more, she was interested in treasure trove, too. In no time at all James was telling Mrs Fenton all about *his* bits of treasure trove, including his prize possession.

At the end of the walk Charity Anstey was impressed by Mrs Fenton's kindness and patience with the children, and grateful to her for keeping them, James especially, so amused. Maria herself was more than grateful. Before she left for home that afternoon, she knew all she needed, about the picture, about where Uncle William had put it for safety, and about how to get in to the East Wing without bothering the servants.

That night, as soon as she thought the children would be in bed and asleep and the servants in their own quarters, she put her plan into practice. It was some time since she had last visited premises without their owner's knowledge, but it all came back to her. And in fact, because it was not often in use, she found the East Wing at Shearings ridiculously easy to get into. In a surprisingly short time she was on her way back home with the all-important picture in her possession.

It was just as well. Kidman arrived the noon the next day with Walter at his side and in no mood for prevarication. He was as tense as she had ever seen him. 'Where is it?' were his first words. With a touch of triumph in her smile, Maria handed the picture to him. But, far from looking pleased, he said grimly, 'Why was I so sure that you would "manage" to find it, Maria? Where was it? Hidden in your room? I warn you, one of these days you will play your tricks once too often.' He looked at the picture. 'What the devil is this? Are you trying to gull me again?'

'No, Kidman. I am quite sure that this is the key, and if you'll come with me to Charlwood I'll show you where you can use it.'

'There's no need for you to come. You can *tell* me where!'

Maria was prepared for this. 'I really can't. It's too difficult to explain, I need to show you in person.'

He looked at her suspiciously, but then nodded his head. 'Walter will keep an eye on you.'

They left for Charlwood.

Meanwhile, Laura had been telling Emily about Maria Fenton's visit the previous afternoon. 'She was really very kind, Aunt Emily. She gave James and me sweets and came on a walk with us, too. But I think she likes boys better than girls. She talked a lot to James— all about his silly treasure trove.'

'James? What's this? I thought your uncle told you not to say anything about treasure.'

'But this was different! Mrs Fenton is a *friend* of Uncle William's. I had to tell her, Aunt Emily! She was really interested. She knows all about Charlwood, you see.'

'She certainly does,' said Emily with a look at Rosa. 'Did you show her your...any of your treasure?'

'Oh, no, I told her I couldn't, because Uncle William had put it away.'

'Good! It's better to be safe than sorry. You didn't say where he had put it, did you?'

James hesitated. 'I...I don't think so...'

'Yes, you did, James!' Laura said decisively. 'You said he had put it in his secit...sectri...secataire!'

Emily exchanged another look with Rosa. 'James,' she said calmly, 'I think I'd like another look at that picture. Would you like to show us where it is?'

James gave a cry of outrage when the secretaire desk was opened and he discovered that the picture was missing, but Emily was not really surprised. It was all too coincidental—Maria's visit when they were out, her desire to spend time with children she had up to then ignored, and her clever questioning. She really was a ruthless, devious and dangerous woman. James was a bright little boy, and fiercely protective of his treasures, but he had noticed nothing odd about her questions. Perhaps Miss Anstey might have, but she had been left to look after Laura, and had not heard all of Maria's conversation.

James was inconsolable, and Emily had a hard job persuading him to wait until his uncle came home before setting out to look for the picture himself.

'I thought Mrs Fenton was nice,' he sobbed. 'I didn't know she just wanted to steal my picture. I know Uncle William told me not to tell anyone, but I thought she was his friend.'

'It was very wicked of Mrs Fenton to take your picture, James, but I think it will be quite safe,' Emily said, wiping his face with her handkerchief. 'There's really no need to get so upset. I'm almost certain it has only been borrowed. When Uncle William comes back, we shall go and get it. He will know what to do.'

'I don't want to wait! She had no right to take it, and I shall tell her so. I want to go straight away. Now!'

Emily pointed out that it would not be long before William returned and worked hard to persuade James that he would have a better chance of recovering his picture if he waited till then. He wasn't entirely convinced, but eventually calmed down enough to go to his morning lessons. Meanwhile, Emily and Rosa had a lot to talk about. They were both amazed at Maria Fenton's audacity. They had known for some time that Edric Fenton had lived on the wrong side of the law, but, though Emily had never liked or trusted Maria Fenton, it had never occurred to her that his wife was just as bad. She said as much to Rosa and wondered, too, how Kidman and the others had found out so quickly where the picture was.

'I suppose we should be relieved that Maria, not Kidman, came to collect it,' Rosa said. 'Things could have been a lot worse.'

Emily nodded. 'I agree. And though I don't know how they found out, I would be willing to wager that if that picture isn't already back at Charlwood it soon will be. I only hope it will be left there.'

James had just finished his lessons and was on his way to talk to Emily again about the picture. Unfortunately his sharp ears overheard this last bit. He was angry and very disappointed with his Aunt Emily. Had she no idea of how much the picture meant to him? 'Hope it will be left there'! If she knew where it was now, why wasn't she taking him to get it back, instead of making him wait for Uncle William? He had a jolly good mind to go himself...

And it didn't take long for James to decide that that was just what he would do. He knew the way to Charlwood. It was a bit too far to walk, but the pony he had been given would take him. One of the stable boys was his friend—Jem would help him to saddle the pony and mount it. No need to tell him he was going for more than a ride round the park. Spurred on by righteous anger, James set off for Charlwood.

Emily was uneasy when James failed to appear for the afternoon walk—he was usually prompt. Laura said she had not seen him since the end of their morning lessons. The feeling of unease grew when she sent several

of the servants to look for him, and was told that he was
nowhere in the house. Philip had been out on business
all morning and was still not back, so James could not
be with him. If he was down at the stables, he was due
for a scolding! She went herself to see, but James was
not there. And neither was his pony.

Seriously worried, she questioned the stable boys
and one of the younger ones, a boy called Jem, told her
that Master James had taken his pony for a ride in the
park.

Emily knew instantly where James had gone, and
it wasn't for a ride in the park! She wasted no time on
further questions, but had a quick word with Rosa,
changed, and, almost before her horse had been led
out and saddled, she was back, ready to set off in
pursuit.

William had finished the business of delivering the
Valleron collection to the strong room at the bank the
day before, but the hour had been too late to set out for
Shearings. He had been invited to spend the night in
Arlington Street, where he brought Lord Winbolt up to
date on developments in Berkshire.

'My congratulations! You and Emily have done an
excellent piece of work between you. And now all that
remains is for you to finish the job and marry her! Don't
stand any nonsense, Ashenden. You're the man for her
and she knows it.'

'I still have to set my house free of Kidman, before
I do.'

'Ah, yes, ah, yes! Tell me, how do you suppose
he would take it if he opened that panel and found
the bag with nothing of value in it and the Valleron
treasure gone?'

William paused for thought. 'I should imagine,' he said slowly, 'that he might well go insane. He has expended so much time and effort hunting those jewels, his mind is so fixed on owning them, that it might well turn his brain to discover they had gone.' He nodded his head, then said reassuringly, 'But for the moment Kidman has no way of finding that out. The picture, the key to it all, is safely stored at Shearings, and without it they can't open the panel. Maria Fenton believes it is lost, and will tell Kidman so. They'll take time to work out what to do, and in the meantime I shall find some way of trapping them. It's no use just frightening them off. They have to be caught.'

Lord Winbolt frowned. 'I'm not happy, Ashenden. We both know that Kidman is dangerous. I don't like the idea of Emily—or her brother and Rosa—being anywhere near him when he discovers he has been cheated of his prize.'

'They won't be! I promise you, sir, that I will make very sure that Emily and the rest of your family are well clear of Charlwood when that happens.'

'And when Kidman has gone, we can look for wedding bells?'

William said calmly, 'I think that is up to the lady, sir.'

'I tell you what, Ashenden. I like you, but if I have a fault to find in you it's that you're a bit over-cool in your attitude, a bit too well balanced. My girl doesn't show her feelings to everyone, but they run deep. I think she would be safe in your hands, but she could be badly hurt by someone who doesn't care enough for her.'

William had been twisting his glass of wine between his fingers and examining its colour in the candlelight.

Now he looked up and saw the anxiety in the faded
eyes looking at him so intently. He met them frankly.
'You may set your mind at rest, Lord Winbolt. I care
more than I want to admit, even to you.' He took a sip
of wine, and leaning back in his chair he went on, 'If
you had asked me six months ago if I would ever marry
for love, I would have laughed at you. And, yes, my
decision to ask Emily to be my wife was eminently well
balanced and, if you like, cool. I needed someone to
create a home for the children, and I thought she would
agree because, in return, I was offering her a home of
her own. We had enough interests in common to make
for a pleasant relationship. And...' He hesitated, then
went on, 'You're right. Emily has a depth of feeling, a
passion that surprised and delighted me.'

'That's not what I meant.'

'I know. I know what you want of me, and I swear
that now, whether Emily marries me or not, I care
for her more than I ever thought I could care for any
other being on this earth.' William said this calmly,
but with such deep sincerity that Lord Winbolt was
reassured, even when William went on with a smile,
'But I would prefer her not to know that. It doesn't do
wives any good at all to know how much we are at
their mercy.'

'Naturally not. You have my blessing, my boy.'

The next morning William finished the few bits of
remaining business, went back to Arlington Street to
bid Lord Winbolt goodbye, then set off for Shearings.
He was glad to be going. Since his talk with Emily's
grandfather the night before, he had felt impatient to
see her again, had even felt anxious about her—for
no good reason, as far as he knew. As the morning

went on this irrational feeling grew, and he wasted as
little time as possible on the road, arriving at Shearings
earlier than he had said, at about half past two in the
afternoon.

'William! William, thank God you're here!' Rosa
met him at the door, her arms outstretched, her face
white with worry.

'What is it? Tell me!'

'It's Emily! And James. And the picture. Oh, I don't
know where to begin.' She burst into tears.

After signalling to the manservant that he should
bring Mrs Winbolt something to restore her, William
led her through to the small sitting room she generally
used and sat her down. 'Now tell me,' he said. 'First,
where is Emily?'

'She's gone to Charlwood after James.'

'I don't quite understand. Why should James take it
into his head to go to Charlwood? There isn't anyone
there!'

'Oh, William, I do so hope not!' Rosa burst into a
fresh bout of weeping.

This was the point at which Philip arrived home and,
after a shocked look at his wife, declared she was to go
to bed immediately. At this Rosa grew more frantic than
ever.

'No, I must tell William all of it,' she said between
her sobs. Philip took her into his arms and after a few
minutes she was calm enough to tell the whole story.

William was appalled. His facile assumption that
Emily and the others would be safe had not allowed
for Maria Fenton's ingenuity and a small boy's determination. If Emily and James were at Charlwood at
the moment when Kidman discovered the loss of the
jewellery, there was no saying what could happen to

them. He shouted for Barnaby Drewitt to join him with fresh horses, and, after begging Philip to follow him as soon as Rosa was properly taken care of, he set off for Charlwood straight away.

Chapter Fifteen

James was damp, shivering with cold, and cross. He had been so sure he knew the way to Charlwood, but he and Jonty seemed to have been plodding on for hours through endless lanes without getting anywhere! And it was raining. Now the pony had cast a shoe, and that meant he would have to stop. It had been impressed on him that a horse could go lame if he carried on riding it after this happened, and he didn't want his precious pony to go lame! Besides, what would Mr Winbolt say if it did? He slid down from Jonty's back and started to lead the pony back towards a farmhouse he had passed a few minutes before.

Here his situation improved a lot. When he told Mrs Pegg, the farmer's wife, that he was on his way from Shearings to Charlwood, she exclaimed, 'Eh, young master, you're a good bit out of your way, and that's a fact! Come on, then, we'll get you warm and then we'll see what's to be done. Mr Pegg's not far away, I'll just send the lad for him. Meanwhile, sit yourself here.' She put him by the fire, and gave him a slice of bread and

butter and a hot drink of some delicious sweet stuff.
James began to feel that the world was not such a bad
place after all, especially as Jonty was taken to a warm
stall to wait until the shoe could be put back on. When
Mr Pegg came in, he wasted no time in arranging for
James to be taken home to Shearings in the gig as soon
as he was warm and dry again.

Emily, of course, knew nothing of this. She, and
the stable lad she had pressed into service as a groom,
were riding to Charlwood as fast as they could, only
slowing down occasionally to make sure they were not
missing James on the way. But they saw no one at all,
probably because it had only just stopped drizzling and
the lanes were very muddy. As they passed the Dower
House, Emily slowed down to see if anyone was there,
but she couldn't see a soul. The place was deserted. The
men had probably given up for the day because of the
rain.

They rode on up the drive, but she drew up when
they were still some way from the house, dismounted
and handed the reins to Jem. 'Wait here,' she said. 'I
don't think we missed Master James on the way—he
must be inside. But I have to check first.' She considered
Jem and wondered if he was sensible enough for what
she had in mind. He was competent enough at looking
after the horses, but he was very young, and not the
brightest lad in the stable. She said clearly and carefully,
'Jem, I want you to stay out of sight of the house under
these trees. Don't let anyone see you. If James should
happen to arrive while I'm still inside, keep him with
you. Whatever you do, don't let him follow me. Do you
understand?'

The boy nodded, and Emily walked on up the drive.

She looked round when she reached the entrance, but there was no sign of any horses or carriage. Maria couldn't have come yet. James was probably in the parlour, waiting for his picture to arrive. The boy had no idea what was at stake or how dangerous it was, and the sooner she collected him and got him away from Charlwood, the better. That wretched picture could and would wait, whatever he said! She walked through the hall to the door at the end and opened it.

'Who's that?'

Kidman! Emily had heard that voice with its strange impersonal overtones before. She froze. Heaven forbid that James was in there with Kidman! Then a man she didn't remember seeing before came out of the parlour. When he saw her he said, 'It's a woman.'

'Bring her in here.' But Emily had already pushed past the man and was inside the parlour. Somehow or other she must get James out of there. If he hadn't already argued with them about his picture, she might still manage it as long as they didn't suspect she knew anything about the Valleron jewels. But once inside she stopped short. There was no sign of James. Maria Fenton was there, standing over by the panelled wall, and next to her was the tall man she had seen by the fountain in the garden.

'Mr Kidman!' she said. 'What are you doing here? It is Mr Kidman, isn't it? Or do you prefer to be called Mr K…Kavanagh when you're in the country?' Without waiting for his reply she swept on, 'And there's Mrs Fenton, too! I didn't know you two knew each other. What on earth are you both doing in Charlwood?'

Kidman and Maria exchanged glances, but they said nothing.

'Or did you think you might find Mrs Fenton's button

here?' Emily went on. 'I suppose it might be—I understand you visited Charlwood quite recently with Sir William, did you not, ma'am?'

They stared at her and she felt cold at what she saw
in their eyes. The masks were truly off, and danger was
all round her. The tension in the room was palpable.
James was clearly not here, and she herself must get
away from them as soon as she could. If she could. She
tried again. Hiding how afraid she was under an air of
annoyance, she said, 'You might at least give me the
courtesy of an answer!' The second man had come up
rather too close behind her, and she moved away from
him. 'Please keep your distance,' she said coldly. 'I don't
think I know you, and if I did, I would have no wish for
you to come any nearer.'

'You've met me all right,' he said, with an inso-
lent smile. 'At a very respectable ball, too. I'm Walter
Fenton.'

Emily ignored him. She turned back to Kidman and
said firmly, 'I'm afraid I shall have to ask you all to go.
Now!' The tension was emanating from him, not the
others. He was almost vibrating with excitement. She
waited, but he said nothing. She went on, 'Very well.
Since I can't force you to go myself, I shall have to leave
you here. But I warn you, I shall be back in half an hour
with someone who can.'

She turned to the door, but didn't reach it. Kidman
spoke at last, but only to say, 'Stop her, Fenton!'

The man behind Emily took her arms in a cruel grip.
Shock and outrage gave her the courage to struggle
furiously. 'How dare you, sir! Let me go this instant!'
she cried. But his grip only tightened until the pain
was so severe she was afraid he was going to break her

arm, and she stayed still, wondering what would happen next.

Kidman was examining the panel in the wall. Without turning he said, 'Put her in the turret room.'

'What'll I do with her there?'

'Whatever you like,' Kidman said indifferently, his attention still on the panel. Then he swung back again. 'No! Wait! I don't want you to waste any time at the moment. I need you with me. Leave her there. I'll deal with her myself later. Just gag her and lock her in.' He cast a glance full of dislike at Maria and added, 'I need you here to keep an eye on this sister-in-law of yours. She's too ready to give in to temptation.' He added, 'Maria, go and open the door for him, then check there's no one else outside. The key is on a hook next to the door. You can hand me the picture. I'll keep it till you're both back.'

Emily was marched out of the parlour to the oak door along the passage. She was being held so tightly that she could hardly breathe. Fenton said, 'Quick, Sis! Don't you waste time, either. We don't want to leave him alone too long in that parlour. Take my cravat.' The cravat was used as a gag, and Maria took her own scarf to tie Emily's hands together behind. Then the two bundled her so roughly into the turret room that she tripped and fell. Then the door banged shut and she heard the key turn in the lock. She heard Maria's lighter footsteps hurrying out along the passage. She was going out as Kidman had ordered to see if there was anyone outside.

Emily lay on the floor in a daze. It had all happened so quickly that she had had hardly any time to take it in, and she lay hoping that Maria wouldn't see Jem, and praying that James was not with him if she did. She strained to hear what was happening, and finally heard Maria coming back along the passage. Her voice was faint behind the thickness of the oak door, but Emily heard her say, 'It's all clear.' Emily breathed a sigh of relief. Jem had stayed hidden.

The sound of two pairs of footsteps hurrying back into the parlour, was followed by silence. After a moment she had recovered enough to try to sit up. It proved harder to manage than she had thought with her hands tied behind her back, and there were some painful mistakes, but she did it. It was easier after that to stand up. In the process she had discovered that Maria and Walter Fenton—she remembered him now, he had been at the Langleys' ball—had been in such a hurry to get back to see what Kidman was up to that they had been careless. The bonds round her wrists were already substantially slacker and after some wriggling and twisting of her hands and wrists she had loosened the knots in Maria's scarf to such an extent that in a very short time she had freed herself. The next step was to get rid of her gag, and her fingers were soon busy loosening the knots. Another few minutes and the gag was off, too. It had been so tight that she had been unable to breathe properly. Once it was removed, she felt much more like herself, and tried to take a cool look at her situation...

It was not a happy one. There was no way of getting out of the tower, no windows or other doors, and she was a prisoner here until someone unlocked the heavy oak door into the passage. The thought was not reassuring. It wouldn't be long now before Kidman discovered that the Valleron treasure was not in its hiding place, and it was almost too frightening to think of what he would do then. She thanked God that he couldn't have any idea who had actually removed it, and wondered who would be his chief suspect. One of the others, perhaps? It looked as if none of the three in the parlour trusted either of the other two. She put her ear to the door and listened, but could hear nothing.

Suddenly there was a howl of rage, more like that of an animal, and then Kidman, obviously beside himself with rage, was shouting obscenities at his companions. Emily could hear Maria's screams mingling with shouts of protest from Walter Fenton, but everything was drowned by Kidman's demented roar. It was terrifying. Emily could not imagine what it must be like to be in the same room with him. Kidman was a villain, but his chief characteristic had been that emotionless voice of his, which always conveyed such controlled menace. The noise coming now from the parlour was the raving of a madman. Emily heard another, louder scream, and Kidman shouting—so loudly she could easily make out what he was saying. She almost wished she couldn't.

'Where is it? What have you done with MY JEWELS? Come here, you harlot!' Another scream from Maria. 'TELL ME! Don't try your lies on me, you treacherous whore, it has to be you! And YOU, Fenton! I suppose you thought you'd share Edric's treasure with his widow, did you? DID YOU? Tell me where she's put them! TELL ME!' There were sounds of a struggle and then another yell from Kidman. It sounded even louder this time. He must have come out of the parlour and was in the passage. Emily shrank back, hands to her ears. His voice came from just outside the door to her turret room as he shouted, 'COME BACK HERE, YOU YELLOW-LIVERED SCUM! You won't get away from me again.' Another scuffle. Then, 'Got you!'

There was a scream from Fenton and a gurgling sound, which was cut short as something heavy fell in a series of bumps. Whoever it was must have fallen or been thrown down the cellar steps. Then someone—she guessed it was Kidman—leapt down the steps, and for a few minutes there was silence. Terrified lest he should take it into this head to look for her, Emily snatched a pike that was hanging on the wall next to the door and cowered in the corner, pike at the ready. She heard a woman's footsteps running past the turret-room door, and then after a pause Kidman came up from the cellar and she heard him take off in pursuit.

They had gone outside. It occurred to Emily that she might see something from the top of the tower, so, though her legs were trembling along with the rest of her, she struggled up the spiral staircase. When she got to the top, she could see the courtyard behind the old part of the building, and a carriage and horses. It explained why she had made the mistake of assuming that the house was empty when she arrived. Kidman and the Fentons had taken the precaution of leaving their carriage out of sight in that courtyard. She craned her neck to see if she could spot anything else, but the tower was on the wrong side of the house. She could hear shouts in the distance, but nothing to tell her what was happening. She was desperately afraid. Fenton was almost certainly at the bottom of the cellar steps, quite possibly dead, and once Kidman had dealt with Maria, he might well turn his attention elsewhere. Would he remember her and come back for her? She almost hoped he would, if that meant that Jem would escape his attention, and have the wits to fetch help. And she prayed harder than she had ever prayed before that James was somewhere safe.

* * *

James was quite safe. The gig had met William's troop and, after a quick consultation and a promise of dire things to come, he had been dispatched to Shearings in the company of one of William's men.

William himself pressed on with Barnaby Drewitt at his side and more men behind, now more than ever certain that Emily was in the greatest possible danger.

When he arrived at Charlwood, the first thing he saw halfway up the drive was Emily's horse with one of the stable lads in charge. 'Where is she?' he asked curtly. The boy was pale.

'Inside, sir. But Master James—'

'Never mind Master James. I know where he is. Who else is inside?'

'I don't know. Miss Emily thought there wasn't anyone, that's why she went in. But I've been hearing a good bit of noise…'

'Why didn't you go to help her, damn you?'

'She told me I wasn't to, sir. Very determined she was. I was to wait here, and if Master James turned up, I was to keep him wi' me.'

At that moment a woman appeared at the top of the drive, apparently running for her life, a man in close pursuit. 'Emily!' William shouted. 'Emily!' He started racing up the drive towards her. But before he was more than halfway Kidman, for it was he, had caught her and, shouting incoherently, was shaking her like a doll. Then, just as William reached them both, he threw her to the ground, where she lay still, an inert, pathetic bundle of clothes. William felt the heart had been torn out of his body. He knelt down and turned her over and his heart started to beat again as, dizzy with relief, he realised that the woman in his arms was not Emily, but Maria

Fenton. She was still breathing, and he jumped up and
gave a look to one of the men to carry her away. He
turned on Kidman.

'Where is she?' he asked fiercely.

Kidman's rage had suddenly vanished. His eyes were
blank, like those of a man in a trance, or otherwise
drugged. 'Inside,' he said indifferently. 'Locked in the
turret room. She was in the way.' His eyes followed
Maria's body as it was carried down the drive. 'I didn't
mean to kill her,' he said. 'I wanted to know what she'd
done with the Valleron jewels.'

William said curtly, 'She isn't dead. With care she
will survive.' He turned towards the house, saying over
his shoulder, 'And she didn't take the jewels, either. I
did. Those jewels are on their way back to their owners,
Kidman. They're in a vault in London.' He started to
race up the drive.

Kidman came to life again. His face contorted with
rage, he snatched a pistol out of his pocket, lifted it and
took aim at William. But he stumbled and fell to the
ground long before he could fire it. He himself had been
shot.

Barnaby Drewett nodded as he put his pistol away
again. He looked unmoved as Jem and the others gazed
at him with a mixture of dread and admiration. They
had never seen anything so quick. 'Is he…is he dead?'
asked Jem.

''Fraid so,' Barnaby said. 'My finger slipped.' Then
he added laconically, 'But better dead, than alive. Very
unhappy future waiting for him.'

Emily couldn't hear much from the top of the tower,
but she did hear the shot. Had Kidman killed Maria?
Was he going to come back for her? She was aware of

footsteps, purposeful and threatening, coming along the passage towards the oak door. So it was the end. Jem had either been captured or he had failed to find anyone to help him, and Kidman was probably going to add her to his victims. But she wasn't going to make it easy for him! She grasped her long-handled pike even more firmly and descended as far as she could without being seen from the door. Holding her pike at the ready, she waited for the door to open. She wouldn't give in without a fight.

'Emily?'

At first she could hardly believe her ears. Then he spoke again, more urgently. 'Emily, are you all right? Kidman didn't say you were dead. Oh my God, Emily, where are you?'

'William! Oh, William!' Emily threw the pike down and, laughing and sobbing at the same time, flew down the staircase. As she reached the last few steps she tripped over her pike and fell headlong into William's arms. He held her, kissing her as if he could never have enough of her, muttering between kisses, 'I thought you were dead, I thought I'd lost you, Emily my love, my only love, never do that to me again, do you hear? I couldn't stand it.' She could feel him trembling against her as he kissed her again and again.

After a while, his arms still wrapped around her, he had calmed down enough to ask again, 'Are you sure you're not hurt?'

She shook her head. 'Only a bruise or two. William, is James all right?'

'He won't be after I've dealt with him. Do you realise that, because of him, I could have lost you for ever?'

'He's only a little boy—' she began.

'Why are we talking about James when I'm desperate to tell you how much I love you?'

'Do you, William? Really love me?'

He looked at her. Then the tiny fan of wrinkles appeared at the corner of his eyes. 'You mean apart from your fortune?'

'William!'

'I worship you, Emily. Surely you know that? You could be without a penny to your name or a rag to your back, and I would still adore you, my lovely Emily. In fact I rather like the idea of loving you without a rag to your back. I would kiss you and you could call me Will in that special way of yours…'

'William! Will you *never* be serious?'

'I have never been more serious in my life. Emily Winbolt, do you love me enough to marry me? For the only reason that makes any sense at all. You can make a home for the children, build up Charlwood, have the establishment you wanted…anything you say. But all that is nothing. The only thing I truly want is that you should love me as much as I love you. That you can imagine life without me as little as I can without you. Tell me, my very dear love.'

Emily took his face between her hands and kissed him long and sweetly. 'William, I love you in every way you say. I really do. And I can hardly wait to start our life together. But now let's go back to Shearings so we can tell Philip and Rosa. I don't think they'll be very surprised, do you?'

There were, of course, a number of matters that had to be sorted out before William could take Emily back. He did suggest she should go back with one of the men, but she absolutely refused. He smiled, mouthed the word 'strong-minded', but let her stay, and Will Darby went alone to Shearings to reassure the household there. Maria Fenton was taken to one of the houses in the village and made comfortable until the question of her future could be decided. And two bodies were carted away to be decently and properly dealt with.

While they waited for the men to finish, William wandered through the house with Emily, his arm round her shoulders, hers round his waist. They even went into the small parlour, though not without some hesitation on Emily's part. 'I rather think this room will never seem the same,' said William. 'Shall we take out all the old panelling and make a modern room of it in the style of the rest of the house? What do you say?'

Emily shuddered and nodded. 'I'd like to get rid of Fenton's secret hole,' she said. 'It's sinister. What was left there cost so many lives. Yes, please, William.'

Last of all, they stood at the window in the salon and surveyed the fountain court. 'That's it!' he said. 'Settled. They've all gone. We can start a new life as soon as you say the word. A month?'

'A month is impossible!' said Emily. 'Of course it is! Just think, William, Charlwood won't be ready, the arrangements for the wedding will have to be done all over again, guests inv—'

Emily was ready to argue further, but William stopped her mouth with a sudden kiss. When she was able to speak again she said weakly 'Whatever you say, William. A month. One month from today.'

'That's better, my strong-minded beauty,' he said.

Epilogue

❧❧❧❧

December 1821

It was just over a year later and Charlwood was humming with activity. Guests had come to stay for the Christmas festivities and William had been heard to complain, though not very seriously, that he could hardly move for all the visitors and their babies, valets, maids and nursemaids. But the house could easily cope with any number of people, and this was a very special Christmas. It was a housewarming for Charlwood, its alterations, extensions and redecorations complete, and now one of the county's showplaces.

Emily stood at one of the long windows in the salon and gazed out at the lively scene before her. The sledging party was on its way back from an afternoon spent on the slope beyond the fountain court. Laura was skipping at William's side, her cheeks as rosy red as her cap, chattering away, nineteen to the dozen. James was more energetic, racing and sliding down the hill with Philip, while Rosa, laughing and calling, tried in vain to keep up. For a while after Baby Richard's birth they had been concerned about her, but it was wonderful to see her now so full of health and energy again.

The sledging party gradually disappeared round the corner, and Emily turned to face the room. The servants had just been in to light the candles, and the crystal chandeliers and girandoles reflected a thousand points of light. The room was bathed in a soft glow, reflected again and again in the mirrors round the walls.

It had been grimy, neglected and half-ruined the first time she had seen it. Now it was as lovely, as light and airy, as she had pictured it would be. Her eyes lingered on its pale ivory walls, its white woodwork, the elegantly beautiful fireplaces at each end of the room, and the soft lustre of silk curtains hanging in graceful folds and gleaming in the candlelight. It was exactly as she had imagined it. There were other rooms in the house she liked, rooms where the children played and William had his hobbies, but this was still her favourite.

She looked round and smiled. At a table at one end, the Deardons were playing cards with Rosa's father, who had deserted his books and come over from Temperley to join the party. At the other end, in the warmest corner of the room, sat her grandfather, dandling his great-grandson on his knee. The advent earlier in the year of Richard, Philip's son and the first of the next generation of Winbolts, seemed to have given Lord Winbolt a new lease of life, and to everyone's pleasure he had made the journey from Arlington Street in the depths of winter in order to be present at the baby's first Christmas. He was chuckling now, as Richard's tiny starfish hands tried in vain to grab his spectacles.

Emily hurried over. 'Shall I take him?' she asked. 'He's quite a handful.'

'A few more minutes, and then I'll have had enough. He's a bonny lad!'

Noises in the hall suggested that the party of sledgers had come in, and for a while the room was full of life and movement. But the children were eventually taken off for supper and bed, and when the baby was carried away by his nurse Lord Winbolt announced he was going to his room for a rest before dinner. Emily walked with him to the foot of the stairs. She smiled. 'Confess, sir! That baby has you under his minute thumb!'

'No such thing. But he's uncommonly bright for a child of his age. Uncommonly.' He gave her a sharp look from under his brows. 'I'd like to see another before very long, though. And I don't mind if it ain't a Winbolt. An Ashenden would suit me just as well.'

William came up behind them and put an arm round his wife's shoulders. With his inimitable grin he said, 'We'll see what we can do, sir. Maybe this time next year?'

'You're not the man I thought you were if I have to wait as long as that, William, my boy. Remember my age!'

'William! Grandpa!' Emily protested. 'This is a highly indelicate conversation.'

'Not to my generation it ain't. Get on with it, girl!'

That night Emily waited in her bedroom in the master suite, waiting for William to come up. She had drawn the curtains back and was standing at the window, entranced by the view. When he came into the room she said, 'Look! This is the sort of thing you meant me to see when you decided that this room was to be mine. Am I right?'

He came up behind her, kissed the back of her neck, then put his arms round her waist and looked out at the moonlit scene. Frost had covered the ground with silver, and hung a cascade of diamond daggers on the statue and urns in the garden. The avenue of trees was a colonnade of white, leading up to the folly and a sky filled with brilliant stars.

'The Valleron jewels and all the gold that went with them, are back with their rightful owners,' said Emily softly, 'and I hope they are pleased. But no jewels could rival that view. And no gold could buy it.'

They stood and watched for a few minutes, then William said, 'I was talking to Philip earlier. He told me that a certain Madame de la Roche has recently opened a very discreet gaming establishment just off Pall Mall.'

Emily looked blankly at him, but, though there was a distinct twinkle in his eye, he remained silent. She said at last, 'How very interesting. How kind of you to inform me! I must make sure to put it in my note book. Why are you telling me this?'

'I thought you would like to know where to find me if and when I go gaming in London.'

Emily knew that voice of old. What was William up to now? 'Thank you,' she said cautiously. 'But why should you want to go gaming? I thought you liked it here with me?'

'I adore it here with you! Particularly here!' He let his eye rest on the bed. 'But I don't like to forget old friends…'

'Who *is* this Madam de la Roche?' demanded Emily.

'She was formerly a friend of yours, too. Her name was once Maria Fenton…'

Emily regarded him with awe. 'She can't be! Really? She is?' He nodded, laughter in his eyes.

Emily took his face between her hands and pulled it down to within an inch of hers. 'Listen carefully, William Ashenden! If I catch you within a mile of that discreet gambling establishment, I shall…' He was holding her close, so close that she could feel every line, every muscle in his beautifully honed body. 'I shall…' He was moving quite suggestively, and she was finding it difficult to concentrate. 'I will…'

Suddenly he laughed and swept her up in his arms. 'Emily, light of my existence, my adored wife, why would I want to go within ten thousand miles of a woman like Maria Fenton, when I have all I shall ever want or need in my arms right here and now? Now stop being ridiculous and set about helping me make your grandfather happy!'

* * * * *